babel

FREDERICK GARCIA

ISBN: 978-0615912158
ISBN-13: 061591215X

DEDICATION

This book is dedicated to my wife Yolanda and our sons, Justin and Kevin -
two great guys that I'm so proud of.
My son Frederick: you always said I had a few books in me - thank you for
your belief.
I love you guys, and I dedicate it to you.

CONTENTS

ACKNOWLEDGMENTS

Thanks to my brother, Hank, for designing such a great cover. You are an artist!

And thanks to my great brother-in-law, David Raney, for being my proof reader and collaborative editor.

PROLOGUE

At the round earth's imagin'd corners, blow
Your trumpets, angels, and arise, arise
From death, you numberless infinities
Of souls, and to your scattered bodies go.
"Holy Sonnets" - John Donne

I LEFT PHYSICAL THERAPY FEELING PRETTY **GOOD** *about the workout, which had gone well, as my sticky, sweaty T-Shirt proved. One reason I felt good, as I stepped into the bright Memphis sunlight, was that I was able to support my weight - sort of - using my right arm and doing a modified push-up.*

This was no mean accomplishment, since I had spent the last few months completely paralyzed on my right hand side. The worst part wasn't even the paralysis - it was being unable to speak or communicate in any way.

I had suffered a form of aphasia, which was even harder to take than being in diapers and being dependent on others to take care of even your simplest wants or needs.

This was the result of the brain tumor that had been successfully extracted by the neurosurgeon who saved my life at the cost of the damage - for which I was grateful most of the time. Especially since it had only put off the inevitable for three to five years.

1

My therapists and doctors were constantly reminding me of how well I had come along - first standing; then shuffling along supported by various contraptions; then by a cane; then walking unassisted; then jogging and running. All the while I was remembering how to form words; then sentence fragments; then whole sentences. (Albeit sounding a bit like Robocop).

With therapy I managed to get fully fluent - although I can still hear the stuttering, hesitancy and lack of confidence in expressing myself. Folks tell me they can't hear it, but I think they don't have anything to compare it to. I know they can hear it, though, when I get tongue-tied. That happens a lot when I get "all balled up" trying to express a complex thought or argument.

That had been my life's work - using persuasion... now I had no life's work - other than to try to get as whole as possible, given my "advanced age."

I reached into my left hand pocket for my car keys. It's amazing how one has to re-orient their world - even with the simplest things - when one has a disability. Not being ambidextrous, and having a right handed orientation, I have carried my keys in my right hand pocket for the 40 some odd years that I have been driving. Same way as I carried my wallet in my right hand back pocket. Now, I have accommodated.

I pressed the key fob to unlock the door, and then I reached with my right hand to see if I could pull the door handle to open the car door. I did this periodically - testing the dexterity of my right hand and arm to see if - today - I would be able to accomplish this small task. I did this because during my recovery - learning to walk and talk again - I took small steps and tried small words. Slow but steady - and surprising - progress. Step by step.

But no joy.

I have control and feeling of my thumb and pointer finger. I can curl my other three fingers, but I can't feel what I'm doing nor do I have control. I can't manipulate objects, I can't write (or type - except one handed, which is slow and frustrating), I can't hold a knife to cut an onion, nor can I twist a knob to open a door. Surprisingly (at least to me), I can't even gain the purchase to open a flat cabinet door. It appears that the micro-muscular control to gain leverage and purchase on a cabinet door is beyond me. Who knew?

So, I am forced to open the car door (trying all the while not to drop the keys) by pulling the latch with my good left hand. Since I drive an SUV, I have to climb awkwardly into the driver's seat by grabbing on to something - usually the steering wheel - with my left hand and pulling myself into the seat. All with accompanying moans and grunts, of course.

I can hold on to a key with my right hand on a key chain, but lack the motor control to insert the key, much less turn it. So I go through this convoluted process where I reach through the steering wheel holding the key with my left hand at a very weird and awkward angle, fish for the ignition, insert the key and turn over the ignition. Like I said, it's a right hand world, and I'm just visiting it with a bum appendage.

Now all of this is complicated by a couple of things. First, in order to provide myself room to wedge my hand through the steering wheel, I have to - after parking - turn the steering wheel left or right until one of the larger gaps (there are five - two very small, two larger, and one largest) is positioned right in front of the ignition.

Second, when I pull myself into the cab of the SUV, I sometimes accidentally "jam" the wheel, which in turn, does not allow the ignition to engage. It is easy enough to unlock the "jammed" steering wheel - merely turn the wheel by applying torque while engaging the ignition and pressing on the brake.

Easy.

If. You. Have. Two. Hands.

Easier, if you are not twisting yourself to put your one good hand through the steering wheel gap, holding the key in an awkward position while holding down the brake pedal. Even easier if you are a Cirque du Soleil acrobat.

Alas, I am not one.

It so happened that after pulling myself up into the cab by grabbing the steering wheel with my left hand, and pulling myself up into the seat, I could hear the distinctive "click" of the steering wheel jamming. I closed my door, while still holding on to the keys, and promptly dropped the keys on the floor between my feet.

Naturally, this caused me to have to open the door again to gain room to be able to grope with my left hand to fish for the keys. This was awkward, given that I could not use my right hand for leverage. After much grunting and groaning (after my "illness" I had gained so much weight that my belly got in the way), I was finally able to hook the key ring.

That accomplished, I was finally able to close the door, fish awkwardly for my seatbelt, stretching it to accommodate my having to fasten the belt on the right-hand side using my left hand. Next came the tortuous twisting of my body to insert the key through the gap in the steering wheel.

Naturally, the steering wheel was locked, so that the key would not turn.

Try as I might, I was unable to turn the wheel or gain leverage to do so with my right hand to un-jam the steering. I was not going anywhere unless I asked for help.

I broke down.

I don't know how to explain it. But I simply broke down. I had these big, honking tears dripping down my face. I was beating the steering wheel with the palm of my hand, and crying out with these big whooping sobs. It was pitiful.

Once I wound down, I thought, "Where was this coming from?" But I knew it was the little frustrations adding up to what I couldn't stand any more. Even at my sickest, I hadn't felt this close to giving up. I just wanted OUT of this pitiful, aging body, and this damaged brain that wouldn't allow me to do all the things I had taken for granted.

And this was permanent. I would spend all my life like this. No recourse - no going back - no reprieve. Little improvements along the way... but not enough.

I leaned my forehead against the hot steering wheel and got myself together. I told myself, "Get your big boy pants on, and suck it up!"

I took a deep breath and tried to figure out what I could do. I tried raising my right knee up to the steering wheel and tried torquing the wheel to free up the key with my thigh at the bottom, and... a click! Success!

I turned the key and fired up the engine. I had to reach across with my left hand to put the gear in reverse, and I backed carefully to the point where I could put the gear into drive and pull out into traffic. I turned right out of the parking lot, going up Poplar Street and heading toward my home in Germantown.

I had forgotten to turn the radio on, and the air conditioning was going full blast, trying to overcome the hot summer air. I could not turn on the radio or adjust the air by using my left hand (I had to steer and keep on the road), so I had to content myself with air conditioner noise to fill the silence.

I considered turning into a nearby side street to park and safely do both... when a strange physical sensation struck me. I had a sense of déjà vu. It felt just as when I was first rushed to the hospital by my wife, where I was diagnosed with a rapidly growing brain tumor.

At that time, I experienced something called "Jackson's March" - a simultaneously creepy-crawly feeling and spreading numbness along my right side, from my jaw, down to my arm, and down my leg.

Only this was different. It was all over my body, accompanied by muscle spasms and flashing lights swimming in my eyes.

I thought, "Oh, no… not in the middle of traffic!"

I just knew that the tumor had come roaring back with a vengeance. I was on anti-seizure medicine, but, apparently it was not enough.

As I lost control of the vehicle, I had time to think: "If I survive the crash, I wonder what hospital they're going to take me to?" I did hope I didn't take anybody else with me… and would they know how to reach my family? My cell phone contact list?

All these thoughts tumbled through my head. I was fairly calm, as I always seem to be in times of crisis or danger, but the muscle spasms really got painful as I lost total control in what seemed to be a grand mal seizure.

A curious thing happened as I tried to focus on the oncoming traffic. Time slowed down, and I could see all the cars on the road were also going out of control.

I swerved over the median. I was going to hit head-on with a car going over that same median. I saw pedestrians falling on sidewalks and crosswalks, twitching and jerking spasmodically. I had time to think, "Nerve gas attack?"

I was now seeing double. This was no surprise, as my eyeballs were convulsing along with my seizure.

But the scene through the windshield - the cars, the pedestrians - became … transparent and unreal. I saw, and felt, myself falling down a long flight of stairs as my body was wracked by the spasms.

My body was jerking so hard that I felt my bones were about to break. What appeared to be concrete stairway was rising up to meet my jerking body. At the same time, the scene of onrushing cars was fading out and receding like an old time black and white TV turning off.

As I was passing out, I could hear the distant crashing of cars fading out like a dream.

When I hit, I heard the violent "oooffff!" of breath leaving my body quite clearly. And I felt the pain of broken bones snapping against the concrete stairway. As I lay slipping into unconsciousness, I could hear the staccato drumming of my head and limbs as they flailed about…

BOOK ONE: FORTRESS

Therefore its name was called Babel, because there the LORD confused the language of all the earth. And from there the LORD dispersed them over the face of all the earth.
(Genesis 11:9)

I. VICTOR

PAIN. There was so much pain there didn't seem to be an end of it.

I was curled up face down.

I could feel every inch of my body as it relaxed from the agonizing cramps that twisted up bone, muscle and sinew. I was taking small sips of air - in agony to breathe.

My first thought was that since I had been flying to New York on a business trip, and coming in to land at LaGuardia, I was now lying in a jumble of smashed jet plane parts in an equally smashed body. But my sense of smell - usually my most reliable sense - did not pick up the hot stink of metal, jet-fuel - or blood.

I smelled... well... dust. And cement. And new paint. And an underlying plastic /rubbery smell.

I couldn't hear the rush of sirens, or screams, or yelling ... or anything beyond the quiet soft sounds that seemed to be a breeze from the air-conditioning - as well as a faint humming sound of background electrics.

My face was pressed against some kind of semi-soft matting. Maybe I was on a gurney in a hospital... but there was no "hospital" smell.

I could dimly sense bright lights overhead from behind my tightly closed eyelids. I resolved to open my eyes as soon as the pain subsided enough to make the effort. The pain became more tolerable and I was able to take deeper breaths without feeling that my ribs were grating shards of bone, rubbing against each other.

But I couldn't open my eyes. They were too heavy.

It reminded me of a recurring dream I have in which I am driving in heavy traffic and I can't keep my eyes open. In the dream, I can't pull off safely because I seem to be in the middle lane of a three lane highway with cars speeding by on either side. Although how I came to be there and how I knew about the cars whizzing by with my eyes squeezed shut, and why it was so darn hard to open my eyes in the first place, could only be explained by dream logic.

The dream always ends when I can force my eyes open in panic and wake up.

...So I'm having a weird dream, I thought, and the pain is bleeding over from the real world. So why can't I wake up?

I gradually opened one eye in a squint - the other was apparently pressed against whatever I was lying on. At first, I saw nothing but a blurry floor. I guessed I wasn't awake yet, and this was part of the dream.

I have heard of people being able to take charge of their dreams if they became aware of being in a dream.

Okay, I thought, let's give it a try.

I forced my body to roll over on my back. It hurt like hell to move but I did it anyway. There was no way I could have done that without using both arms as support (I quit having abs about twenty years ago), but that's how dreams are, aren't they?

I opened both eyes now, but they were blurry. I blinked rapidly to clear them. Could you do that in a dream? Obviously so, but it was decidedly weird.

I looked to a ceiling that seemed improbably too high and far away. It was very "industrial-looking" with clearly visible duct-work and pipes going all over the place. It resembled a loft you might find in New York City in a "trying too hard to be trendy" condo.

The lights I sensed overhead had no discernible source or fixtures. Rather the ceiling seemed to glow, giving the clarity of light that I automatically associated with outdoors and sunlight.

Nice view… but boring. Dreams should be exciting.

I decided to look at my hands in order to change the focus of my eyes. I raised both arms up until I could see both hands.

Only they weren't my hands. The arms were too toned and fit, and so very long. The hands were definitely larger than my stubby paws. I saw that they were wrapped with boxing workout wraps - although the left hand wrap was partially unwound and hanging loose.

I recognized the wraps because, until just a few years ago, I had religiously worked out in kick boxing, having, in my teenage years, obtained the rank of black belt in … and I drew a blank.

I couldn't think of the word. It was a Japanese word for a striking and kicking martial art.

Common word. Everybody knew it. There was even movie called "The _____ Kid." I could not for the life of me remember - or even think about - the actual name. It was as though my brain skittered around that one word.

This sent scared tingles up my spine.

I knew the feeling of not being able to come up with a word. Right before my illness, I had a few, then-unrecognized, symptoms. I was lying in bed trying to get to sleep. My thoughts were a jumbled, tired mess. I was, for some reason, thinking about an old movie I had not seen in years. The main actor was a very famous old time movie star. I could not think of his name.

I could picture the actor's face, his mannerisms, and even his walk. I could almost quote the dialogue. But his name was simply an itch on the top of my brain.

I tossed and turned, unable to sleep. It was driving me crazy.

I got up without waking my wife, and went to my office to Google the movie. And there it was: the name of the main actor was John Wayne. I almost slapped my forehead, thinking "How could I ever forget that?"

This was a little like that.

I was in a very weird dream but my body seemed to be recovering. I already felt better - except for the itchy part of my brain with the missing words. Odd that they seemed to be foreign words.

8

I was scared that I was having a brain hemorrhage in the waking world and that this was a part of that. I needed to wake up.

Right now!

II. SAM

WHEN SAM WAS ABLE TO MOVE AGAIN (hours, minutes, days, later?) he slowly unclenched from the fetal position that he wound up in. His thoughts were pretty scrambled and he couldn't seem to concentrate on a damn thing.

Every single muscle and ligament was locked in excruciating spasm.

As the pain of the... (attack? Fit? Just what was that?)... event... started to subside, Sam was able to concentrate on one thing at a time.

First, it was obvious that he was lying on his back on a very hard surface.

It felt like concrete.

His office, where he been (minutes?) before, didn't have concrete floors. It was appointed with rather plush retro carpeting which was in clashing opposition to all the large monitors surrounding the room.

The single, specially built chair (it reclined and swiveled 360 degrees to take in all fifteen, 90-inch HD monitors surrounding the office walls) sat in the middle of the room.

It had old-fashioned input devices (keyboard and mouse, voice command input, etc.) as well as more esoteric, not yet publicly available I-devices: gesture-readers, touch pads, eye-controllers, and floating virtual controllers.

No desk. No other furniture. No CPU, as he had gone cloud, years before.

It was obvious that he wasn't in his specially built electronic cocoon at Google HQ, where he served as "Chief of Cyber-Research."

That made-up title had been bestowed on him to satisfy the board and to "clarify" his role (and justify his ridiculous salary). Google hired him instead of prosecuting him for cyber-terrorism when he had brought down the entire Google search engine. He had legendary status in the hacker community.

The Fed also wanted his services at the NSA, even after the FBI tracked him down and arrested him as the infamous "xeroman" hacker.

The next thing he noticed was that he had his eyes tightly closed and that he didn't have the wherewithal to unclench them.

From the sounds, smells and noise, it seemed like he was outdoors. He could smell concrete and oil and grass - and oily smoke.

It was hot on the concrete - it was radiating heat against his back - while relatively cooler air washed over his body in fits and gusts of a breeze.

Ergo: outdoors.

And he could hear what seemed to be multiple car alarms (earthquake, maybe?)

He remembered seeing a movie where a massive earthquake had set off car alarms over the entire city. But that wouldn't explain being outdoors.

It's not like he had been in a high-rise building that had shattered like the Twin Towers and deposited him (miraculously) on the street. He had been sitting in his office, on the ground floor, smack dab in the middle of the Research Lab Building.

So that left... what? Memory loss after a terrorist attack? That didn't explain the severe cramping.

Sam forced his eyes open and saw that he was, indeed, outdoors. It was nighttime, and he had the sense that he was lying on a sidewalk beside a low stone retaining wall. Above the wall was greenery - manicured and trimmed bushes. He sensed a fairly tall building just beyond the wall and bushes. It was a dark shadow with no illumination.

He saw street lights, illuminating the corners of the street. Across the street, he saw more lights. It looked like a chain link fence surrounding an open green field, kind of like a kid's ball field. The street lights were lighting up the border of the fence.

He wanted to get a better look, so he struggled to sit up. But something was pulling on his hair. That was pretty unusual, as he had very short hair. It was as if his back was trapping something lying around his head. Like a hoody, or something. It did feel like long hair.

He managed to get his hands flat on the gritty sidewalk and sat up. He looked down to see bare legs. Shapely legs. Running shorts and shoes.

What the?...

And an overflowing bosom encased in a cleavage enhancing sports bra!

Holy shit! He thought. I'm a girl!

III. VICTOR

I CAN'T TELL YOU WHEN I first realized this wasn't a dream or hallucination. I came to it slowly and gradually. I can't even say what my alternative idea was. Something about another reality or something.

But I had to operate on the premise that this was all happening and real... and that I had no memory or knowledge of this reality. I have a bias for action. Do something... even if it's wrong. Just do something.

I started by assessing the body I was in. It was quite obviously young - not the old fart's body I had "groaned" into over time - and very fit. I could also sense that I was much further from the ground than I was used to... maybe by as much as five to six inches.

So, I was way taller.

Okay. Good data.

I was wearing Under Armor shorts and shirt. While it supposedly "wicks away" sweat, it was apparently not doing a good enough job, based on the whiff I caught of myself. I desperately needed a shower. I was also barefoot.

Okay. Now what?

I began to look around, assessing my surroundings.

I saw that I was in a vast indoor space. Much larger than I could have imagined. I turned and looked at the place I had apparently fallen from. There were low steps leading to a slightly raised platform. But not a ring or a cage, as I had expected. But rather a fairly large matted area, like a wrestling or grappling platform.

What was puzzling was that there were "heavy bags" for punching - and kicking - and various striking dummies surrounding the platform.

I could also see various "fighting sticks" with taped and wrapped handles, as well as what appeared to be old fashion police batons and some of the more modern telescoping batons.

That gave me a clue. This was a "Combatives" gym, probably serving cops and/or military. This was starting to make sense.

I turned and looked to the right of the platform. It appeared further away than seemed possible (in fact, it looked like a waste of space. This place must be a bitch to heat and cool!) There, in the backside of this cavernous room to the right, the space was filled with exercise and weight machines, kind of like a fully equipped Gold's Gym, or something.

Some of the equipment was only partially assembled. There were several weight benches. Some free weights lay scattered on the floor, waiting to be organized on racks.

So this is a new facility. That explained the paint and cement dust smell.

I turned back around and saw that there was a pitiful attempt at filling the front of the training facility with counter-tops, display cases and some office furniture and couches and chairs. There was just too much room for this to be effective.

There were cardboard boxes, as well. Some had been partially opened, showing garments… t-shirts, workout pants, grappling and/or boxing shoes, more fighting sticks and what appeared to be edged weapons.

Okay. So, a newly opened, or soon to be open, facility with too much room.

I again glanced overhead to get a clearer picture of the WAY too high ceiling. Again, this was disproportionate. Why so much height? And the light source was still puzzling. It seemed too "natural."

I turned to my right and saw newly painted walls. I'm a genius - I saw the signs taped to the wall reading, "wet paint."

I also saw two doors - the nearest labeled **OFFICE** and one wider door branching to a corridor labeled **LOCKER-ROOMS AND SHOWERS**. Just how BIG was this place?

I decided to walk over to the office, which had an inset window to the right of the door. I was at the wrong angle to see much in the window other than the opposite wall.

I walked to the door and saw a desk, an office chair, a computer monitor on the desk, and a desktop computer lying unconnected on the floor, trailing the electrical cord, and with a loose blue Ethernet cable hooked to the back of the CPU.

There was an old sofa (it had seen better days - and clashed with the newness of this place) placed on the opposite wall, facing the desk.

I walked into the office and saw opened boxes labeled "office." I could see why the computer wasn't set up: the Ethernet connection was on the wrong wall for the way the desk had been set up. Also, an extension would have to be set up to get power to the equipment. That wire would have to trail awkwardly along the floor in front of the desk.

I also noticed a fist-sized hole driven into the plaster board.

Temper, temper!

I could almost picture it: somebody (movers?) had set up desk, chairs, sofa and computer equipment willy-nilly.

The owner (presumably me) walked in and saw what the lazy movers had done and hit the roof (or more literally, the wall) in frustration.

That said something about his (my?) short fuse. It seemed a trivial thing to me. Maybe he had faced other frustrations I didn't know about.

I looked on the desk and saw three items. One was a framed magazine article from Texas Now magazine and the other was a color print-out of what was apparently an online news story. The third item was a large picture frame that was apparently being prepared to display the news print-out.

The magazine article was titled "*Victor Vega, Bexar County Sheriff's New Top Dog at the Bexar County Violent Criminal Apprehension Unit.*"

It showed a picture of imposing figures in the background dressed in those black SWAT uniforms wearing all the armaments usually associated with that profession. Off to the side was a picture of an intense-looking guy with his muscular arms folded in an obviously posed position with the caption reading:

> *"Vega is a native of San Antonio who has been with the sheriff's department for eight years."*

Here's what the article said:

> *In the sheriff's department most deputies start out working in the jail, and then take a test to come out on patrol.*
>
> *Vega, a former Army Special Forces captain who served two tours, each, in Iraq and Afghanistan, skipped that part. But the deputies who serve under him don't seem to resent that at all.*
>
> *As a winner of two Bronze Stars, two Purple Hearts, and a Silver Star for bravery under fire, Vega joined the Bexar County Sheriff's Department as a lieutenant commanding a unit of SWAT, using his vast experience to rapidly modernize and improve the Department's Special Weapons and Tactics Unit.*
>
> *He soon gained a reputation for not only leading the best SWAT team in the nation - gaining that title ahead of LAPD's famed SWAT unit and the FBI's Hostage Rescue Team (HRT) - but also for modernizing the tactics and weaponry used for Bexar County and throughout the San Antonio Metro area.*

Vega used his status and reputation gained as a genuine military hero to lobby for a Federal grant to purchase the latest armaments, tactical gear, armor and gadgets.

Vega also introduced the concept of "Ready Response" to the department, and used his experience in the Combatives Arts to introduce a Combatives Training regimen similar to that used by the military's special forces.

When more violent crime began to filter up from the border towns, the Sheriff's Department began fighting against a level of criminal not realized in US history.

"We're fighting a real war - not unlike what we faced in the Middle East - with criminal cartels that are trained," says Vega. "They show up with gear. They have ballistic armor. A lot of the men they recruit are ex-military, ex-police. They know SWAT tactics. They know counterintelligence."

Vega was tapped as the Commander of the newly formed Violent Criminal Apprehension Unit, changing the face - and effectiveness - of modern day law enforcement. The Unit is charged to arrest, stop, and put away the most violent criminal offenders by any means necessary - including very effective deadly force.

The ACLU, never known for its love of…

HMMM… INTERESTING. Apparently, from all indications, I am now this "Vega" person and, apparently, "I'm" in Texas.

The second news print-out was a bit more informative, in its own way.

Here it is, in part:

By John Estas   Published 6:48 pm, Friday

A new Martial Arts center is coming to Leon Springs, Texas to teach the official self defense system of the Israeli Defense Forces, _____ _____, the Russian Special Forces

Combat System, _____, Filipino Stick Fighting, _____, and a mix of kickboxing and grappling (_____-_____) with the best of professional MMA (Mixed Martial Arts.)

But not everyone can attend. Victor Vega, chief instructor and majority stakeholder of the Combatives center says membership is restricted to law enforcement and active duty military. Vega also happens to be the Commander of the Bexar County Sheriff Department Violent Criminal Apprehension Unit (VCAU).

Vega, a highly decorated war veteran, holds three black belts in traditional martial arts, was a Golden Gloves boxer, a college wrestler, and a professional MMA fighter with a record of 8 and 1, before joining the Army Special Forces. He served in Iraq and Afghanistan. Vega also earned the distinction of being the All Army Combatives Champion while stationed at Fort Hood.

Vega said there is a difference between traditional martial arts or self defense and "Combatives."

"Traditional martial arts schools, self defense schools and fighting schools all offer something - but that is not enough for what law enforcement and the military need," he said.

"The idea is not to defend yourself - but rather to make sure the bad guys don't get up to hurt you or anybody else."

Vega said he decided to bring the center to the Leon Springs area, near Boerne, because he wanted to bring Combatives Training to the northwest side, in Bexar County but just outside SA city limits.

The unspoken implication was the history of political conflict between the mayor of San Antonio and the highly effective Bexar County Sheriff Head of the VACU.

Vega said it was a matter of finding enough space at a low cost so Combatives could be offered to anyone in law enforcement, "- including my brothers in arms of the SAPD who wanted to take it, despite any objection on the part of the mayor and his liberal minions."

The 40,000 square foot facility is located in the now infamous Alternatives Green Technology Complex - a "green building experiment" that has become known as "Gore's Folly" - even though the environmentalist ex Vice President had nothing to do with the costly failure.

As reported in this paper, the AGT Complex was an experimental building design that was supposed to lead to an "energy-independent, fully sustainable and renewable building complex for business and residential living alike."

Cut into a massive hillside in San Antonio's hill country, the multi-billion dollar "experiment" was a complete bust - having ignored the timeless real estate wisdom that says, "location, location, location..."

Despite the promised energy savings, both businesses and potential residential tenants stayed away in droves - apparently not interested in the massive in-ground (in hill-side, actually) hard to get to, extremely ugly fortress.

Attracting only three businesses - now four with the Combatives school - it became a laughing stock and left people scratching their heads. "This might have gone over in 'keep it weird' Austin," says business developer Mark Goodard, "but San Antonio?..."

THE ARTICLE WENT ON IN THIS VEIN for a couple of more pages, only going back to the Vega story in closing. I needed to find a mirror to determine if, indeed, I was now this "Vega" guy. I'd worry about the "how," later.

Feeling disoriented and slightly dizzy, I set the articles aside and went to sit on the ratty sofa.

I noticed that all the foreign names of the various martial arts were a vague blur to me. I couldn't read them, as my eyes kept dancing and skipping over them - not comprehending them. I knew what they were in context, but my eyes refused to make sense of them. Apparently aphasia could be visual, as well.

I was also wondering about my family. Are they doing okay? What do they think has happened to me? I had to find a 'phone. Maybe in Vega's locker.

I felt weary, but decided to have a look beyond these walls… after going to the locker room and taking a hot shower - if there was one.

IV. SAM

WHEN SAM WAS ABLE TO GET OVER THE SHOCK of discovering he had swapped bodies with a hot chick (presumably hot, although she could be a complete butter face) ala Freaky Friday, he decided he needed internet access, right away.

He looked around for a phone she could have dropped. No luck. Not even an iPod. Who the hell goes running without ear phones and a way to call for help? It seemed reckless to him.

No ID, either. He was hoping to find a driver's license tucked away somewhere. He did find a house key tucked into one of her shoes, between the laces. But there were no identifying marks.

Now what?

He decided to walk over to some cars that had apparently gotten in a fender-bender. Due to the "event", maybe? Walking lent itself to some uncomfortable bouncing and jiggling he wasn't used to.

There, upwards of ten or so cars were strewn about the street; some over the curbs and sidewalks in a tangle of crumbled fenders and chrome. There was one car directly across the street that had crashed into the chain-link fence and was partially on the grass, having ploughed gouges in the turf.

Some car alarms were blaring (although, fewer as time went on.) He could see air bags deployed and what appeared to be slumped bodies. It was hard to see, as some of the headlights shone directly at him.

He also noticed several bodies lying in the street. They seemed too still and silent to be anything but dead. They didn't appear to be victims of any of the crashes - although he couldn't be sure this far away.

Sam decided to approach a car that was nearest to him. It seemed undamaged, although it had swerved over the curb and past the sidewalk, onto the grassy area surrounding the stone wall.

He called out, "Hello," surprised at the girlish voice that came out. Crap, he thought, one more thing to get used to, as if having boobs isn't enough!

As he approached the car, he seemed to hear a voice respond in the distance. Too far away to distinguish words, but definitely a human voice.

A sense of relief washed over him, realizing that he was not the only person alive in this world. It made him want to get to a phone even more. The driver of the car in front of him was bound to have one. Who didn't?

He finished the trek to the car and saw the driver, who was being held up by the seatbelt. It was an older black lady, and her face was frozen in a horrible rictus, and her body seemed twisted up and cramped.

Kinda like what I felt... he thought... only I survived. But WHY??

He decided to open the car door and look for the lady's phone to at least call 911. If it was a smart phone with a browser, he could gain web access to find out what was happening and why.

As soon as the car door opened he caught the stench of loosed bowels and bladder. He had to cover his nose with his elbow to keep from tossing his cookies.

Sam thought he heard the voice coming nearer but still couldn't make out words over the noise of car alarms, but he yelled out, "Hey... Over here!"

He looked in the car and saw the lady's purse lying on the floor on the passenger's side. He decided to go around to the street side and open the passenger door, rather than reach out over the dead lady.

As he did so he called out again, "Over here! I'm calling for help!" He heard the voice nearer but couldn't distinguish the words. It was a man's voice, though.

He hoped that anyone that came up to him would not think him a looter. He reached the lady's purse and saw the cell phone in one of those holders some women use that clip on to their purse for easy access. He began to dial "911" as he stood up and called out to the approaching voice, "Over here! I'm calling 911 for help!"

He thought he heard an answering growl. Odd. But then 911 began to ring… and ring… and ring before he got the dropped signal. That didn't bode well. He hit redial, only to encounter the same thing.

Damn!

He saw a dark figure approaching in the distance and called out, "Hey! Over here! I'm dialing 911 but no answer!"

That's when he saw - and heard - the man running to him. He was yelling some angry sounding gibberish in a foreign tongue. He could see the man's face contorted by anger and rage - and that's when his own anger and rage hit him with a surge of adrenalin.

He wanted to KILL this damn foreigner! He wanted to tear his throat out with his teeth to stop the ugly foreign words coming from that foul mouth and spit out the flesh and gouge his eyes out with his fingers!

Sam could feel his own face contorted in savage hate and started toward the man, dropping the cell phone to form his hands into claws.

That's when Sam saw the man raise a gun while still running. He heard the cracking noise and saw the gun muzzle flash. The guy was trying to kill him!

Sam felt the urge for fight or flight.

He chose flight.

V. VICTOR

MY EXPLORATION OF THE LOCKER ROOM, and finding a mirror there, helped solidify the reality of my... what? - transition? ... more for me.

The locker room looked like all the locker rooms I've ever been in - the ubiquitous metal lockers, the vented and slotted doors, the looped latch on which you can hang a padlock...

There were also the usual wooden slat benches lined up in front of the lockers. To the right, in the back, I saw some shower stalls lined with tile, like all gym showers seemed to be.

A door was open on one of the lockers. I assumed this would be where I could find "my" clothes and stuff. I walked over to it and looked inside.

There were metal shelves built in - one at the top of the locker, about 18 inches in height; one at the bottom about 24 inches. That left just enough room to hang clothes on the provided hooks.

The top shelf held wallet, keys, what I assumed to be a badge and credential folder and a cell phone.

The bottom shelf held black combat boots, various cop tools - all in black leather belts - holster and gun; a mace or pepper spray in its own holder; spare mag sheaves (four of them, presumably holding said loaded mags); a heavy flashlight (in black, of course); and an unusual looking clip holding a small wand. No stun gun or Taser. I thought those were pretty standard, but I guess not.

I assumed the wand wasn't a magic Harry Potter wand, so it must have been a telescoping baton.

The clothing was all black Battle Dress Uniform (BDU) - a "SWAT" uniform, obviously. Cool.

I examined the BDU shirt. It had black on black uniform patches with raised black thread. The patch read "Bexar County" on the top of an inset circle and "Violent Criminal Apprehension" on the bottom half with a Texas map in the middle of the circle and the words "Deputy Sheriff" arching over the top of the patch.

There were two raised stars made of black thread, on each of the collars.

Pretty snazzy looking.

I reached in to get the cell phone. It was an Android phone very much like mine. I "woke" it up and hit the green handset icon to bring up the dialer. I couldn't bother with his contact list, since I would not recognize any of the names, anyway.

I closed my eyes, trying to remember my wife's number. Contact lists have been pretty destructive to the memory. People tend to rely too much on them. But I had a pretty good head for numbers.

I punched in my wife's number - not knowing what to say when she answered.

After ringing a while, it went to voice mail with her usual cheery greeting. Man, at that moment I missed her with a sudden ache that left me dizzy.

I debated whether or not to leave a message. She wouldn't recognize the name on caller ID nor the number calling - and certainly not the voice. What could I say anyway that wouldn't sound crazy? "Hey babe, it's me... calling you using a different number and different voice...?"

I disconnected.

I then tried both my sons' numbers and my daughter's. Same thing.

Damn! Now, I was worried for them. What if...?

I looked at the phone's date and time. It was still today as I remembered it, but I had lost a couple of hours in the agony of what I was beginning to think of as "The Transition."

My wife would be home by now, but my kids... who knows? They were adults with their own lives and concerns.

I decided to go online to check the newsfeeds. There were no updates since a couple of hours ago. Hmmm.

I sat down on the bench and reached into the locker for the pistol. It was encased in a black, tough, fabric holster with Velcro straps to accommodate tying to the thigh area like a military tie-down. The belt and the accompanying accessories were about as heavy as you would expect.

Old habits kicked in as I un-holstered the weapon and hit the magazine release button. I then jacked the mechanism to clear the chamber. The bullets were unfamiliar to me (they looked "pointy" like a rifle slug), as was the gigantic magazine that must have held up to 20 rounds.

The pistol was something I hadn't seen before. I trained with the old army 1911 when I was in the service. Practiced and carried, but never shot one in combat, relying on my army-issue M16 and then a CAR 15, which had about the same number of rounds in it as this pistol. This was serious firepower.

I looked at the stamping and saw "FN Five-seveN." Specialty gun, if I recall, only available to military and special law enforcement units. This baby fired the 5.7×28mm bullet that could pierce most body armor. I'd only seen this gun in pictures, and most certainly never fired one. Must kick like a mule.

I thumbed the round back in, and replaced the magazine, thumping it home. I automatically jacked in the round. I looked for a safety, but there wasn't one. Scary.

I put the gear away into the locker. I tried the phone again. Same results.

I stood up and walked to the row of sinks lining one wall. I looked in the mirror.

First time I'd seen "myself." Tall, dark and intense, judging by the eyes glaring back at me. Or maybe that was just worry about my family and the craziness going on here. It matched the picture in the article.

The guy looking back at me in my reflection was totally unfamiliar. Athletic, very fit and with rangy musculature. Long arms that I associated with fighters, quarterbacks, running backs and other athletes.

He was just the type of guy that caused me to quit kick-boxing. When athletes had gotten into the martial arts, my "superior" technique and martial spirit were not enough to over-come reach, speed and stamina. Don't believe the movies: spunk and spirit are not enough to keep from losing.

I decided to take a shower, then get dressed in "my" uniform and gear; try the phone again; then go outside to see if the world was any different.

It was.

VI. SAM

SAM WAS SLIGHTLY OUT OF BREATH, but still surprisingly able to continue at this blistering pace. This gal must be a serious runner!

So must his pursuer, who had quit firing (ran out of bullets, or put off by the impossibility of hitting a running target while running himself? Who knows?) He was still running after Sam shouting obscenities, presumably, and threats in that foreign language that so enraged Sam.

But why? Sam was no bigot.

To react so viscerally to hearing a foreign tongue was not like him. He considered himself a tolerant liberal... well, except for the occasional joke. But honestly! To react with such violent intent (even though he ran away) was just not like him!

Now, he was running like a scalded cat and cursing himself for dropping the poor lady's phone.

He first ran in zig-zags, and back and forth, crossing streets and avoiding the occasional wrecked car. Then he ran full out, attempting to put distance between him and his pursuer. He was aided by the girl's running gear - which the guy back there didn't have. The guy was probably running in street shoes.

Sam decided to run to where it was darkest and maybe find a place to hide. He was running past a fence that seemed to surround an apartment or a condo complex. He came to a gated entrance, and he grabbed the gatepost to do a 90 degree turn into the complex.

This gained him a few steps. He could hear the puffing and growling man pound the sidewalk in his dress shoes.

There! Sam spotted the perfect hidey hole. There were pole lights on, highlighting the parking lot full of cars. Here and there Sam saw fallen bodies in the agonized position that he had become familiar with.

One of the bodies was at the back of an SUV that had its back gate open. The woman was apparently unloading groceries when the event struck. There were plastic grocery bags strewn all over. Not a familiar sight in California, where he been when... snatched?... transported?... Plastic bags had been outlawed there. So data point: Not in California anymore!

Sam dove into the back of the SUV and eased the hatch shut, just as he caught a glimpse of the pursuer.

Sam held his breath and peeked out the back window, praying not to be spotted. He saw that the man was still carrying the gun, which irrationally enraged Sam - enough to want to go out and confront the man and beat his brains out with his own gun.

Fortunately Sam retained enough rationality to know that it would be suicide. Even as an out-of-shape male computer geek, he couldn't have tangled successfully with the physical presence standing there, glaring into the parking lot. Much less as a girl.

Although the girl seemed much stronger than Sam had been and was in way better shape than Sam ever was. Still...no.

The man glanced angrily about, cursing (presumably) and casting about for any sign of movement. He walked over to some of the bodies just to make sure, but covered his nose with the crook of his elbow as the fecal and loosed bladder smell that seemed part of this death event lingered.

He looked in some of the cars closest to the entrance. He also got down on one knee to look under the cars, in case she was hiding there.

Sam saw the man glance up and to the right as if he had heard something. Sam realized that he heard what seemed to be angry screaming coming from his right, far away, but echoing. It was faint in the interior of the SUV, but was probably louder outside in the parking lot.

Sam looked up and to the right where a weird, massive building complex was illuminated against a rather tall hillside. Next, he heard two booming sounds in rapid order and saw spears of light that looked like fire coming from the hillside.

The man, obviously reacting to this, took off running, back to the entrance and off to the right.

Sam breathed a sigh of relief.

But what was that?

VII. VICTOR

FRESHLY SHOWERED and dressed up in sheriff's battle dress - complete with the trimmings, including gun belt - I stood ready to go. It was funny how I knew exactly how to put the gear on and how to strap the low slung thigh holster. It felt - right.

It seems that muscle memory may be a function of nerve and organic brain inputs. It got me to thinking about the nature of this "transfer."

Why did I not have access to any of the memories of this man? And why, having learned 3 languages - including Japanese - was I not able to process the foreign words?

I spoke and read Spanish to some degree, but when I tried to access common words and phrases, I ran into a brick wall. It stood to reason this Vega character - even as a born and bred American - would have had some familiarity with the language, being a San Antonio native where even the whitest of the white were exposed to it on a daily basis.

Strange.

I picked up the phone again and tried my family's numbers one more time. Same thing as last time.

I went into Vega's contact list, but of course did not see any familiar names. There were entries of "Office" and "VCAU Desk". Obviously work related. No pictures associated with his listings. Not a very sociable guy, apparently. His call log was mostly to the office and work.

I pulled up a browser and logged on to newsfeeds. There was nothing unusual. Just the latest news about the sad state of affairs on the political scene, the usual "entertainment" junk, and such. The odd thing was that the latest updates were over six or seven hours old.

I then logged onto a live video news feed that I have membership with, and got... nothing. There was a live video stream that showed the news desk and fake backdrop, but no talking heads reading the news. There were news crawls at the bottom, but they were hard to read on this screen. No audio. Strange.

I got the nasty feeling that this "transfer" involved more than just me.

As I stepped out of the locker room, I brought out Google Maps on the browser and had this location spotted on GPS. If I was going outside, I needed to have some idea as to where I was.

I was familiar with San Antonio, having spent some time at Fort Sam Houston and Camp Bullis during some firearms training while in the Army forty years ago. I had the opportunity to later vacation here with my wife and to travel here on business.

I marveled at how the city had grown over the years, extending beyond Camp Bullis, which had seemed to be backwoods country back in my Army days. Now there was a Six Flags nearby, giant malls and housing developments.

My wife and I had vacationed at a nearby Westin Resort, when the kids were all off to college. We enjoyed the sun, Tex-Mex food and the cool hill country weather while playing golf.

It seemed I was pretty near there - according to the GPS - and just up the road from IH-10, a major highway leading west to El Paso and east to Houston. This location was pretty much located up in hills with only greenbelt surrounding it. Seemed a bit odd for an office building as this appeared to be.

I decided to go out the front door, which had a frosted glass insert panel. I stepped out onto a softly lit balcony/corridor that had a safety limestone wall and open black wrought iron rails at chest height. The long open corridor stretched out quite a distance on either side, which made it difficult for me to make out other doorways or branching corridors.

The walls, which looked to be bare concrete, were lit with soft, glowing sconces, rather than brightly lit fluorescents, as some office buildings often were. This meant I had to let my eyes adjust to the dimmer lights after stepping out from the brightly lit gym.

I'll try to describe what I saw at that time.

I stepped up to the safety wall, noting the soft echoing sounds that my footsteps made bouncing off those concrete walls. I looked out into the countryside and saw that I was on a hilltop looking down on greenbelt. Far away, I could see crisscrossing streets and lights - some seemed to be major roads, while others were leading into sparse homesteads.

There was a major highway about a mile away, easily seen from this high up - IH-10, presumably. But there wasn't any traffic whizzing along at highway speeds.

Instead, there were bunched up headlights shining every which way all along the highway and some along the access roads.

Something was burning all along the way - casting dancing shadows against the highway illumination. From this vantage point, I could also see what appeared to be massive fires in the distance, scattered around the landscape. Some of the buildings seemed to be burning, as well.

I could hear the faint noise of car alarms beeping and sounding horns amongst the lights. It was a scene out of some apocalyptic movie. Only, in this case, I could hear the sounds and smell the burning wreckage.

AFTER SOME TIME, I came away from the view, determined to go down there and find out what was going on.

I noted that I appeared to be about five or six stories up from ground level. But that was hard to determine, as the overhang roof of my balcony seemed at least two stories high itself, and there was no way of knowing how many layers were beneath me. Also the greenery and the broad roadway below appeared to slope downward.

Off - some unknown yardage away - I could see a thick, stone wall fence surrounding this place. The roadway led to a metal, double-gated opening that you see in guarded complexes and residential communities - only bigger and more massive. No telling from here how far away that gate was, really.

I attempted to lean out over the railing to look up at what was above me - but my balcony roofline overhang seemed to be offset to a wider degree than the balcony, hence blocking my view. So I had no idea as to how high up this complex was. This could be a skyscraper, for all I knew.

But it was a WIDE sucker, based on the long corridor I could barely see the end of. It looked to me to be all of two city blocks long on either side. Or that could be an illusion, given my perspective.

I decided to walk down the corridor to find a stairwell exit or an elevator to go down and explore.

I noticed my boots gave off a muffled sound, even bouncing off these concrete walls. I guess that's an advantage when you're a SWAT guy. Don't want to warn the bad guys that you're coming.

I walked along at a fairly rapid pace, anxious to find an exit. I came to another doorway, far along the hallway. It had a big sign on it that said "SA Restaurant Supply Company" and a logo that I thought was understated and well done. No cutesy chef's hat or checkered aprons; just "SAR" in embossed gold 3D lettering.

Looking down the rest of the corridor, I could see a faintly glowing sign that read "**EXIT**". My goal.

But first, I decided to see if the restaurant supply house was inhabited. There were lights on, similar to the gym, behind the frosted glass door. This door had their company logo etched into the glass. I grasped the handle and the door swung open, freely.

I peeked in and saw an office behind a service countertop. Behind that was what seemed to be endless shelves going back into the dimly lit, cavernous room.

The shelves were stocked with what I could only presume to be "Restaurant Supplies" and equipment of various sorts.

There were also, against the back recesses of the dimly lit warehouse space, what appeared to be giant double doors leading to who-knows-what.

No one seemed to be inside, but I called out, "Sheriff's Department."

I felt like a fraud. "Is anybody in here?"

I stood stock still, as I thought I heard a sound in the back.

I held my breath to see if I could hear it again. Nothing.

I called out once more, "Hello?!"

Again, nothing. I decided to close the door and move on toward the exit sign.

I got about 25 or 30 steps when I heard running footsteps echoing behind me and what seemed to be angry, foreign-language cursing. I recognized Spanish as the language but didn't understand anything he was yelling.

This was my reaction:

I turned around and crouched in a combat stance. My adrenalin was instantly high, as I reacted with cold, ferocious anger and hatred. Time slowed down for me as I saw a man running toward me with a giant cleaver raised above his head to cut me down.

As the man got close, I lashed out with a push kick, stopping his progress. At the same time, my right hand reached down to draw my pistol and I shot him, rapidly, twice in the forehead, losing sight of him in the unexpected flashes and the thunderous sound of this massive weapon as it bounced off the walls, deafening me.

I stood very still in a crouched position with the pistol extended in both hands ready to fire again.

I CAME OUT OF THIS BERSERKER MODE, with ears ringing from the weapon's discharge. I realized two things:

One: I could not have reacted that quickly to a threat in my "former" life. I was never that good. I probably would have frozen for an instant, giving the attacker time to cleave my skull. Apparently this body was trained and honed to react with deadly efficiency without conscious thought.

Two: While I spoke Spanish - and I recognized the tone and phrasing of that language enough to distinguish it from anything else - I simply could not recognize or understand anything he was saying. My brain skittered around the meaning in a way that infuriated me beyond all reason.

That was the thing: I was still raging. I found myself wanting to attack this guy with a ferocity that transcended the fact that I was reacting to an attack. I HATED!

When my vision cleared fully, I saw the body slumped backwards in boneless death that is never really duplicated in movies. I smelled the cordite and coppery blood smell that I have always associated with combat.

I had fought in Vietnam, but rarely this close up. I knew the limitations of the average soldier in combat.

Few could have reacted so quickly and expertly delivered a precise double tap to the head. Most people are taught to shoot at the center mass of the body in order to maybe be lucky enough to hit their intended target. Surprise and adrenalin cause severe "buck fever" that causes people to miss even a broad target from mere feet away.

I - that is, this body - managed to fend off an attacker while drawing a holstered weapon and placing precise kill shots to the head while raging mad.

That was impressive.

I walked over to the body, suppressing the urge to kick him uselessly in the balls. He was most definitely dead, missing the top of his head from the bridge of his nose on up. There was a spray of blood, bone and brains behind him past the doorway he had come from.

I felt nothing but satisfaction.

I looked down at the pistol in my hands in wonder. Outside of some big caliber weapons I had shot in the past, I have never seen that big a flash from this size frame. I was deafened by the report, even behind the weapon, and could imagine how it must have echoed off this building, down into the streets.

I regretted not putting in earplugs. I now knew why the belt had earplugs lashed to it. I would put them in, just in case, when the ringing in my ears subsided. I didn't want to be attacked and not hear somebody sneaking up on me. Made me wish this weapon had a suppressor. It had the threads for hooking one up, but I didn't have one on Batman's utility belt.

I decided to slide my way to the exit sign by putting my back to the wall and keeping my head on a swivel, looking both ways for signs of movement.

When I got to the exit sign, it led out to a broad corridor that branched out from the balcony. I cautiously peeked down the deep corridor and saw the same softly-glowing sconces lining the walls on both sides. They provided just enough light to make out some details.

On the right were two banks of passenger elevators while at the back of the extra wide hall there were some heavy-duty, super-wide freight elevator doors.

I stepped out to the middle so I could see the left-hand wall. In the middle of that wall I saw a door and a mark with the universal sign for "stairs."

I opted for the stairs.

I WAS RIGHT about this being a multistory building with extra height thrown into the mix.

When I passed the elevators on my way to the stairwell, there were indicator lights above the elevator doors that showed the building to have two sub-floors, six real floors and a floor marked "Garden at the Top." I figured one or both of the sub-floors to be parking and perhaps serving as a loading dock.

I was proved right, as I moved cautiously down the metal stairs that zigzagged back and forth five times per floor, due to the unusual height of each floor in this weird building. Each floor landing had a metal door marking the floor number.

I stopped at the door marked "SB-1" and went through it. I entered an enormous underground parking garage. It only had three cars and what I presumed to be Vega's sheriff's SUV, since it had the markings and logo of the Bexar County Sheriff Department on the sides of the vehicle. It was a black Escalade with all the chrome blacked out, and an enormous black deer catcher grill in front. It also had cop lights unobtrusively mounted on the dash.

I extracted Vega's keys, hit the unlock button and was rewarded with a beep and flashing parking lights. This was it.

I went to the back of the SUV and holstered my weapon. I saw a car, two spaces down from mine, and saw a contorted body next to it. It was a man lying face down in a twisted fetal position. He had apparently had his keys out to open his door - presumably going home after work - when he had been caught in the same event that had made me spazz out.

Only this poor guy hadn't made it. He was definitely dead and he had voided his bladder and bowels in death. The stink was pretty harsh. I went over to check, anyway.

Yep. Dead as disco.

I decided not to go through his pockets looking for ID. I wasn't really a cop, anyway.

I stood up and opened the hatch on the Sheriff's SUV and looked in the back. There was a broad, black plastic equipment case. I opened it and found what I was expecting.

A treasure trove of weapons, body armor, a helmet, goggles, tactical gloves and knee pads, infra-red and low light viewers, a butt load of ammo, an M16A4 rifle; a Colt Commando 733; a SIG-Sauer MPX-S (Submachine Gun); two shotguns - both Remington 870s - and a half dozen flash bangs. I also noticed some fragmentation grenades that are definitely not standard police issue.

The armor - black of course - was not of the type I was familiar with. But - looking at the label - I remembered reading about experimental body armor called Dragon Skin. It has been around for a while, but was now using piezo-electrics and intelligence to enhance the armor's strength - which is derived from an arrangement of overlapping ceramic and titanium composite discs. Not a normal law enforcement standard.

Reading about this made me jealous at the time, thinking that if we'd had this technology in my days of soldiering, we could have prevented the casualties we took. This armor made someone virtually bullet proof.

Cool.

I decided to put this armor on and take the MPX SMG and some extra mags.

I put on the knee pads - it seemed like a good idea - and put on the tactical gloves. I cleared and checked the weapon (again, relying purely on muscle memory, as I had only seen this compact submachine gun on TV), made sure the magazine was seated properly and closed the SUV hatch.

Ready to go, I climbed in the driver's seat and started up the vehicle. It was time to get out there and find out what was happening.

VIII. SAM

SAM CREPT OUT OF THE BACK of the SUV warily. He hated to do it, but he had to search the dead lady's purse for a phone, an ID (maybe it had her address with what apartment she belonged to), and, hopefully the keys. If not, he'd have to search the other bodies lying around the parking lot. He really didn't want to, as it meant actually touching the bodies to get to pockets and such.

He saw the lady's purse on the ground beside the body, and said a silent prayer. He reached down and opened the purse. Phone. Wallet. Keys. Bingo!

First, the wallet had a Texas Drivers License that showed an address that meant nothing to him, but also had an apartment number listed. Hopefully she wasn't just visiting.

He dropped everything but the phone and keys, feeling like a thief, and mouthed a silent, "Forgive me."

He looked at the buildings which were numbered on the front, and he found the apartment he was looking for directly above on the second floor right where the SUV was parked.

He saw two flights of metal stairs and saw that the apartment was just to the right of the stairs in an inset alcove. He decided to risk being seen by his erstwhile attacker as the stairs were highly illuminated. He just had to get somewhere safe to think and figure out some options.

SAM VERY QUICKLY made his way up the stairs and was able to make out the apartment key, open the door, and breathe a sigh of relief when he closed it behind him.

The apartment was dark and silent, with very little light seeping through the curtains in the main window. He saw a couch and collapsed on it - stifling a sob. He closed his eyes and put his now feminine forearm over his eyes. He still clutched the phone in one hand.

After a while, his breathing slowed and he was able to try to think coherently.

Okay, he thought, first things first.

He sat up and looked at the phone. It was an iPhone. He could work with that, but he preferred a larger screen. To that end, he looked around for a computer, a laptop, a pad, or anything that would provide him with broadband access. He spotted a newer looking notebook on the counter that divided this room from the kitchen.

It was a touch screen Windows 8 notebook. Bad news, because it would take him a while to bust through the lock screen password. Doable, but he didn't want to take the time.

He turned to the iPhone and noticed a password keeper app that permitted people to access forgotten passwords. Stupid.

Sure enough, when he pulled up the app, he immediately found the notebook unlock code.

Sweet.

He entered the password and pulled up a browser. The first thing he did was tunnel through, using his private VPN, to reach a backdoor into the main Google server access. He entered a series of complicated passwords that changed based on an algorithm that depended on a five minute span of time, based on the current Network time (GMT). Virtually impossible to break.

He accessed the root on the Linux server and then accessed his own personal virtual control panel. He had designed this to be able to reach into any feed coming across the network. He also obtained his location using GPS locators.

Apparently he was now - in this girl's body - in San Antonio, Texas. No wonder it felt so damn hot! He looked for the feeds...

The streams were... quiescent. There was no activity at all. As far as he was concerned, the world was dead.

He felt numb.

He stopped to think a moment. He then entered a series of commands. This allowed him to access all street video feeds that were scheduled in real time.

This was a project that was designed to take over the Google Maps static "street view" produced by the Google car cameras over the next quarter. It was an experimental system that sought to take advantage of all the high-res traffic cams being put up by governments everywhere, in addition to all the private security cams, etc.

He set the program to start accessing the 'cams geographically starting from his California office and heading East and South to where he was now.

IT WAS HARD TO DESCRIBE what he was seeing.

His view began with the cameras inside the Google complex. In all of the buildings, where there were cameras, there was no movement. He saw twisted bodies in room after room.

He peeked into his office. This required him to unblock the webcams peeking into his office using commands he obviously knew and... there was his body. His real body - in the same twisted death-thrall he was becoming so familiar with.

It hit him. He was really dead - in that body.

It was real, and now he was in a different, and female, body a thousand miles away. He hung his head and sobbed.

AFTER A WHILE he began to run the camera skipping program.

Mile after mile he saw tangled wreckage along the major highways. At airports he saw the flaming wreckage of planes. Using traffic cams, he saw whole neighborhoods burning - and some city streets and buildings as well - as it appeared that air traffic came raining down during the event, or right after.

On some camera shots he saw movement - or shadows of movement - that made him realize that there were other survivors like him, but not many.

Sometimes the movement was violent, as bodies seemed to clash in anger. Some views appeared as though weapons were flashing - but it was hard to tell without sound.

A security cam in Las Vegas caught various people fighting and killing each other in seemingly random ways. Thousands lay in the streets and sidewalks with neon lights playing over the dead.

Mile after mile. Death and silence - or deadly encounters highlighted by flickering flames. It was a nightmare in hell.

HE SKIPPED THE SMALL TOWNS, viewed all the large cities and finally reached downtown San Antonio, slowing the camera jumps.

There were surreal lights twinkling merrily in the night along the River Walk, reflecting along the San Antonio River, with drifting canal boats breaking the reflections and filled with dead tourist bodies.

Hundreds of bodies lay on the sidewalks lining both banks of the river - but here and there, he caught sight of people moving about, bending and searching. He saw one man beside a fallen police officer take the pistol from the officer's holster. He began to fire at someone on the other bank - mouthing and grimacing in hate.

Is this what it came to? The world has died and the survivors fighting and killing each other? Were they in hell?

SAM STOPPED THE PROGRAM and accessed cameras near his GPS location.

There were no cameras at the apartment complex, except for a pair of cameras mounted on the entrance and exit gates - apparently designed to record the comings and goings of vehicles. The focus was weird because they were designed to capture license plates.

He decided to look for cameras along the way where his attacker had run. He had the system search.

He got up from the couch, suddenly thirsty and very hungry. He went into the small kitchen to open the fridge. He found bottled water and an apple. He drank the water thirstily and ate the apple with gusto.

But then he felt pressure on his - actually her - bladder.

Man, he didn't want to deal with his - her - new body in that way! He didn't know what to do, or how - well, he did, but didn't want to think about it.

The urge came on too strong, so he looked for the bathroom praying that "she" would do the automatic thing...

BOY, THAT WAS WEIRD!

Luckily, her body knew what to do (like sitting down)... and ... stuff. Anyway, definitely weird.

Washing his hands, he got a good look at his new (female) body. She was REALLY good-looking. Fit and curvy with long dark hair, with an Indian (not feathers, but curry) cast to her features. Like a really attractive Bollywood star.

Even flushed, sweaty and with no make-up she was STILL a knockout. Great. Just great. It was not easy to get used to.

He walked out of the bathroom, back to the computer to see what the nearest cameras would show. The map showed cameras in a rather large building deeply inset into the woods and up on a hillside.

Most of the interior cameras were off in that building, where they showed up on his tracking program, except for surveillance cameras on the rooftop looking down to the entrance, as well as some cameras surveillancing two levels of parking.

The rooftop cameras were low light and were focused to see the road leading down to the entrance gates. There were two inactive cameras mounted outward from the gateposts, but he was unable to activate them.

He saw movement coming away and down from the building. It was an SUV. A cop car!

It was driving to the gate and it opened. The car disappeared down the road.

He pulled up a static satellite map and saw that the long road running by the apartment complex led to that strange building on the hill. That was where the booms and flashes came from.

A cop might be just what he needed.

But to intercept the car and flag it down, he'd have to risk going down there where he could run into that maniac. He looked around for something that he could defend himself with. Even if the dead lady owned a gun - and if he did find it - he wouldn't know how to use one in real-life. Clicking a mouse in a video game just wasn't the same.

Sam saw a knife block on the kitchen counter. He decided: I'm going to take the biggest knife I find and go down there. And, if I run into old foreign-language face, I'll gut 'im like a fish.

He grinned a very feral grin at this. He thought, Let's go!

IX. VICTOR

I DIDN'T GET VERY FAR.

I went through the gates down a road that was surrounded by fenced-in pastureland with fully grown mesquite and live oaks. This soon gave way to a wooden fence on the left side of the road. I could see what appeared to be two story condos or apartments peeking over the fence line.

I looked down the roadway and jammed on my brakes.

There, illuminated by my headlights, was a young lady waving her arms above her head for me to stop. She was quite striking and seemed to be out for a jog. Except that I spotted a rather large knife in one of her hands.

I opened my door quickly, after throwing the SUV into park, and placed my submachine gun in the crook of the door frame to steady the weapon. I activated the laser target directly on her forehead, just where a Hindu girl would place the dot on her own forehead. This struck me as quite apropos, as she looked like a beautiful Bollywood dancer.

I yelled, "Drop your weapon or I'll drop you!"

Her eyes widened in fear as she realized what the laser light on her forehead meant. She was one twitch away from getting her pretty little forehead split and splattered by bullets. I saw her stiffen in fear.

She screamed, "Please don't shoot! Please…"

I stood up and cleared the door while holding my target. I stepped sideways and growled, "Put your weapon down, now!"

She flinched, looked at her hand, and realized what she was holding. She immediately opened her hand, stiffly widening her fingers and the knife clattered to the ground, narrowly missing her foot. She looked back at me in fear. "Please don't shoot me!"

I said, "Now back away from your weapon and get on your knees."

She looked confused. I yelled, "Do it - now!"

She dropped to her knees. I felt a little bad because that had to hurt, given her bare legs. She must have skinned her knees something awful. I also opted to forgive her for ignoring the letter of my command to back away, and gave her credit for honoring the spirit by immediately dropping down on her bare knees.

"Now put your hands behind your head and interlock your fingers. Do it!"

She complied while babbling, "Please, officer! Please…"

I stepped up, while keeping the weapon pointed at her and kicked the knife away. I stepped back and brought the weapon down in the ready position using the chest sling.

"Now," I said, "what are you doing out here with a knife in your hand?"

She started to babble. Something about waking in the street, wrecked cars, bodies in the streets, cameras…

I yelled, "Stop!"

She immediately closed her mouth. I said, "Stand up and walk over to the car."

I sidestepped to her right. She stood up to comply, and I could see bloody abrasions on both knees glistening in the headlights. She limped over to the car, glancing at me uncertainly.

I motioned for her to sit sideways on the driver's seat looking out towards me. She hoisted herself up, and sat as indicated. I followed and stood facing her, ready to react. She would be pretty much hampered by her position, and, in any case, I figured I would be able to handle this girl, especially given the new body I was operating in. But better to err on the side of caution.

Anyway, I thought I was doing a pretty good job at imitating the tough cop.

I told her, "Now, let's start over. Take a deep breath, slow down. Tell me who you are."

I saw her take a breath - which caused some interesting and distracting pneumatics - and she began to speak. "My name is Sam."

"Well, Samantha, where did you come from and what were you doing?" I asked.

She looked up sharply at me and said, "It's SAM - not Samantha! And I'm not me... her... That's just it! I'm a dude, for crying out loud! And I don't know what's happening to me..."

She began her story...

"... AND THAT'S WHEN I RAN OUT HERE ON THIS ROAD. I saw your truck on the surveillance cam, and I knew you were a cop. At least, I hoped so." She looked up at me. "What's happened? Do you know?"

I listened to her - him, if she, or he, was to be believed - and saw the parallels in our experiences. It must have been really terrifying for her - him.

Damn, I'd have to pick a gender to think about this person. My eyes (and nose - she smelled like a sweaty woman - definitely not like a guy) was telling me that a very attractive girl was sitting in "my" cop car. Her experiences - not withstanding my shooting some guy - were worse than mine.

At least I had had the opportunity to "assimilate" to this new reality in a safe place - and with a hot shower. I had a name and some idea as to "my" new identity - while this poor dude didn't even have that. I had armor to protect me as well as some pretty nifty new skills and weapons.

She had running shorts, a sports bra, and a cheap kitchen knife.

I admired the way she adapted and overcame.

"I believe you, Sam," I said quietly. "I don't know what's happened, or why. But we need to find out."

Out of the corner of my eye, I saw some movement to my right, deep into the darkness. While the headlights reflecting off the road were highlighting me in the dark, the faint red glow from the parking lights in the rear helped illuminate the slight movement that I saw.

I started to turn to bring up the Sub-machine gun, when I heard popping sounds and saw flashes of fire coming from that source of movement. I felt a light punch on my side, and heard what sounded like Spanish cursing.

For some reason, the Spanish angered me more than the gunfire. I quickly knelt down, illuminated the target behind the flashes, and put three three-round bursts into the target, going from low to high.

Since the MPX was flash- and sound-suppressed, the rounds sounded like air bursts from a pellet or a paintball gun. I saw the immediate splash of red as all of the rounds found their mark.

More proof that I had acquired the abilities of this new body. I didn't think. I just acted.

I moved in a crouch, rapidly shuffling my feet and went over to the target. I put two rounds into his head while standing over the body. That's something I probably would do as a soldier - given my experience - but was surprised that a cop would do that. Apparently Vega's Special Forces training and experience took over as well.

I looked back at the sheriff's SUV and saw Sam standing there, crouched over with hands formed into claws and a face twisted by hate. The look wasn't for me, as she was looking at the body on the ground.

Suddenly she stood up, composed her face and gulped. I saw her looking at me. I realized my face was equally ferocious. I stood up and tried to smooth out my expression, as well.

"God," I said, "why do we feel that?"

She shook her head and said, "I don't know. Hearing a foreign language?"

"Bit of an over-reaction, don't you think?" I said with a grin.

I WAS PICKING A FLATTENED SLUG out of the armor on my right side (lucky shot, I thought, snarkily) and said softly, "Damn. This armor really works!" Up this close, that should have at least bruised or broken ribs, and maybe knocked me down. I barely felt it.

I told Sam, "That has happened to me, before - up there." I motioned my head toward the barely illuminated hulk of the building. "A guy came at me with a cleaver on the balcony. I shot him - and I felt nothing but hate."

Softly, "He was also yelling at me in a foreign language. So… why the extreme feeling of hate?"

"So that's what I heard coming off that hill," Sam said, quietly.

"Yeah, probably." I looked at her and said, "I need to tell you my story, and then we can compare notes and try to figure out what this is all about… But it's not safe for you - or me - here, so let's drive and do some scouting."

"No shit," said Sam, "but I have a suggestion…"

I looked at her with a raised eyebrow. She - he - whatever - seemed remarkably calm after seeing a person so violently torn apart by SMG fire. For that matter, so was I.

Was this guy - and the last one I shot - a regular person, just like us? Were they scared and confused, just as we were. I had the feeling that it was so.

Sam said, "Look, I've been out there a ways. There are wrecks blocking the way and dead bodies all over. The highways are a nightmare. I saw all of that on the cams I accessed 'coming' from the West Coast. I can't imagine it will be any different in the city - or any other cities, for that matter."

"Okay?...so…?"

"Well, I just think it would be better to do some exploring virtually - not put ourselves in any more danger," she said. "Anyway, I'm beat. I'm hungry and thirsty and damned tired.

If I can get to a computer, I can do all the exploring that we need to plan a route and to sniff out any danger. Any computers up there?"

I grinned, "Well, you'll probably be disappointed. I saw a computer in… my… in Victor's office. But the power and Ethernet cord weren't set up. Should be easy enough to do, though."

"Who's Victor?"

"Well … Me, I suppose. This body I'm walking around in."

"You mean you aren't you also… er… as well!? Then who are you? I mean… who were you?"

I shook my head, barely smiling. "Doesn't really matter, at this point." I motioned to the car.

"Get in. We need to get out of here. Come on, I'll tell you my story driving to the building."

She nodded and went around to the passenger side, opened the door and climbed in. She sat back wearily as I walked over to pick up the gun the dude used. It was a nine mm Cop's gun. A Glock. I racked the slide part way back and saw a round chambered, then dropped the mag. One more in the magazine. I reseated the mag and walked over to the car.

I handed the Glock to Sam and said, "Here, hold this." She took it awkwardly and looked a little afraid to hold it. I started up the car and did a "U-ie," heading back to the building on the hillside.

She sighed and asked, "What is that building, anyway?"

"I don't know, really," I replied. "A news clipping I found inside called it 'Gore's Folly'..."

"WHAT!" She sat up suddenly. "THAT's Gore's Folly??!!" She chuckled, excitedly.

I looked over, puzzled. "Yeeaahh?... So you know the place?"

"Man, oh man! This is perfect!"

"What's perfect?"

She laughed delightedly. "Man, only the answer to our dreams! The perfect place... probably the ONLY place ... for long term survival in this... this... apocalypse!"

"Yeah?" I was puzzled.

"You'll see. I'll tell you all about it - after you tell me your story." She looked up at the building, ducking down to get a better view through the windshield.

"But I'll tell you this... it may mean our salvation, and a way to find out what's happening." She turned and looked at me. "It will be our protection... our Fortress..."

BOOK TWO: BOOK OF LISTS

See, the Lord is going to lay waste the earth and devastate it; he will ruin
its face and scatter its inhabitants—

(Isaiah 24.1)

They have given the dead bodies of your servants as food to the birds of
the air, the flesh of your saints to the beasts of the earth.

(Psalm 79:2)

I. SAM's LOG

THE BODIES.

It was time to do something.

Look - with several million dead bodies in the metro area, rotting in the
Texas heat, it was going to get toxic really, really fast.

But I better start from the beginning - what Victor and I agreed upon,
speculated about, and confirmed that first night in Gore's Folly. Victor
didn't agree we should call the building "The Fortress." He said it was too
melodramatic. He said, "I know how you girls like melodrama…"

I looked up and yelled, "Hey! I told you I'm not…"

I saw his smirk and realized he was busting my balls… so to speak.

41

Besides, I could guess at his politics, and he liked the idea of tweaking my liberal sensibilities, and liked the idea of calling anything "Gore's Folly." So, I just shut up about it. Anyway, this was much later on.

As we drove up to the building, we were both lost in our thoughts. I considered what I knew about this building. My employer had sunk about a billion into the development, so I actually knew quite a bit. What I didn't know fully, I could find out with a little digging with a computer.

Gore's Folly - or the Alternatives Green Technology Building - was designed to be the proving ground for all kinds of experimental technology. From advanced bio-mass energy production, to solar-power and wind, to advanced recycling, manufacture, and reuse, to 3D printing parts production... to... just about everything you can think of ... short of nuclear power ... to colonize Mars, survive on the moon or go into interstellar space. It was AWESOME!

And an awesome failure.

Not the technology - just the intent. It was thought businesses would flock to it. But... no. The location was just too out of the way. While energy production was essentially "free", the initial investment was costly, and the investors had to recoup.

So the building sat idle, until a few specialized companies (and apparently "Victor's" gym) were offered bargain-basement pricing. They did not depend on location. Just space. And when the investors were looking to recoup any of their investment, the price on that space began falling.

I looked at Victor and said, "You didn't happen to see the building control room or utility room when looking around by any chance?"

"No. Like I said, I only saw part of the third level, the stairs and the parking garage." He glanced at me. "Why?"

"I believe we may have access to some of the most advanced computing power and wide band access in the area," I told him. I grinned, "No need to set up the computer in your office if we locate the control room."

He grunted.

On the way there, he had told me what was, I presumed, a shortened version of his experiences. He wasn't much for details, but I got the gist enough to see parallels and to begin drawing some conclusions.

As we pulled into the parking garage, I got a sense of just how BIG this place was! The ceiling of the garage was at least two stories high. I also saw a ramp and signs leading to what was apparently an underground section.

He said, "Let's drive down there and see what's what, before doing anything else."

THE RAMP CURVED DOWN and switched back four times, but didn't give me the claustrophobic heebie-jeebies since it was really wide and the roof was way up. The curves were such, and ramp so wide, that an eighteen-wheeler could easily come down here, without hanging up on the curves. I noticed the down ramp was one-way, so there must be an up-ramp, elsewhere. I figured that we would find the loading docks and freight elevators at the bottom of this ramp and, maybe, equipment room access.

I was proved right, as we came to the bottom level. It, like the previous level, was enormous. I could see loading docks on the back wall of this giant cavern. There was also one lone truck - or van - I couldn't decide which - parked in the back next to the loading docks.

The van - or truck - was black and looked like an oversized bread truck. As we pulled up beside it, I could see large, reflective decals that read "Bexar County SWAT." I turned to Victor and asked, "Yours?" He shook his head, "I don't know. The article said Victor was head of 'Criminal Apprehension' - not SWAT. Maybe they share stuff?" He shrugged. "Don't know why it's parked here. Maybe ol' Vic was using government property as a moving van. Dunno."

"Hmmm."

We both opened our doors and stepped out. I was still holding the gun Victor had handed to me. It made me a little uncomfortable, but I didn't want to look like a weenie. So I held it with both hands, like I've seen cops in movies do it, and pointed it down and away from me, at the ready. It was lighter than I imagined.

"Um… you might want to take your finger off the trigger and lay it on the slide. You might shoot yourself." I sort of flinched and complied. He was, of course, grinning.

We walked up to the van and "Victor" (he still hadn't told me his "other life's" name) pulled out his keys. There were only three keys on the key chain besides the electronic fob. One was for the SUV. That left two. He tried the other two keys on the van door - no luck - and then went around to the back door. It was secured with a sturdy-looking padlock on the bottom latching-handle. He tried both keys, again with no success.

He went around the side, climbed up on the panels, and peeked in.

"See anything?"

"Nah…" he shook his head and jumped down.

"So?" I asked.

He didn't answer and moved to the loading dock stairs. "Stay behind me." He paused and looked at me. "Just don't shoot me."

I think he was serious.

We climbed up the left hand set of stairs. There were three over-sized doors I presumed to be freight elevators; a smaller door to the right of those (a passenger elevator, obviously,) a clearly marked stairwell door, and a door with no markings. All were deeply inset under a slight overhang.

There were a couple of forklifts backed into their charging stations, and some hand-trucks and assorted dollies. I could also see - to the right of the loading docks - what appeared to be a business front, which was odd to me. But not apparently to Victor, as he grunted, "A custom-car shop. Makes sense to set up down here."

It didn't to me. What the heck for?

I could see a large, metal hatch to our immediate right labeled "Bio-Materials Loading." It was built to have trucks back into it and deposit whatever they were meant to deposit. I bet I knew what, and I was about to mention it to Victor, when he interrupted - apparently focused on the car shop.

"Let's go check it out," he said.

AFTER CLIMBING DOWN THE RIGHT hand stairs on the far right of the loading dock, we went about a 100 yards to where the shop was. There, a bunch of cool-looking cars were parked in front (again, it seemed odd to me to see a "building in a building" in this underground garage) and there was one twisted body by the parked cars.

Inside, after carefully easing our way into the interior via the open car bays, we found a lot of neat machinery, machine tools, lifts, and cars (some in the throes of disassembly or, perhaps, re-assembly, I don't know.)

And bodies. Lots of them.

I assume mechanics, machinists, laborers and the like. Inside the office part, we found clerk types, as well. They were all dead.

"Man," I breathed, softly.

Victor seemed less... moved. Distant from all the death around us. I began to wonder about this guy.

He cocked his head, curiously and asked softly, "I wonder why?" He looked up and said, "Why they are dead... and not us... or the guys I killed out there?"

I knew what he meant. "I've been thinking about that. I have a theory."

I didn't tell Victor my theory just then. Only later when I was able to check some facts, do some observation and some - if I do say so myself - outstanding computing.

AFTER CHECKING OUT THE CAR SHOP, Victor and I made our way back to the loading docks.

We went up to the passenger elevator door, and Victor said, "I propose that we explore, level by level, beginning on the first level, and then - depending on what we find - we can go back to 'my' gym. Are you up to it?"

I felt bushed - and hungry. But I smiled gamely, "Sure. Let's go. We need to find the control room, though. I would have thought it would be on this level. Doesn't make sense that it's not."

"Maybe it's behind 'Door Number Three'," Victor said, motioning with his head toward the unmarked doorway.

I looked up, innocently, and said with a straight face, "Three? But there're five doors…"

He shook his head and said, "No… it's an old game show reference…"

He stopped when he saw my grin and said, "Quit tryin' to make me feel like an old man! In this body, I'm not much older than you!"

We moved to the door. It was one of those metal doors that have a thick glass inset at head height. But this one was frosted and had metal rods crisscrossing through it.

I grinned and said, excitedly, "This must be it!" I recognized the "look" of the secured doorways that we often used at Google HQ for computer rooms, and such. Pretty non-descript.

I tried the handle - and of course it was locked.

I looked up at Victor.

He looked down at me and said, "I suppose we could use C4 and blow it open."

"Really? Cool."

"No. Don't be silly," He said scornfully.

"But we gotta get in there," I said.

He looked thoughtful for a minute, then said, "Hmmm… wait here, little lady," and jumped off the loading dock and took off at a trot.

Little lady! "Hey! I TOLD you I'm not…"

Grrr! I vowed I'd kick him in the balls when he got back!

II. VICTOR

VICTOR STILL HADN'T GOT used to this girl - who claimed to be a guy - and was fairly uncomfortable even thinking about the subject.

Victor still felt "60 plus" inside, despite his transition into this younger body, and he felt protective of this younger girl. She was the age of his youngest daughter, and so those fatherly feelings were understandable. But "she" was a "he" inside - just as Victor was an old man inside. Confusing, to say the least.

Victor trotted up to the Sheriff's car and, once again, opened the back hatch.

He placed the MPX SMG and the extra mags in their place and secured them. He then took one of the Remingtons and extracted the rounds from the shotgun, then placed them in a shell-holder on the strap.

He then looked for the shells he needed and loaded two of them, just in case.

He also pulled out a couple of presents for Sam.

He went back to the loading docks and walked up to the door. He ignored the evil eye Sam was giving him.

"Here," he said, "for you."

He handed her a pair of pink foam earplugs and safety glasses.

He took the Glock from her hand and ejected the magazine. He took out a fully loaded mag and inserted it. He then handed the weapon back.

He looked back at her and said, "Cover your ears and step way back," before inserting his own earplugs. He also donned his protective goggles. He waited for her to do the same.

He racked the breaching load and aimed at the door lock. He had never done this in his life, but knew the procedure from watching The Military Channel on TV. There was not much call for breaching flimsy hootch doorways in 'NAM.

He looked back at Sam, who was covering her ears, despite the ear-plugs, knowing what was coming - probably from playing video games, no doubt. He mouthed, "Ready?" to her. She nodded.

BLAM!

The round did what it was supposed to do. It blew the lock off. He also felt the thud of metal fragments hitting his armor AND his goggles.

He also felt a sting on his cheek. Good thing he had been smart enough to use the protective gear.

He looked back to Sam to see if she was Okay. She was grinning ear to ear and said, "That was totally AWESOME!"

At that moment, Victor was struck by the fact that this person - this very pretty girl - was really a young guy. He felt genuine sorrow and empathy for the changes this poor kid was going through. He thought of his own boys, and wondered if they could have adapted so well.

Sam saw him looking at her and said, "What?"

Victor shook his head and said, "Let me go in first. You follow, and back me up."

He then ejected the remaining breaching load, and inserted the man-killers. He said, "Ready?" Sam nodded and Victor went in.

III. SAM's LOG

WHAT WE FOUND INSIDE THE door was a wonderland. A veritable playground to warm the cockles of any nerd's heart.

Victor seemed less than excited as he shuffled up and down the hallways with his shotgun at the ready, and peeking in at the various glass-enclosed rooms lined with racks and racks of servers, monitors and blinking lights.

It was much colder down here - in fact, too cold for my flimsy outfit. I hugged myself for warmth. I shivered and said, "Man, it's cold here!"

Victor glanced at me - then down a bit - and said, "Yeah. I can see that." Before I could react to his grin, he said, "Wait here..." He hurried down the hall, turned the corner and disappeared from view.

Man, now I REALLY wanted to kick him.

I took the opportunity to look into the room I believed was the control room. I saw large monitors and keyboards. I thought I should be able to reach the 'Net from here, provided there was access. My experience told me that there would be.

I went to the doorway. It had a numbered keypad, but no card swipe. Apparently, to gain access, I would have to figure out the code. Sometimes easy. Sometimes hard. It was better than having to hack a card swipe with no equipment, so I counted my blessings.

I saw that the keypad was lined by touch sensitive Gorilla Glass. I went up to it and breathed on it. Sure enough, the steam from my breath highlighted distinct smudges on three numbers: one, nine and zero. It was highly unlikely that they would use a three number code. Maybe four to six, but not three. So some numbers would repeat. This made the combo more difficult, but not impossible, to figure out.

If it was a three number combo, there would be 27 permutations. For a four number combo, 81 permutations. For five - 243 and for six - 729. Nice. Could be done. I used to do this in my hacker days with... ahem! ...borrowed ATM cards.

I was willing to bet on human nature, which leans toward laziness with just enough attention to "complexity" to assuage guilt. So four numbers would be just lazy enough. Besides, most PINs are four digits, and people are creatures of habit, so go with the norm.

So, 81 permutations.

I bet myself I could, with a little thought, get it on the first or second try.

No need to go through any permutations. I entered "zero nine one one" and... Yahtzee! I was in!

I smugly stepped through the open doorway. Let's see Mr. Muscles get in without breaking the door down.

I was afraid he'd do just that, so I looked for something to prop the door open. I saw a large printed binder that would do the trick. Now, to look around at the goodies available.

I WON'T BORE YOU WITH THE DETAILS of the control room - except for one thing. It had the usual large screen monitors and input devices. The monitors were, of course, touch sensitive to take advantage of the latest fad of wipe-able iconographic activations and motion sensing.

One very large monitor had thumbnail representations of what appeared to be security cams in the building. Just as I had seen remotely on the dead lady's notebook, the only 'cams that were active were the two on the rooftop looking down on the driveway, leading away from the parking structure. The rest of the thumbnail views were black.

There were over eighty thumbnail cam views. I ran my finger over the blank ones and they activated, one by one - with a couple of exceptions. There must have been an electrical or mechanical problem on those. It was, of course, difficult to see any real detail on such tiny representations.

They were either programmed to cycle through large views (probably to reduce boredom) or the "watcher" had to expand the views manually. Probably both. There was a fairly large empty part of the screen at the bottom.

I experimented by dragging four "tiles" or thumbnail views to that part of the screen. Sure enough, the cam views popped into place at a consistent size to make detailed viewing possible. There was enough room to expand four more views.

Cool.

A ghosted menu appeared at the bottom, offering set-up choices. I set the choice to "Cycle'" and pulled down an "Interval" setting and chose the "Every 30 secs." by highlighting the choice.

That done, I moved to the other console and monitor. It was running a version of Windows on top of Linux. I brought up a browser and got to work.

I LOST TRACK OF TIME until I heard Victor clear his throat behind me to get my attention. I turned around quickly and smiled excitedly.

"Ummm..." he said, "Nice work getting the door open."

"Thanks!... but get a load of what I've found!"

"OK," he said, "But I have some presents for you."

He handed me a bunched-up jacket with bottles of water wrapped up in it, along with some vending machine sandwiches, assorted chips and some nut bars. My mouth watered instantly. Man! I was hungry, cold and very thirsty. I looked up in gratitude.

"Where'd you find this?"

"I found the employee locker-room and the break room. There were vending machines there," he said, "along with three bodies."

I said, "Ummm... this jacket didn't come from...?"

"No, no," he said quickly, "I found that in the locker room."

"Good." I put the jacket on gratefully. It was warm.

We both uncapped the water bottles and drank thirstily. Then we tore into the sandwich packages and chips. I don't really remember what they were, but they tasted mighty good to me. We wolfed them down.

Swallowing, I said, "Where'd you get the change for the machines?"

He grinned and lifted the butt stock of his shotgun. "Who needs money?"

Figured.

We were silent for a while (well, except for the chewing, swallowing and gulping.)

Victor unwrapped a candy bar, stared at it a while, and set it aside, distastefully. He said quietly, almost to himself, "I guess I don't eat sugar. God. I hope this guy's not a health nut!"

Having a different body with different wants and needs was definitely going to be strange.

He looked at me and said, "OK. Tell me what you've found."

I explained.

LOOK, I DON'T WANT to recount what I said to Victor. Frankly, I don't remember my exact words, or the order I explained my doings and findings.

Here is the gist of what I told him:

I had accessed the Google servers and controlling software, virtually duplicating what I could do from my erstwhile office. I then tapped into every social media outlet and forum doing two things:

First, I planted a 'bot to "listen" for any chatter on those sites - kind of what Homeland Security does to listen for any terrorist activity - only mine was a whole lot easier. I didn't have to provide a lexicon of keywords - just "listen" for ANY activity or access to the sites. (No wonder the NSA wanted to "hire" me.)

Second, I posted a "push-banner" to all the sites that - upon login - would "push" a message to the user to respond to #BodyTransferEvent. It asked people to post their experiences, what they knew, what the effect was in their part of the world, and so on. The banner would funnel all the input to a site I could control and filter.

Next, I wrote a little routine that would access all of the secret intelligence organizations' spy satellites. That included all imaging satellites that were filtered by the (again) secret AI (artificial intelligence) routines to capture any "anomalous events."

These "events" were pre-defined by a set of menus I had hacked earlier in my career (in fact, that's what got me busted by the Feds.) I set the parameters to look for traffic tie-ups (including car crashes), airplane crashes, big fires, explosions, "mass casualties" - which should fit the bill when looking for dead bodies in the streets, and so on.

... "and that should calculate the number of deaths associated with whatever is happening out there," I said, "and tell us how extensive this may be."

Victor yawned loudly and said, "Well, we know the 'Net newsfeeds are silent, but we haven't checked 'old school' into radio and TV."

I stared at him and thought, "Duh. How could I have missed that?!"

That turned out to be a dead end, as well. We looked for a radio or a TV, but none was to be found. We needed to see broadcast and/or cable to be sure this wasn't just a 'Net glitch. Even radio apps were not a good indicator, as they could be compromised.

But, just in case, I used the phone I had which had an iHeart Radio app on it and went to "local stations". I found dead air or automated programming - but no "live" broadcasting.

Victor, still yawning through his words said, "Look. I saw some couches in the employee lounge. What say we try to get some shuteye and go fresh in the morning? I'm about dead. You can tell me your theories when I'm less brain dead."

I agreed to that wholeheartedly.

We walked wearily to the lounge and said, mostly to myself, "I wonder if, when we wake up, this will all have been a dream?"

It wasn't, Auntie Em. It wasn't.

IV. VICTOR

VICTOR WOKE UP CRAMPED and with his legs folded on the way-too-small couch. There was a definite disadvantage to extra height. He sat up and stretched to get the kinks out, feeling every sore spot from the seizure event yesterday.

Sam lay snoring daintily on one of the other couches. She lay huddled up underneath a first-aid warming blanket that Victor had found while searching one of the cabinets. She would definitely be disappointed to wake and find that this was, indeed, not a dream and that this was their new reality.

It had taken some convincing to get Sam to use the employee lounge after she saw the three bodies near the cabinets that held a coffee machine and all the fixings. Victor had to drag the bodies out by their feet to a far corridor around the corner, wincing every time they bumped their heads on a threshold.

It was undignified, especially for the one female that was wearing a skirt that kept hiking up to her waist. It made him sad, and he thought of what his wife and daughter might be going through, if they were alive.

By the time Victor was finished with the last body, Sam had fallen asleep.

Victor had removed his equipment and armor, but left his BDUs on for warmth. He had been too exhausted to even remove his boots. He fell asleep almost instantly.

Now that he was awake, he needed to think about what needed to be done. He sat with his face in his hands, rubbing his face in an unconscious habit that had been part of his "previous" life.

He got up and decided to make some coffee. As he was doing so, he could hear Sam stirring. Then, he heard a groan. He turned around and saw her looking at him.

He said to her, "Sorry. Not a dream... Coffee?"

She groaned again and plopped her head on the couch. "No... thanks."

Victor nodded his head and turned back to make the coffee.

As he took his first sip, he asked, "Hungry?"

She shook her head, no. "What time is it?" She asked sleepily. He woke up his phone display and showed her the time. It was 6:00 AM.

He said, "You probably need to clean up. There're showers in the employee locker room, and maybe you can find something else to put on by rummaging in there."

"What are you going to be doing?" she asked.

He motioned with his head and said, "I'm going back out there and see what I find. You need to see what your computers have found, and when I get back we can talk about what we both think is going on - and what to do next."

He picked up a phone, went to the 'Contacts' to display a number and showed it to her. "I picked up this phone from... one of the... um... people I found here and added my number in the contacts - call me if you need me, or anything." She nodded.

Victor put on his equipment and armor, then left the room and went back out to the loading dock. He went to his SUV and put the shotgun away, opting to carry the Colt Commando and extra ammo in case he needed to take a longer shot than the submachine gun would allow. He briefly considered taking the M16, but the Colt was equipped with a suppressor and had pretty fair optics, so he chose that.

He once again drove out through the gates and then stopped. He got out of the car to look back at the building - this time in daylight. Man, was it big! It seemed to recede into the hilltop, and he couldn't see the roofline from this vantage point.

He got back in and cranked up the AC - it was really starting to warm up out here - even this early.

He drove on down the road and came to the place where he had first spotted Sam. He stopped.

There was a body on the road - obviously the guy he'd shot - but it was hardly recognizable as human. There were vultures all around the body doing their thing. They had the body stripped to the bone, making it look like road kill dressed in rags and shoes. The vultures were so full that they didn't even take off when he pulled up.

He drove on, going around the vulture feast. One less body to be concerned about. From what Sam described, there would be a whole lot more.

WHEN HE GOT TO THE ROAD after going a couple of miles, he saw that it teed off right and left. The GPS Map showed that the left went toward IH-10, while the right led to some winding ranch roads. He chose to go to the right, past the apartment complex he had seen, and that Sam had mentioned. The gates were open, leading to a parking lot with a few cars and some dead bodies. There were a few vultures, feasting.

He drove on and came to a tangle of cars. They were strewn about the road and some over the sidewalks. All had bodies inside. This part of the street was impassable.

He thought about getting out and driving some of the cars out of his way, but he decided that, after spending the night in this Texas heat in enclosed cars, the bodies would be pretty ripe.

He decided to push what cars he could, using the reinforced grill "deer catcher" mounted on the SUV. That might not work with the big pickup trucks that were pretty prevalent here. But he would do what he could, and pick his spots and go over sidewalks, or whatever worked.

Using that technique, he got to some clear roadway where some cars were askew on the road, but not blocking it. He stopped when he spotted an SAPD cop car with its driver side door open and a uniformed figure hanging halfway out. He picked up the Colt and opened his door to go over, cautiously, to the car.

He moved up to it, always vigilant for any movement. His senses heightened in the familiar way they had some 40 years ago when he had been in combat. He had forgotten how much of a rush it was. Like most combat vets, he would never admit to this atavistic feeling, except to those that had similar experiences - and then only with trustworthy comrades in arms. Certainly never to his family or friends.

He shuffled over in the crouched posture assumed by soldiers, cops and others accustomed to impending violence. He got to the car and saw that the cop - an Hispanic looking man - had been partially pulled from the vehicle just enough to remove his gun from its holster, which was unsnapped. The cop's extra mags and his Tazer and his mace were still on the utility belt. Victor suspected that this was the gun Sam's attacker had found and used.

Victor looked at the cop's name tag, which read "Tellez" and said, "Sorry this happened to you officer Tellez." Then he reached over to pull the mags, the Tazer and mace from the belt. He didn't bother with the cuffs. He didn't plan on arresting anyone soon. He put the mags and the other equipment in his car.

He then went back to the cop car and popped the trunk from the inside. He went around to the trunk and found what he expected - an M4 and a combat shotgun, along with the respective ammo. He also found some road flares and took these as well. He placed the items in his SUV, got in and drove off.

When he came to the highway access road, he could see that the highway crossed over an underpass. He was stopped at a four-way stop sign at the access road facing the overpass "tunnel" formed by the highway. What was unusual was that the access road was a two-way, which he wasn't used to. Across the highway overpass, he could see another four way stop sign, with that access road being a two way as well.

Blue and white highway signs pointed to "IH-10" going east toward San Antonio and west toward someplace called "Boerne." He remembered this town from his Camp Bullis days as a very small place out in "the sticks." Apparently San Antonio had spread its urbanity toward Boerne, as he could see signs of restaurants and businesses all along the highway.

He couldn't see what was directly on the highway ahead of him due to its height, but he saw down the highway as it sloped down to street level. What he saw was a tangled mess of cars and trucks - all smashed in and some smoke rising from some of the smoldering hulks.

He noticed movement coming from his right, going west.

It was a car.

The driver stopped at the stop sign and his passenger, a blonde woman, looked directly at Victor with her mouth opened in surprise. The driver turned to look, equally surprised.

They sat there, stunned. Victor hit the gas, got right in front of the car blocking it.

Victor quickly got out of the SUV, got behind the hood, and pointed the deadly looking Colt directly at the driver. He yelled, "Turn off your car and get out immediately with your hands up, or I will shoot you!"

The next few moments he would know if they spoke and understood his language, and whether they would live or die. It scared him that he was thrilled to have the latter possibility come true. It scared him how much he wanted that.

V. SAM's LOG

VICTOR STILL HADN'T gotten back by the time I showered and took care of ... other business. This being a girl thing was WAY weird!

Luckily, I found some (at least I hoped) clean sweats in the ladies' locker room that were a bit big for me, but not too bad. But, unfortunately, no undies.

I decided to wash the (shudder) sports bra and panties (and my grungy socks) under very hot water with a little shampoo.

I dried them under the wall-mounted hand dryer, put them on, and put on the too-big sweat pants, having to roll them up a bit at the cuff.

I put the sports bra on (THAT takes some getting used to), but decided not to use the sweat shirt - opting for the jacket that Victor had found for me.

I tried brushing my teeth with my finger and some shampoo, but that was disgusting. I rinsed out my mouth thoroughly, but the bad taste of the shampoo lingered all day.

NOTE TO SELF: Get some toiletries and clothes that fit!

I looked at "myself" in the mirror.

Her (my) hair was loose, wet, and looked a bit curly. I (she) was a babe. I wouldn't have stood a chance with me - her - in ANY reality.

Yeah, I (the former male "me") was pulling down some very nice scratch being a big-wig at Google, but even with the nerd-chic trend going, I wouldn't have dared talked to this babe.

This kind of circular and confused thinking was driving me nuts! We needed new pronouns!

I decided to do what I do best.

I went back to the control room and looked at the data my 'bots had gathered.

[I need to stop here and add a parenthetical. I'm sitting here recording on video, but my early descriptions of Victor's and my initial experiences were "written" - electronically - and I haven't gone back to record that transcript on video.

Hopefully it won't get lost - given what we know now - but I'm not too worried about what wasn't videoed. Everyone that has gone through this experience knows what we went through in terms of coming to grips with our circumstances... Not to mention surviving those first few months. And that IS everyone - except for our future descendants, if we survive to have any.

We decided to use video as a storage medium for a lot of reasons. There are consequences of living in this new world and the long term resources that are available to us. I am going to cover things we came to know as we experienced them, and as we came to some realizations about the LONG term implications of the "Event."

I will be recounting some things, but not necessarily as they happened. This is the value of hindsight. So here goes.]

One of the first things I checked were responses or pings of any login activity or postings on the "banner-push ads" on all the social media sites.

I don't know what I expected since these sites were worldwide, but certainly not the mere thousand or so logins and the mere hundreds of responses to the posting request. Even posted in English, pushed banner ads should be generating millions of responses, worldwide!

I noticed that the response to the banner push somewhat equaled the English logins. The logins in foreign languages (even though they were gibberish to me) were not responding to the banner push request at all.

As I thought about it, that made sense. Since WE couldn't read foreign words - maybe foreigners couldn't read English, either. Maybe their minds skittered around the words like ours did.

Secondly, the views through the 'cams made me think that a great percentage of the population had died - either coming through the event, in accidents - or by violent action afterward.

If Victor and I were a representative example of survivors, we had -

well, Victor had - accounted for the death of an equal number of survivors.

The violence I had seen on the street 'cams in Vegas and on the River Walk 'cams in San Antonio showed that the small number of survivors seemed prone to violent action against others.

I was guessing this was triggered by a kind of xenophobia. A linguistic, violent kind of xenophobia.

I gathered, and sifted through, the various postings. Most of the postings were from people that were in a fairly "safe" place - mostly in the U.S. and the U.K.

Very little violence was taking place in those areas - although some. And the violence that was reported was as we had experienced it - violence AGAINST and FROM people of other linguistic... persuasions.

But all of the people described their inability to speak, comprehend, or even read, other than their own native language.

Most of the people posting had, in their "former selves," spoken, or could read, a smattering of other languages - but they could not now.

Even "common" foreign words that had become a part of the English-language idiom were now unthinkable.

One of the posters had an example: "We all know the word for the dish of Japanese raw fish, rice-and-seaweed-wrapped rolls - so why can't we say or read the word? It's on a lot of menus! It's driving me nuts!"

Now, it was driving ME nuts!

Oh. And that other... "small"... issue: all the responders reported having gone into another body and geography.

Here's what we know, now:

By some act of God, space-aliens, government-experiment-gone-wrong, magic spell or odd quantum event - ALL the population of the earth had their minds (or souls, or whatever) RIPPED from their own bodies and scattered willy-nilly across the planet to land in OTHER bodies, not their own.

The consequences of this were varied:

First: this transference was so traumatic that all the people transferred (apparently EVERYONE in the world) instantly went into violent grand mal seizures. A very small number, according to what we have seen in the streets, survived this.

Second: Even if you were "lucky" enough to survive the event itself, there was a possibility that you died falling down stairs, traveling by car, boat, train or plane (think about the loss of control of driver, pilot, or whatever), having a plane drop on your house, a fire due to crashes, while swimming etc. It was a dangerous, active world.

Third: By all reports (even of those encounters with "foreigners") only a narrow band of "receiving bodies" seemed to have survived the transfer. There were no children, no elderly, no sick.

In fact, it was easier to describe the survivors: generally young - between 18 to 40 - and athletic or physically fit. That's it. No others. Anywhere.

That was a lot of people who wouldn't fit the criteria.

Hence, a lot of people dead.

There was a lot of visual evidence, as well. Detailed satellite images showed scores of dead bodies in the streets, busted up cars along superhighways, as well as on dirt roads, buildings and whole neighborhoods razed by plane crashes, and out-of-control fires raging worldwide.

Where the world had been in the middle of sleep-time, there had been fewer people about at that time and hence less traffic - and, therefore, fewer accidents visible on the streets.

Presumably the majority of people had been in their dwellings, so that accounted for some of the nearly body-free streets.

People had died in the transition most likely in their sleep. Those that survived (the young and athletic) were now out and about in the daylight trying to make sense of their world.

And now, we could see more evidence of violence, with large groups clashing. It was odd.

This is the theory we (the posters) came up with to account for the strangeness of the "linguistic xenophobia":

Now, please bear with me. This is simple - therefore more difficult to explain, simply. That's the paradox of ideas.

We're going to concentrate primarily on the top eight languages spoken natively across the globe.

These are: Mandarin; English; Spanish; Hindi; Russian; Arabic; Portuguese; Bengali and French in that order (There are really 30 some-odd languages, but for the purposes of this thought model, this is simpler.)

Picture the world map laid out before you. And let's assign colors to the countries and continents where a language has predominance.

For example: the Western Hemisphere would have only four colors dominating the continents. North America would be tinted BLUE for English, from the border of Mexico well into Canada - with the exception of the Province of Quebec, which is predominately French-speaking. Let's tinge this anomaly RED.

Central and South America we would color Green for Spanish - except for another anomaly, Brazil, where Portuguese is spoken. Let's use Yellow for this.

We move on to tinge Australia BLUE, along with England and some parts of Africa, where English is the official language. I hope you're getting the picture: Asia would be dominated by four other "colors" - or languages - Russian, Mandarin, Hindi and Bengali. The Middle East, Arabic. Europe and Africa would be a mishmash by country. French would hold sway not only in France and Belgium, but in large parts of Africa.

Realistically, the map would not be so pure, as in any given moment there are immigrants (legal or otherwise), visitors (tourists, business people,) and so on, living amongst these pristine "colors."

For example, the Southwestern borders of the U.S. would be "tinged" by the Green - especially as there are millions of Spanish speakers spread out around the Southwest. It would be the same for Canada, with the French language encroaching beyond Quebec.

But here's a look at how the native-language speakers break out around the globe by continent. Believe me, I was VERY surprised!

North America		South America	
English	70%	Spanish	58%
Spanish	9%	Portuguese	33%
French	3%	English	1%
Mandarin	1%	Other	8%
Other	17%		
Europe		Africa	
Russian	22%	Arabic	17%
English	8%	French	6%
French	8%	English	4%
Spanish	6%	Other	73%
Other	56%		
ASIA			
Mandarin	33%		
Hindi/Bengali	20%		
Other	47%		

Now, by POPULATION, these numbers come to mean something as to the DENSITY of the different "hues" on the map. Take a look at this:

Native Speakers Globally	
Mandarin	1,151,000,000
English	1,000,000,000
Spanish	500,000,000
Hindi	490,000,000
Russian	277,000,000
Arabic	255,000,000
Portuguese	240,000,000
Bengali	215,000,000
French	200,000,000
Other	4,328,000,000
Total	8.656,000,000

Again, I was surprised by these numbers. I would never have thought that English was JUST under Chinese, and that Spanish was in the top three!

That said, we used a thought model to picture what had happened - but not why. Cause is unknowable and really not germane to our situation.

(Makes for great late evening philosophizing, though. I'm more in the Space Alien or Quantum Event camp, while Victor is more of an Act of God kind of guy. He calls it "The New Tower of Babel.")

Here's the thought model that serves our purposes:

Now, I gotta credit Victor, somewhat, for this idea, since he brought it up.

It was bolstered by a friend of mine - in my previous geek life - that collected antique, esoteric toys. I thought of that when Victor talked about remembering a Cracker Jacks toy from his childhood.

I'd actually seen something like it in my friend's collection. This was a skill toy that was a flat piece of cardboard with a flimsy transparent plastic dome covering it. The cardboard had several colored dimples in which corresponding colored "b-b's" could rest.

The idea was to shake the toy up and down, mixing up the "b-b's" and trying to see if they landed on their matching colored dimples.

It was an exercise in probabilities.

Now think of the world map with the colors corresponding to the "density" of native languages spoken - the "dimples" if you will.

The colored b-b's are the 8.5 BILLION people that speak their own "hard-wired" native tongue. The world gets shaken up (aliens, God... who knows?) and the minds of 8.5 Billion people are thrown up into the figurative air and... come down who knows where.

What are the odds, given the disparity of native languages spoken, coupled with the geographical density, that any one b-b would "land" on their own corresponding color? That is - a body that would match their own hard wired tongue? And what if this "match" accounted for survivability?

OK. So now, this becomes a matter of calculating the probabilities of "the event." That's MY world.

So using the loose observational parameters (and admitted guesswork) of a narrow band of "18 to 40 year-olds" surviving; relative fitness or athleticism; accidents taking the life of potential survivors; the language populations and geo-density to match up minds to bodies - I was able to establish a set of criteria upon which to build an algorithm to calculate the NUMBER of POTENTIAL survivors.

Easy Peasy.

Except that I needed a huge amount of calculating power. So I turned to the MIT Statistical Computing Mainframe that I... ahem!... had unauthorized access to, and planted my little program there to calculate freely and happily as good, tight little programs all should.

What we didn't account for were those that didn't match "language colors" - yet still managed to survive the transition. That was a later discovery.

But for now, let me present to you, my invisible audience, the exacting fruits of my labor and genius.

I won't "show my work" because most of you- to be blunt - are incapable of understanding the math. Those of you that are - much love.

But you can do your own damn calculations. One hint, though: it would help if you had access to population, health, language density and actuarial tables. Here's the bottom line:

Survivors	
Mandarin	19,555,500
English	15,120,000
Spanish	2,575,600
Hindi	2,447,000
Russian	273,000
Arabic	592,700
Portuguese	361,000
Bengali	257,000
French	440,000
Other	1,385,000
Total	43,006,800

There were, according to the program solution, only 43 Million people left on THE ENTIRE PLANET - out of almost 9 BILLION! That was a 99.5% death rate from one event.

It made the images seen on the satellites just the tip - hell, just ONE ICE CRYSTAL - on the iceberg. That was truly Armageddon.

And more bad news was coming.

VI. VICTOR

VICTOR LOOKED AT THE YOUNG MAN riding beside him, and at the blonde woman riding in the back seat through the rear view mirror. It had taken a surprisingly short amount of time to come to trust them - just as he and Sam seemed to trust each other.

After being confronted by him, they got out of the car. The driver - a 20-ish looking young man, long and lanky - and black - in a baseball uniform - and the woman - a stylish and trim blonde in expensive slacks and blouse - were made to sit on the slick hood of the car. It must've been uncomfortably hot (after running the engine, especially in this heat) but other than wincing, neither one complained.

They both had looked at him with cautious eyes - wary, but seemingly not surprised at having a high-powered assault rifle pointed at them from a menacing, black uniformed figure. He admired their poise.

He had told them, "Sit there, and don't even think about moving." They nodded their understanding, and the blonde woman said, in a strangely-accented, almost fake British accent, "Wouldn't dream of it, dear."

"Any weapons in the car?" he asked, while moving around to the driver side door.

The young guy, in an also strangely accented voice - not quite British - answered, "Yes. Two. Revolver on my seat and an automatic pistol on hers. There's also an empty pistol in the boot."

Boot?

Victor walked to the open passenger door and glanced in to make sure. He then walked over to the front of the car and slung his rifle at the ready. "You can come down now. That must be hot."

"Thank you, young man. It is rather uncomfortable," the woman answered.

Young man?

Even if she were judging him by Victor's appearance, she had no reason to call him young. She had that "gym-fit" and tanned look that made it hard to judge age, but she appeared no more than 40, if that. She jumped off the car in a smooth, athletic movement.

The young dude slid off almost languidly and stood looking at him with sharply inquisitive eyes.

"I would guess you two are not - or were not - the people you appear to be," Victor said. The two exchanged quick glances.

"You are correct, young man," the woman answered, "and I would assume you are not, either." She pronounced it "eye-ther."

Victor relaxed, grinned and said, "Not hardly. But let's exchange stories out of this heat…"

WHEN THEY WERE FINISHED TALKING, out of the summer heat and in the cool air conditioning of the SUV, he felt like he knew these strangers.

They exchanged histories and experiences of coming through the event. Each had theories about that event, but what little information they had gathered made them realize that survival was going to be difficult in this new world.

Each of them had been attacked by - or had attacked themselves - people speaking another language. Each of them had been multi-lingual in their previous lives, but reported not being able to conceive of those other languages. They both admitted to being irrationally - even homicidally - enraged at hearing another language spoken.

They each considered English to be their native tongue - that language that they were "hard-wired" to think in - and translate "learned" languages into. They noted that reading foreign words (Spanish-language signs and ads were everywhere in this part of Texas) was impossible. The woman spoke about her mind "skittering" away from those words, and the words becoming an unfocused blur. That echoed Victor's own observations, and he said so.

He told the woman, "You tell your story first."

She complied.

JANIS

MY NAME IS - WAS - Janis Juma-Peterssen.

I find false modesty tedious, so I do not mind telling you that I am - or rather, was - a recognized authority in the application of science and technology to sustainable agriculture and that I was named one of the most influential Africans in 1990 by the New African magazine.

You see, I was "Professor of the Practice of International Agri-Development" and Faculty Chair of the "Innovation for Economic Development" at University of Pretoria, South Africa. I am - I was - Director of the School's Agricultural Science and

Technology Curricula and Head of "Agricultural Innovation in Africa" Project. Rather pretentious titles - but such is the world of academia.

I grew up on the Kenyan shores of Lake Victoria where I was raised by British missionaries when I was orphaned as a babe in arms. My mother and father were both killed in tribal violence. God chose to spare me.

I loved my adoptive white parents - and they adored me. I first worked as an elementary school teacher at my adoptive parents' missionary school before becoming Africa's first black science and environment journalist at Kenya's Daily Nation newspaper. My parents were responsible for my confidence in accomplishing whatever God set before me.

For them, I received an MSc in Science, Technology and Industrialization and a Doctorate in Science and Technology Policy from the Science Policy Research Unit at the University of Sussex.

For them, I have written widely on science, technology and sustainable development. For God brought me to them so that I might accomplish works thought impossible for a Black African woman.

For them, I survived the savage attacks by Afrikaners that took their lives in apartheid South Africa, just it had my birth parents 30 years, earlier.

I survived for 84 years.

And for them, I will abide this Act of God's will.

Jonas, my erstwhile companion, here, does not hold much to what he calls "superstition." But what other explanation could there be? I find myself at a loss to explain such an event - other than to see God's inestimable hand in it.

(Jonas, I see you shaking your head and smiling at a daft old woman's musings. Do not deny it!)

We are both scientists, though from much different disciplines. We both come from a world as far apart as Texas is to us both. I, from Africa, and Jonas... Well, I will let him tell his own tale.

As for the "event" itself, I found myself at the end of my years, and was lying awake in my bed at 3:30 in the morning. I know this because, annoyingly, as I have reached this age - as the Bible says, "being full of years" (a delightful phrase) - I ALWAYS wake at this hour.

I think this is so because God wants to prepare us for our time ending on this Earth. Statistics tell us (Jonas, you will appreciate this) that a greater percentage of deaths occur between the hours of 3 am and 4 am. This is regardless of time zone - it is a worldwide phenomenon.

(Superstition, my dear Jonas?)

In any case, I thought my time had come at last.

But this was not the Rapture I had come to expect - nor was it quite the up-drifting of my quiet soul to my Father's heavenly arms.

Rather it was a violent shaking off my old, withered husk and just as violently entering a new body.

The Bible never described THAT experience. And I would not have thought to be transported into a young, female, white body in the middle of a seizure. But you must have some idea as to how that felt. The confusion. The mystery of the event, and the change in yourself.

And all of the dead.

I shake my head because I keep seeing all those dead children - and their parents, presumably - surrounding my slowly recovering body. We were in a grassy playfield, illuminated by bright lights mounted on poles. They were apparently playing football - what Americans call "soccer," for reasons I have never really understood - when they were all struck down.

I came to the realization that something evil had happened to my world.

You must look at this from my point of view. I came to, groaningly recovering from the fierce cramping and twisting of my limbs, and found myself in a new, young and supple body. The Bible tells us that we are to be given "a new, incorruptible body" in heaven, free from pain and the weakness of this sinful world. I could tell right away from the pain I was suffering, that this was not it.

And the bodies around me stunk of violent death. I have smelled that noxiousness many times in my long life. I fell to my knees to pray aloud for deliverance from my ignorance, and for God to save me from this world that I suspected to be Hell.

But it just turned out to be Texas.

SHE CONTINUED WITH HER STORY, which, for Victor, confirmed what he thought was going on.

She described her initial confusion about what was happening and where she was. She left the grassy field seeking help or information. She described the expected car wrecks and bodies laying about, and seeing signs written in English - and what she presumed to be in Spanish. But she couldn't seem to focus on the foreign words.

On much of the signage, she saw advertised telephone-number sequences she was not familiar with. And a billboard advertised "The Best Car Repair in San Antonio." Since it was in Americanized English, she presumed it to be in the U.S., but could not be sure because of all the Spanish signage around her. Did Spain or Mexico have English adverts? She thought perhaps not.

But that didn't matter as the strange thought struck her that she been transported anywhere and not in her own, failing body.

Victor asked her, "So why didn't you just find somebody's cell phone and GPS to find out where you were?"

She looked at him and sniffed, "Young man, I presume you mean one of those mobile gadgets my granddaughters are always forcing upon me. I am 84 years old! And though I am a scientist, I hold those "Facepage", and "Tweetybird" gadgets in the highest contempt!

Also, I would not presume to go through someone's personal effects without permission!"

Victor smiled and thought to himself, "So where'd you get the gun you're packing 'grandma'? Did you 'get permission'?" Seeing those piercing green eyes glaring at him, he could almost picture the old, stubborn - and very accomplished - black woman inside.

He kept silent and waited for her to go on.

She wandered through the suburban streets in the deepening gloom - the weather not much different than in her own native Africa. It became readily apparent to her that she was lost and alone.

Seeking help, she came upon a young man sitting on the curbside by a wrecked car.

It was fully dark by then, but the man was illuminated by a streetlight that was casting shadows outside of its influence, making it hard to see anything outside its circle of light.

She saw what appeared to be blood running down his face from his scalp. The blood looked like dark oil in that yellowish light.

She stepped out of the shadows with relief. The young man looked up sharply at her with widened eyes, then broke out in a relieved smile.

He, as she was also, apparently happy to see another live, human being.

He appeared Asian or Coloured to her.

She saw Victor's startled look.

She explained that "Asian" - or "Coloured" - did not mean what it did for most Americans.

In her land, the term "Asian" is more commonly associated with people of South Asian origin, particularly Indians, Pakistanis, and Bangladeshis.

"In South Africa and Zimbabwe, the term 'Coloured' refers to a specific ethnic group of complex mixed origins, neither black nor white. It is not considered derogatory," She explained.

She went on.

She had stopped as she entered the circle of light. The young man immediately stood up, swaying before her.

He appeared hurt, but was holding a large revolver in his hand. He did not appear to be threatening her with it, so she reached out her hand soothingly, and said, "Are you hurt?"

His expression immediately changed. He went from smiling sweetly in relief to a ferocious rage, snarling and bringing the weapon up - all the while spitting out curses in a language Janis could not decipher, but whose intonations she recognized as Hindi.

She had spoken Hindi fluently, but, as of that moment, could not.

"I felt a towering rage upon hearing that language… and I had that rage and anger course through my body in a way I have never experienced…" she looked up at Victor with enormously saddened eyes.

"Please understand… I have seen more than my share of savage violence in my lifetime.

I have seen the aftermath of that violence.

I have had my birth parents taken from me by violent, angry men - and my adoptive parents ripped apart by bullets.

I have seen women and children raped and hacked apart by savage strangers just for speaking a different tribal dialect and being identified as a people apart.

I, myself, have been the victim of humiliation and violence by men - both black and white.

All the while I have been able to depend on the Grace of God to reach for, and find, forgiveness…"

Her eyes glistened in sorrow, and her voice broke apart quietly. Victor felt his own eyes sting in response. She said, with a voice thick with choked-up sorrow, "But never have I felt the sheer ANGER and HATRED that I felt at that moment for another human being.

I could have killed him - torn him apart with joy…

But at that moment he fired at me…"

Her voice fell silent. She looked down while tears dropped from her eyes.

JONAS SAID, "I feel it best if I tell my story, now."

Victor looked at him and said, "The lady hasn't finished."

Jonas smiled and replied, "Well, she's not full of holes, is she, mate?"

JONAS

MY NAME'S JONAS SKINNER, and I live - used to live, I should say - in Brisbane, Australia.

I'm divorced and have no children. I'm 54 years old.

I know. You wouldn't think that looking at me now. But I ask you to think of me as a bloody, paunchy Aussie. Ruddy good looks, if I say so myself.

But now I'm this bean-pole of a young black man. Bloody disconcerting. But we probably share a similar experience, so I won't bore you with details.

Like Janis, when I came to awareness after the agonizing cramps, I was lying on a grassy field...

(What's that, Janis?...

I'm not being overly modest. I'm well sure this bloke isn't interested in my resume...

All right... all right... I'll fill him in.)

Fine.

I am an engineer by background - and a bloody paper-pusher by necessity. Despite Janis' assertions, I do not consider myself a scientist. While I do hold a double doctorate in Electrical and in Structural Engineering, I simply do not fancy the theoretical. I do the practical.

I work - or rather worked - for AussiEnCo Limited as President for Program Management. We're a global engineering, construction management, and operations service for the energy industry.

Good Advert, eh?

We have five lines of business: Energy, Environment & Sustainability, Minerals & Metals, Process Infrastructure, and Program Management. I've worked in all of those, at one point or another, but I've always considered myself a practical "grease monkey," as you Yanks say. Always liked working with my hands. Now, it's all politics, paper and bullshit.

(Is that enough, Janis?)

Anyway, as I was saying, I came to my senses in a baseball field, wearing this bloody awful baseball uniform and inhabiting this strange body. I can tell you, it took some time to come to grips with all that.

I know about baseball from my time in Japan. Aussies play baseball, too, did you know? But not as Little Vegimites. So I really didn't grow up playing baseball - and, truth to tell, I find it a bit pointless. Like Cricket. I prefer Ruggers, myself.

But in Japan, they're all crazy for it. So, there you go.

In any case, I found myself facedown in this grassy field, as I said, surrounded by all these dead buggers. We were apparently all dispersing from a finished game. I had on these runners, you see, and not the spiky things. I also found an equipment bag by my side I had apparently dropped as I fell. The field lights were on despite it not being pitch dark, so I knew it was the end of the day, wherever I was.

I tried to get my bearings, going through all the "Am I crazy? Am I dreaming? Oh, my God, this can't be real!!" type of thing. You probably experienced some of that.

Anyway, I tried to pick myself up, but had some difficulty walking after recovering from the seizure. It felt as though my body had been torn apart at all the joints.

I saw a baseball bat sticking out of the bag beside me, so I pulled it out (not with a little difficulty, I can tell you) and used it as a crutch to hobble over to a bench on the side of the field. I rested there for a while, trying to work out the lingering cramps from my muscles and the mental agonies I was going through. The mental took much longer than the physical.

I must've stayed on that bench a long while trying to work out what I had just experienced.

After that, I decided to go over to check on the bodies lying on the field and on the concrete parking lot. They were all dead.

As I entered the parking lot, I saw some of the cars had run into each other while, apparently, driving away from this park. There were other bodies laying about by the parked autos and lorries, as well as in the cars, themselves. Pretty obvious they were deaders.

As I walked to the entrance, I saw two blokes wrestling violently on the ground. They seemed to be fighting for something. Turned out to be a gun, but I didn't know that at the time, else I would not have run - or hobbled hurriedly - up to them to break it up. I still had the bat in my hand.

As I got to them, I could hear them grunting angrily as they tried to wrest what was now apparent to me to be a large revolver. But then, they began to curse at each other in different languages.

I don't know if you, like Janis, have run up against a foreign language speaker, but... oh! You have?

So you might have experienced what we both did. Utter rage. A killing rage. I see that you have - is that why you threatened us like you did? If we hadn't responded in English...? Hmmm. Well. I see.

In any case, at that moment, they weren't people to me, but rather animals deserving of my hatred. I wanted to hurt them...kill them... both of them.

You know the feeling don't you? I can see that.

Anyway, this happened so fast that I only had time to register it in my mind after it was over. I see it in freeze frames, like a comic book.

I was raising the bat in my hands to chop down on their bodies as one of them gained control of the gun and pumped two bullets into the other. The flash and loud blasts startled me, so I stepped back and I probably yelled something - I don't really know what, but I was probably cussing out right well.

The gunman looked up at me with utter hatred, snarling at me. I, snarling back.

He raised the gun, and I swung the bat at him just as he shot. Apparently my swing threw off his aim. I didn't think anyone could miss at that distance. My blow struck him glancingly on his head. I could hear the "thunk."

We both ran in opposite directions, he firing on me one last time. I saw the flash and the boom, but I didn't feel anything. Luckily, he was apparently a really bad shot.

After he disappeared into the surrounding gloom, I followed, cautiously.

I can't believe I was still raging. I didn't even stop to see if the other bloke was a deader. I wanted to bash some brains in!

I came to a street, when I spotted the bloke sitting on the curb at the edge of the sidewalk, holding his bloody head in the palm of one hand. He still held the revolver in the other.

I began to sneak out to him, grinning with anticipation. Just then, I spotted some movement out of the corner of my eye. He must've, as well, for he looked up and he spotted this blonde lady walking up to him, saying, "Are you hurt?"

He stood up and snarled curses in a foreign tongue at the lady extending this kindness. He fired at her twice.

I swung the bat at his head and connected, satisfyingly. I saw a splash of blood as he fell into a boneless heap. He must've died pretty much as he went down, but I kept chopping down on his head 'til it was a bloody mush.

I was panting as I looked up at the lady, still standing there. Remarkably, she was unhurt. He must've been a really, bloody bad shot. He missed completely with both shots at less than a meter and a half!

I said to the lady, "Hullo."

That's how I came to meet Janis.

VICTOR, SHOOK HIS HEAD in wonder.

"Okay. So how'd you end up with three pistols?"

Jonas said. "Well, the empty one was the bloke's I… uh… hit with the bat. The others we picked up at a place down the way called…?" He looked at Janis for help.

She said, "Bass Pro Shop, I think…"

"Yeah, right. That's it. We thought it would serve us to be armed, based on our recent experiences."

Victor frowned and said, "Bass Pro SHOPS," he emphasized the plural, "carries a TON of armaments, AR15's, automatics, shotguns and a whole lot of associated ammo. Why just these dinky pistols?"

"Well," answered Jonas, "I felt like a thief as it was. I had to break a countertop and display-case to get to these.

I just felt it best to keep it simple. I picked a revolver for the lady, since she told me she was uncomfortable with magazines and safeties, and whatnot. I figured a .32 revolver was just the thing for her.

As for me, I happen to own a Beretta 9 mm, so I was comfortable with that."

Victor frowned and said, "Still... you only took a single box of 9 mils and NO extra mags. What's up with that? And no shells for the .32!"

They looked at each other sheepishly, then Jonas said in a subdued voice, "Well... truth to tell we were both feeling a bit crook bein' in the place. It was all a bit spooky in there.

Not only seein' all the carnage about the parking lot, but when we entered the store there was a SMELL about the place..."

"A death smell..." Janis interrupted, agreeing.

"Yeah... just that," Jonas said nodding his head. "We had to wend our way through aisles of merchandise, surrounded by dead bodies. And we had to climb up a wide stair case that was made out of simulated wooden logs, with creepy mounted animal trophies staring at us while we found our way, and this country music song playing cheerily from the speakers...

Well... it was a bit much.

So we got what we came for and got out of there as quickly as we could.

Understand, this was in the morning, after having spent the night talking and coming to grips on things AND trying to sleep in a hot car. We were a bit grungy, but only 'til later did we realize we could have taken some clothes from the store to change into - there were plenty on the racks, but..."

He shook his head, sorrowfully.

"Anyway," he continued, "We were in this rather large shopping arcade or centre. It had a very large cinema theatre and restaurants, as well as assorted shops. We were hungry, but the idea of eating amongst the dead... just wasn't appealing."

Jonas went on to explain that, by using a smart phone they picked up amongst the fallen at the park, they had previously determined they were in San Antonio, Texas USA. They were apparently in the northwestern part of that city.

Neither had ever been to Texas, so did not know what to expect. They had pictured all flat plains desert and cowboys. The urbanity and greenery were a bit disconcerting.

They searched for the nearest large roadway - this turned out to be IH-10 - and they appropriated the nearest car they could find (the driver lay on the ground beside it with keys clutched in his hand) and began to drive.

Their loose plan was to drive on the major artery to see what they could see and follow it to a less populated sub-urban area to find a place to stay, eat, and rest - while making firmer plans. Jonas admitted this wasn't the best of ideas, but given their confusion and grogginess, it was the best they could do.

They drove using the map on their phone, avoiding cars that were crashed and strewn about the roadways as best they could. Once they reached IH-10, they decided to turn right, arbitrarily. That headed west, as far as they could tell, but the compass on the car dash seemed to point mostly north - which was confusing. Maybe Americans did things differently.

Winding their way on the highway through cars and trucks crashed every which way was more difficult than on the less crowded streets. They sometimes - when the highway was divided by grassy mounds, rather than concrete dividers - went "off road." At other times, they had to backtrack to an exit and follow a path on frontage roads until they could get on the highway. Sometimes, the cars were piled up on the frontage roads, and they had to enter business parking lots to get around the snarls.

It was at one of these car pile-up snarls that they found themselves in the shopping center parking lots, and they came upon the giant "outdoor sports equipment" store. They decided to go in and arm themselves if they could. Jonas looked up the store on the phone's internet browser and saw that they sold shooting equipment.

Upon leaving the parking lot to get back on the highway, they spotted housing developments - apartments and residential homes on the surrounding hillsides. They were surprised by the beauty of the hills. Jonas offered that this place reminded him of Italy, with the Mediterranean feel of the architecture.

They decided that their best bet was to find - hopefully - an empty dwelling in one of these neighborhoods to rest and make plans - and to try to find some news. Jonas had suggested that he locate a nearby grocer's to get some fruit, water, cheese or bread to eat. They were very hungry at this point. Jonas looked up "Nearby Grocery Stores" on the voice search and was rewarded with a map pinpointing a big supermarket on the other side of the highway frontage road a couple of kilometers away.

They then drove back up the frontage road paralleling the highway and looked for a cross road to get over to the other frontage or access road that paralleled the highway. They found it and turned onto the other access road, still heading in the same direction.

They had gone about a kilometer, when they were accosted by this dark SUV, whose driver blocked the road and pointed a very scary looking machine gun at them and yelled a warning and a threat to them - in ENGLISH!

Despite the threat, they were relieved. They had found a uniformed authority, at last.

VII. SAM's LOG

I WAS STILL ABSORBING the sobering survival projections when I got a request for a Skype session from one of the social-media posters in Canada. He provided me with his user name and asked that I establish a link. I didn't have Skype loaded on this machine, but it was easy enough to get from the web.

I had Cisco TelePresence available to me, but I wouldn't know if that guy had a link available. So, go with the lowest common denominator.

I downloaded the software, installed it and called up my personal account. My avatar was a geeky "pencil sketch" of me - that is, the "old" me. I entered the guy's user name (it was "floozer", whatever THAT meant) and requested a video call. He had no picture or avatar - only the generic grey silhouette.

It rang with the peculiar "Skype Ring" and I heard the answering "bloo-blee-boop" tone.

A video box came up showing a middle-aged guy - slightly above the mean age of survivors, I would guess - wearing a full headset and mic. Since we both apparently had really high bandwidth, there was no lag or skittering. We were both using high rez HD cams.

The dude sat up straighter when he saw my image and said, "Well... Helllooo theerrre!"

I frowned and said, "Easy there, dude. I was a guy at transfer." Man, this being a chick was a pain!

He said, "Um... sorry. Uh... how are you? You're... Sam, I take it?"

Still cold, I said, "Yeah. You're... Floozer? What the hell's that mean?"

He grinned and said, "Long story... and from another life."

"Did you post your own story? I haven't had time to read them all." I was still cold. His reaction chapped my ass.

Did all hot chicks get off on the attention? No way to tell. The new "me" found it uncomfortable and a bit... perverted, somehow. "You seem to fall outside the parameters identified for survivors."

He smiled and said with good cheer, "Yeah? You shoulda seen me beforehand! WAY past my expiration date." He chuckled, as though he was pleased to find himself in these circumstances. Who knows, maybe he was.

"Okay. So what did you want to talk about that required 'face to face'?"

He smiled. "I'm just old fashioned that way. And I need some info to make a decision."

"Okay. Shoot."

He stopped smiling and paused. He looked more serious.

He said, "I... um... read your banner and postings about where you are."

"Okay...?"

"I used to live down there, and know the area pretty well. I remember the hype about where you're holed up, and know what resources you might have there."

"And, so...?" I asked, meaning, 'get to the point.'

He paused. "So I want to know if making the trip down there is worth it, and what the reception will be?"

Oh.

WE TALKED A GOOD LONG WHILE.

He told me that he had found himself in Canada, going through similar stuff we all have - and coming to the realization that survival was going to be dicey - especially in the long term. He had had encounters with "xenolinguals," - his term, not mine - but I think it's a pretty good one - that had gone into unbelievable violence.

He was in Montreal, and so was outnumbered by the surviving "Franco-phones" and with Paki- or Hindi-speakers, given Montreal's population make-up and immigrant patterns. He was currently hiding in an office building with a few other surviving English-speakers.

They had had to defend themselves with sticks and knives, initially. Canada - the urban part, anyway - wasn't much comfortable with guns. The cops carried guns, of course, but finding police cars and bodies was a matter of luck. They did manage to arm themselves, eventually, but a lot of survivors died along the way.

He and six others had found each other and co-operated to shelter in relative safety.

"The problem is we're outnumbered, and behind enemy lines, so to speak," he said, "not to mention all the signage and directions are in frickin' French! It's damned uncomfortable. I never liked the French much, anyway."

I asked why he didn't just find a car and simply drive down through Ontario to Ohio or Michigan.

He said, "You kidding? I hate the cold... and when winter comes it will be nigh on impossible to survive."

I asked him why. Canada - especially Montreal - was a modern city with plenty of resources.

He looked at me soberly and said, "Apparently you've not thought this through.

The first thing that will go down 'by natural causes' is the North American Electrical Grid. Niagara may keep generating for a long while, but transmission lines WILL go down.

And without the organized effort of co-operating skilled individuals, they will STAY down. And even electrical generation will halt without routine maintenance, eventually. Nuke plants will meltdown without somebody to SCRAM them; coal plants will stop when automated feeds stop..."

Actually, I HAD thought this out, but I was interested in what he had to say.

He went on to say that, as the grid failed, so would communications. Landlines, cell phones, radio - not to mention the 'Net.

"I saw your projections on survival rates," he said, "and even if you're off by as much as 30% - civilization is at an end. The tipping point of skill sets to maintain infrastructure is at nil. Modern agriculture, transportation - the whole shebang requires a certain level of cooperating population."

He was exactly right.

When he had logged online to find news, he saw the banner-push ad that I initiated on all social media sites. He posted and followed all the threads... including my own, which had mentioned us holing up in Gore's Folly.

He said, "I don't know of a better place to gather a new society in the long term and to build out from. Besides," he said, "with enough water you can survive a brutal summer in Texas with or without power. Not so sure about surviving a brutal winter in Yankee-land."

He had a point.

And, obviously, he was smart.

I asked, "So what are you asking?"

He looked at me without the humor that had been present in his voice.

He said, "I think you should put out an invitation to all --- 'Anglo-Phones' --- to join in Texas to organize and survive to build again.

And Gore's Folly is probably the one place on Earth to do it in."

VIII. VICTOR

VICTOR TOLD THE BARE OUTLINES of his story - not even mentioning his past life.

He DID mention Gore's Folly, as Sam had explained it to him, and what he had read in the article about "himself." Both Jonas and Janis reacted. They both, almost simultaneously, asked, "Do you mean the Alternatives Green Technology Complex?"

Victor said, "Yeah?... Why do you both know about it? You're both foreigners. I am an American. I've never even heard of it."

Jonas said, "I had forgotten it was in Texas! My company bid on that project. I worked on the RFT - 'Request for Tender'. I believe you Yanks call it an RFP.

I was sorry that we lost the bid, of course, but the lack of commercial success impacted all Green Building planning and set us all in the 'Green Energy' contracting business back a bit."

Victor looked at Janis with an upraised eyebrow and said, "And you?"

Janis looked at him with her calm eyes and said, "My interest was on the effects on sustainability. I was hoping to gain some lessons from the green-agri experiments that were a component of the project."

Victor pursed his lips and said slowly, "Okay, let's talk about what happens now."

They nodded, a bit unsure about where he was going with this.

Victor took a breath, looked them directly in their eyes to show his seriousness, and began this long monologue:

"Okay. I will offer you sanctuary at Gore's Folly. I think you will agree that this is your best option for long term survival.

I will arm you and teach you how to best defend yourselves. I will ensure your protection, and provide you shelter and provisions - as well as meaningful work. I will provide the means to conduct any research or information-gathering that will benefit us. You can use all the resources at Gore's Folly.

In exchange, I expect you to do your share. Planning, grunt work, fighting - whatever I deem necessary.

This WILL NOT be a democracy.

I WILL allow thoughtful and reasonable 'devil's advocate' questioning and suggestions. But in the final analysis, what I say goes.

I will be your boss.

Not a dictator, but your... 'Sheriff,' if you will. I will be the law, but I will pledge to you to keep my motives clearly on group protection and survival.

If you can't agree to that, then I will let you get on with your business freely, and I will wish you well."

Victor paused and saw them exchange "What the?..." looks.

Jonas was opening his mouth when Victor interrupted him, looking at him severely in the eye, saying, "Before you say anything at all, you need to hear this - and heed this - very well.

I'm not asking for absolute obedience.

I'm asking to be recognized - for the foreseeable future - as the leader of the group that will settle at Gore's Folly.

But this is a one time, once offer. If you do not wish to take the offer, you can be on your way. If we run across each other, we will say 'hello' amicably, talk about the weather, and how foraging is going, or whatever. We can exchange friendly pleasantries.

But please hear this: if, having turned down my offer, you ever come to Gore's Folly, except by invitation - or you interfere with me or mine on whatever mission we are on...   I won't hesitate to fire on you. Is my meaning clear?"

Wow.

Janis and Jonas just stared. Nothing was said for a few minutes.

"Now, why don't both of you go back to your vehicle and discuss this? If you want to - just keep on driving - no hard feelings. If you want to come along with me under these conditions... well, just come back to my car and we can discuss what to do next."

They sat silently for a while. Then Janis nodded and opened her door to step out into the heat. After a few seconds, Jonas followed.

"CRIKEY!" JONAS EXCLAIMED. "What the hell...?"

Janis turned back to look at the SUV. The windows were so darkened that she could not see inside. The car somehow radiated real menace.

"I believe he was serious," she said.

"Hey. I vote we just mosey on down the road," Jonas said. "And why the hell is he so mysterious? You notice he didn't tell us about his past life?"

"I noticed," Janis said, "But I don't think we have much choice but to accept his... 'offer'."

They both turned away and watched the vultures - or whatever they were in this country - feeding on the dead lying all around.

It was not so bad on this crossroads that had little to no pedestrian traffic - unlike the parking lots full of the dead.

But there seemed to be plenty of cyclists on this busy thoroughfare, strewn about the sides of the roads alongside their fallen bicycles, dressed in their silly spandex outfits with their even sillier helmets.

Apparently 'cycling was very popular in this part of Texas. (And wasn't that Lance Armstrong cheater bloke from hereabouts?)

Jonas had never been attracted to that particular activity.

The one thing that irritated him about the "sport" - besides the silly outfits - was the general attitude (seemingly shared around the world, he noticed) that they were somehow invulnerable to 2 or 3 tonne vehicles speeding around them.

They "forced" vehicles to swerve around them dangerously as though they (the 'cyclists) had the absolute right to the road above all others. That people going to and from work were somehow subservient to their hobbyist enthusiasms.

As a working class bloke (ignoring his educational level and income), he mostly resented these people because he found them to be a pampered leisure-class.

Now, he was watching several of these 'cyclists providing a meal for vultures and other carrion eaters. He noticed several crows amongst the feeding vultures.

He didn't know the natural feeding habits of the indigenous fauna in this part of the world, but he would bet that the crows would likely wait for the giant vultures to finish and be contented with the scraps.

Now, there was just such a feast available that all hierarchy was ignored. They also seemed unafraid of the humans moving about in their midst.

"Your carcasses will be food for all the birds of the air and the beasts of the earth, and there will be no one to frighten them away," Janis quoted, apparently thinking along parallel lines. He looked at her, surprised. She smiled, faintly and said, "Deuteronomy 28:26."

"Humph," he turned back to look. He hated to admit it, but that was eerily appropriate.

"Jonas." He turned to look at her. "I think we had better accept his offer," she said quietly.

"Why??!" he said, surprised. "You heard him. We can't agree to that kind of blind obedience... no matter how fine a face he put on it!"

"I do not think we have a choice," she said. She turned back to the vulture feast, and with a gesture of her head said, "We must consider the long-term, as we discussed last night."

She turned to look him in the eyes. "These are only 'the birds of the air.' Have you considered what we will face when 'the beasts of the earth' come down from these hills?

Boars, coyotes, big cats - and pet dogs gone feral, especially after feasting on their master's dead flesh?"

The rotting, carrion smell was getting much stronger as the day wore on and the heat increased.

Jonas stayed silent.

"I've seen this in my own native Africa," Janis said.

Jonas nodded his reluctant agreement.

She went on soberly, "And, Jonas..." He looked up at her. "As in my country, I am much more concerned with the two-legged variety of beasts."

She continued, sadly, saying, "I believe we need HIS kind to defend us from THAT kind..."

Silent, heads bowed for a moment, as if by silent consent, they turned and walked back to the black, menacing SUV.

VICTOR DID NOT SHOW any emotion as they re-entered the cool interior of the SUV.

They sat in the back. Victor turned around to look at them as he said - as though continuing a previous conversation, "I've been studying the SUV GPS map on my dashboard, and I can see where the grocery store is. It's on this side of the highway access road at the next intersection, about two miles up.

I don't know about you guys, but I haven't eaten, today. And I'm getting pretty thirsty from sweating under all this body armor. What say we take time to eat?"

Both looked at each other surprised. Not at WHAT he said, but rather HOW he said it. Gone was all the growling menace in his voice, and he came across as neutrally friendly.

"Um... sure," Jonas replied. "I could do with a bit of fodder. What'ja have in mind, mate?"

Victor said, "Well, there's a Subway about a mile up the road..." Victor paused. "Uh... that's a sandwich shop..."

"Sure. We gottem Down-Under. I imagine they're even in some parts of Africa..." Jonas said, and Janis nodded her silent agreement.

"Well, anyway," Victor continued, "I figure we can stop in, have a meal and a drink; then we can talk about next steps. I've got some ideas I want to discuss with you."

Jonas grimaced. "They're all dead in the shops. I don't fancy eating meats and cheeses with rotting bodies lying about. Not my idea of appetizing."

"Jonas," Janis said, "Nobody said we would have to partake IN the shop itself. I am willing to go in and bring out what we need. I am used to seeing dead people.

Besides, I imagine the refrigeration cases have kept the... smell... from permeating anything."

Jonas nodded his assent.

Victor turned and put the SUV in gear and drove up the road. Very few vehicles were about, until they reached what he thought of as a "strip mall" containing a medical clinic, a nail salon, a Thai Restaurant, an outdoor furniture shop and, more importantly, the Subway Sandwich shop.

As Victor turned into the parking lot he said, "Remember this emergency clinic. We might need the equipment and materials in there." They nodded, agreeing.

Victor parked right in front of the shop. There were no bodies lying about the parking lot despite the goodly number of cars present. The dead must all be in the stores.

He turned around and said, "I'll go in with you, Janis, just to make sure. Jonas, you stay out here and stand watch. Let's go."

He clicked the switch to raise the SUV hatch. They all stepped out into the bright sunshine. They instantly began to sweat in the blistering heat radiating from the parking lot.

Victor went around to the back of the SUV, opened the equipment box and reached in to get the Colt Assault rifle. He handed it to Jonas and said, "Think you can handle this?"

Jonas nodded, inspected the weapon, ejected the magazine, popped it back in, jacked it and made sure it was ready to fire. "Yah... I served my time in the 2nd Combat Engineer Regiment, mate." He grinned. "I'm not just another pretty face, you know - even if it's not really mine."

Victor grinned back. He then reached in to get the Beretta M9 out of the case and said to Janis, "Here," handing her the pistol. "Take this. I don't want you walking into anything unarmed."

Janis looked at it, uncertainly. "It's really simple to operate," he told her. "Just keep your finger off the trigger until you have to shoot. Don't try anything fancy like a two handed grip. Just point where you need to shoot and keep shooting 'til it's empty."

He grinned at her wide eyed stare. "Don't worry. There's plenty of firepower there: you've 15 in the mag and one in the chamber." He grinned again and echoed what he'd told Sam, a day ago. "Just make sure you don't shoot me."

Janis nodded soberly, looking down at the weapon.

Victor handed her a empty knap sack. "For the provisions," he said.

"Jonas, stand on this side of the SUV and keep your head on a swivel. Come running if you hear trouble."

"Righto, will do... Hey, mate!"

Victor looked up. Jonas said, "Make mine a ham and Swiss on whole-wheat." He grinned.

Victor smiled back and led the way for Janis.

AFTER ALL THAT HOOPLA, it was fairly anticlimactic.

There were only two deaders - obviously customers - in the eating area, collapsed in front of the serving line. It was easy enough to drag them outside and deposit the bodies on the sidewalk. The AC was cranked way up in the Subway, and there was condensation on the windows from the cold air. So the bodies were not so ripe.

Jonas looked up and tried to act nonchalant.

Victor intoned gravely, "From earth you came, and to earth you shall return... 1st Opinions 32 verse 8, I think. But maybe not. I'll ask Janis." He grinned as though this was funny. Janis probably wouldn't appreciate it.

But again, maybe she would, given her calm spirit. Victor was one weird bloke!

Victor went in once more and went behind the counter, where Janis was gathering up sliced meats, cheeses, breads and so on. He found two dead uniformed fast food workers, one behind the counter and one in the back room where Janis was gathering the food from the refrigerated units.

As he started to drag the bodies outside, he reminded Janis, "Don't forget some bottled water and soft drinks."

Janis nodded distractedly, keeping busy in order to ignore the goings on.

By the time Victor was done, Janis came out. She had the knap sack by the strap in one hand, and the Beretta in the other.

Victor said, "Good girl... Sure you want to eat in the car? The restaurant's empty."

She nodded. "Let's just leave here."

They ate contentedly in silence with the AC going full blast in the car. Victor had drained two bottles of water before eating the sandwich Janis had handed him. They ate in silence, lost in their own thoughts.

Finally, Victor finished chewing, gulped and said, "Here's what I'm thinking...

We'll go to the Supermarket - that's what we call them here - get some gas (we're running on empty) and go in the store to look around.

I also think there's going to be a bunch of dead bodies in there. These places stay pretty busy. So be prepared for that.

I'm also thinking we don't need to 'grocery shop' for produce or for loose items on shelves. There's probably a small warehouse in the back that has items bundled up for distribution in the store. Maybe large refrigeration for produce, dairy, etc. Probably be some hand trucks and forklifts too.

If we're lucky, there may be a refrigerated truck or delivery van we can commandeer. If not, there'll be plenty of pickups in the parking lot. This IS Texas, after all.

All right, so far?"

They both nodded, but a bit unsure.

He continued. "So, okay... we're gonna take a leisurely drive around the lot and get the lay of the land. We'll go in expecting trouble - locked and loaded.

We have to watch out for each other, and shout out warnings if you notice something wonky.

I go in first and cover you both. Janis, you go last. Go in low. We go in the front and work our way to the back. Let me move and take all the chances. I've got body armor and lots of heavy firepower. Got it?"

Again they both nodded, but Jonas spoke up. "I'm familiar with small squad tactics - but that usually requires more than two people - sorry Janis - to set up Bounding Overwatch."

Victor grinned to show his appreciation. "Well... we'll do the best we can."

After a little more instruction, Victor put the car in gear and drove to the Supermarket.

IX. SAM's LOG

HERE'S WHY I THINK FLOOZER thought that "Gore's Folly" was salvation:

As I had told Victor, I knew about the AGT Complex because Google had made a substantial investment in the construction, and in the advanced technology.

I wasn't a part of Google when they began the project, but when I "joined" Google I had become very interested in all the cool technology being used on the project. So I read about it, and did some... ahem!... "experimental security checks" on the installed core systems.

The powers that be at Google found out about my active "interest" and objected. (I wasn't the only "reformed" black hat hired by Google - only the best.) So, I shut down my exploration - for now.

But when the Complex had gone bust, I had forgotten all about it and lost myself in other "interests."

Now, I was looking at crucial data about the building, FROM inside the building itself. I didn't have to hack in - I just logged into the main terminal station.

I'll lay it out for you, as best I can, using "big animal pictures."

LOCATION:

The Texas Hill Country starts at approximately just north west of San Antonio and continues for hundreds of miles past north west of Austin and into the deepest part of West Texas before running into what most people think of as "typical" Texas geography - flat and desert-like.

This part of Texas has deep water aquifers, lakes, great groves of cottonwood and "live oak" trees and the dreaded Ashe Junipers, commonly called "cedar trees" in Texas (they soak up all available water and put out pollen that - literally - makes people ill.) But more importantly, the area has thousands of hills - some small - some large.

CONSTRUCTION:

It was at one of these hills Northwest of San Antonio, and just west of what I now knew as Interstate Highway 10, where they decided to build the Alternatives Green Technology Complex. They began by deeply, and carefully, honeycombing out the hillside, starting at the top.

They first "flattened" the hilltop, and laid a complex pattern of ducts, conduits and structural material. Then, using the flattened hilltop as an anchoring point, they brought in specially designed boring machinery to dig out the top story of the building by digging deeply into the limestone and rock face.

They used artificial, high-tech support beams made of compressed carbon-fiber and ceramics shot through with "buckyballs" (buckminsterfullerene - look it up) to shore up the "ceiling" of this newly formed cavern and to be able to conduct VAST quantities of energy. They also laid similar structural beams on the floor and laid in conduits, supports, tracks (for constructing "walls" or dividers, as needed) and finished by spraying down the whole construct, floor to ceiling, with a layer resembling concrete and with a special hardening agent.

Each "cavern" was two stories high, a half mile deep and 3/4 miles wide.

They repeated the pattern seven times to build the floors and the parking structures. Then they used "normal" construction techniques to build the building face front, to lay in concrete slabs, and build the oversized elevators and shafts, stairwells and such.

But this was just the shell. What they put INTO the shell was way more exciting.

"GREEN" TECHNOLOGY:

We'll first go to the top of the flattened hill where they installed ACRES of some newly developed, high output, thin film and "stack compressed" solar panels. The energy output of this was enough to fulfill the needs of a small manufacturing plant and a couple of residential neighborhoods.

These, of course, fed storage "batteries" which, in turn, FED, not drew from, the commercial power grid.

Two advanced wind power generators augmented the solar grid, producing over 6000 kW per hour. Again, these fed storage batteries against usage peak needs, but fed the grid with the excess.

Those "buckyball" construction beams were used as superconducting pathways to feed the internal building energy needs.

Now, let's go to the bottom of the building. Below the deck of the primary parking structure (where the loading docks and the "equipment" and computer rooms were built), they drilled an "environmentally sound" access point in to the Edwards Aquifer that is the primary water supply for the region.

Now, ordinarily, that would raise the hackles of the card-carrying members in good standing of the Tree-Huggers Club, but the advanced technology provided for extra purification of all run-off, AND the actual addition of pure water into the system!

The OTHER thing that was done was to drill a shaft PAST the bottom of the aquifer where the temperature was cooler by 20 or so degrees than the surface temperature. This took advantage of the unique superconducting properties of the "buckyball" construction beams and exploited the energy-harvesting properties of temperature differentials to generate electricity.

Ordinarily, these "temperature differential" electrical systems produce mere trickles of energy. This was no ordinary system as it used the HIGHLY superconducting "buckminsterfullerene" construction beams to use the temperature differential and boost the electric generation and wattage.

Yeah. I don't know (or care) how it works, either. It was basically a way to draw "free electricity" from the construction beam materials they were using anyway and use it to power things, store the electricity for later use - or feed it back to the commercial grid. Pretty neat.

Like someone said, "Any sufficiently advanced technology is indistinguishable from magic."

'Nuff said.

Next, a very elaborate, high capacity (and need I get repetitive here by saying "highly advanced"?) bio-mass conversion system was installed on this bottom floor.

It converted ALL waste material - regardless of composition - into its component parts and produced enough thermal energy to help boost the temperature differential energy system by orders of magnitude. It also produces or extracts water; filters out solid chemicals, metals and minerals; AND produces enough methane gas to power SIX turbine engines to generate - you guessed it - electrical energy!

All brought to you by the power of poop!

The intent was to provide the County with sewage and runoff treatment; the outlying septic-tank-served communities with septic tank effluent disposal and treatment; the County and city with solid waste disposal; raw material reprocessing; and - oh, yeah - Methanol Fuel for FREE!

Beauty.

Wasn't done, but the intent and capabilities were there.

It did not end there. They also built an irrigation system that utilized nitrogen-enriched fluids to go to the top of the hill, should anyone want to plant ACRES of farmland on the "roof".

They also installed "sunlight gathering" conduits, augmented by LEDs, that filtered and spread out "natural light" throughout the building.

Even here, in the bowels of the computer room, the light was so natural looking that you could almost hear the birds sing.

INFORMATION AND OTHER TECH:

My world.

The computer room itself had all the bells and whistles - just not up to par with the stuff I had in my Google office - but still plenty good enough.

It had a mainframe (I prefer distributed computing, myself); lots of powerful Intel-based machines running Windows on top of Linux (so why the big iron?); and multiple MILES of servers in racks that consumed electrical power at about 600 megawatts. (A mere pittance for this building.)

The combined processing power of these servers reached up to 100 petaflops.

This may not mean much to you, but gave me a nerdish stiffie. (That is, it would, if I still had a... you know.)

The communications systems were also awesome.

Several SONET rings (fiber access for the telecoms) run around the building with multiple entry points. Also connected to the system is the building's own cell tower and several Ku band satellite dishes to provide telephony, imaging and back-up Internet access.

Too bad that there would be nobody to call and, when the power grid wound down, that there would be no more internet - and, therefore, no more access to distributed knowledge.

But - we COULD download the entire Library of Congress and store it with room left over in a matter of hours. We might also be able to download specific "wikis" of information if we were careful about what knowledge we really needed access to. That is, basic agronomy rather than house painting; medical treatment texts, as opposed to "psychology" information.

You get the picture.

Next comes the part that was not generally thought of.

THE TENANTS:

Ignoring Victor's irrelevant (in my opinion) combatives training gym, there were three businesses that could provide both short and long-term survival assets.

First was the Custom Car Shop on the bottom level. It had VERY advanced machining, welding and forming tools. It contained a large machine shop that could fabricate just about anything - from metal, ceramics, carbon fiber, etc. A mechanic could fix just about anything mechanical.

Next, on Victor's Gym floor, there was a Restaurant Supply House that didn't just sell pots and pans (although they had plenty of those, too). They also had an installed, and fully functioning, display of restaurant-grade walk-in freezers and refrigerator units. Additionally, they had two fully functioning restaurant-level kitchens with all the appliances.

They had full butchering equipment - bone saws, slicing machines, the works.

Lastly - and this would warm the cockles of Victor's "badass" heart - there was, on the second floor, a fully stocked gun-smithing and weapons manufacturing company.

Apparently, they could fix, build, customize or manufacture ANY type of weapon (according to their website.) They had "shell casing manufacturing and custom stamping" (whatever that means), reloading equipment, and a whole lot of guns of every conceivable type in their backrooms. They also had a full indoor shooting range that accommodated every type of weapon.

All of this was why Floozer was so anxious to get here. There was no other place like it except for super-secret military bunkers.

X. VICTOR

IT ONLY TOOK 5 MINUTES TO DRIVE THERE, despite weaving around wreckage on this more congested road. He saw the big red sign sitting in the supermarket parking lot advertising the logo of the store. It also displayed logos for other businesses, including a bank and (of course) a Starbucks.

Victor knew he wouldn't be ordering a Grande Dark Roast anytime soon - or ever. (Could they tear out the coffee machines at Starbucks and install them at Gore's Folly, he wondered? He thought that might be a "must-have" for survival.)

On the southern-most corner of the vast parking lot, he spotted a stand-alone gas station with signage tying it to the supermarket brand. Apparently this regional grocery chain was big enough to have its own branded gasoline.

Victor decided to pull in to the gas station, since the SUV was pretty much running on fumes. Hopefully the gas pumps were still running. He pulled up to one of the two available pumps (there were eight pumps). Vehicles were parked beside the other pumps. Victor stopped and gave Janis and Jonas these instructions:

"Alright. We're gonna fill up the car - we're practically on empty. This will be a pretty good spot from which to reconnoiter the parking lot and supermarket.

We'll all get out - but be prepared for the smell. There're bodies all around the cars, and some inside the cars. They'll have been 'cooking' all day in this heat.

Janis, I hate to ask a lady to pump gas, but I want Jonas' eyes on me as I do recon.

Jonas, stand behind the car to give you some cover, but I want you to have a clear line of sight to be able to use the Colt. I'll be making my way through the parking lot, and I will be looking for any signs of life - and trouble.

After that, barring any difficulties, we pull up by the store and enter it like we talked about.

Any questions?"

Janis said, "I DO have one. How do we intend to pay for the petrol?"

Victor barked a laugh, "Pay?? Why do yo…"

Oh. He paused, and took her meaning. These were automated pumps that took credit or debit cards. Authorization - apparently even in Africa - required some identifying code. More and more, here in the States, that required a zip code entered into the number pad matching the billing address.

After thinking it over, he said, "Well... we'll just pull a wallet from a... customer... and use that ID and credit card."

"I just hate the indignity of robbing the dead," Janis said quietly, almost to herself.

Victor moved to open the car door, when Jonas piped up, "Ummm..."

Victor looked at Jonas and said, a bit irritated, "What is it?"

"Well," Jonas said, "umm... I'm not a very good shot, mate - especially with a short-range carbine."

"Okay...?" Victor said.

"Well, if I'm to 'cover you' at all, shouldn't I have the long gun?"

Good point. Victor traded weapons with him and said, "The optics are pretty good on the M16, but if you're that bad, please put it on 'semi.'

I don't want you to 'spray and pray' in my direction. I've got armor on, but I don't want to test it by receiving 'friendly fire.' These weapons are both loaded with armor-piercing rounds."

"Aren't those illegal in the U.S.?" Jonas asked.

Victor grinned, "Apparently not for 'Victor Vega, Master of the Violent Criminal Apprehension Unit.' " He raised his eyebrows in mock pride.

They stepped out into the heat and Victor handed Jonas a pair of binoculars.

Jonas looked them and understood. "Use these to scan - NOT the 'scope."

While Jonas stood practicing sweeping over the parking lot with the binoculars, Victor bent to search one of the bodies that had collapsed by the nearest car. The smell was overwhelming, but luckily Victor didn't really have to go through a dead person's pockets.

There was a wallet beside the body, apparently dropped when the "event" caused the killing seizure. He opened the wallet and took out a VISA card, and the driver's license bearing the address of the owner.

He popped the SUV gas cover from inside, went around to it and unscrewed the cap. Then he went to the gas pump, slid the card into the slot, and was authorized to pump right away without entering a code.

He unhooked the gas pump handle and hose, selected 'premium' and handed the handle to Janis, who was standing by, watching the proceedings, curiously.

"Think you can handle this?" Victor asked. She just looked at him, scornfully and jammed the handle into the gas intake and began pumping "the petrol."

Victor just smiled and unscrewed the suppressor from the Colt Commando. He looked up to Jonas and asked, "Anything?"

Jonas looked back and shook his head, no. He noticed what Victor was doing with the Colt and frowned. "You sure that's a good idea, mate?" His black face somber.

Victor could hear the older Aussie in this nice, young man. "Don't really see the need for stealth... and I want to make sure you hear me shooting if I get into trouble."

Jonas nodded his understanding as Victor threw the suppressor tube on the front seat.

"Now remember," Victor said as he passed Jonas on the way to the parking lot, "No full auto, try to keep me in sight, watch for any movement, and most importantly - DO. NOT. SHOOT. ME.

Got it?"

"I'll try not to, mate. But I ain't promisin' nothin'." Jonas exaggerated his Down-Under accent.

Smiling, Victor moved on under his companions' worried gaze.

Victor estimated the lot was about 150 yards deep. But by cutting in from the diagonal, it was even a longer trek. (Basic geometry.)

He figured he would have to cross more than 200 yards to get to the front entrance. There were HUNDREDS of cars and trucks parked closer to the store. The parked cars were sparser closer to the street, therefore, he would have to cross open territory at the start.

He knew that the effective range of the M16 was about 500 yards, but that would be determined by the marksmanship of the shooter. "Effective" didn't mean everyone could shoot, and even come near, a man sized target. The 'scope on the M16 he had given Jonas was plenty good, but he only hoped he wouldn't be shot in the back by this amateur.

He had to smile at himself. Without Victor's "muscle-memory" and finely honed skills, his "previous self," who hadn't handled such a weapon in 40+ years, would be just as much an amateur as Jonas.

Now, he fast "duck-walked" in a crouched position to quickly cover the distance. It was a good thing that his Victor body was in such good shape, else the heat radiating off the parking lot would have killed him, wearing this hot, heavy armor. As it was, he would have to replenish liquids when he could.

Even after drinking two whole bottles of water, he felt no urge to pee. He was sweating it out so rapidly that it had no time to reach his bladder.

He held the Colt in the ready position, swiveling back and forth as he crossed the distance. He crossed the first hundred yards and stopped behind a Lexus parked at an angle. It was taking up two spots, as though the driver didn't want anybody parking near and dinging up the gleaming black finish.

He wiped the sweat streaming down his face with his sleeve, and squinted over the trunk of the Lexus to take in the entrance to the store. So far, nothing.

He stood once more and moved around the Lexus. He walked the last few yards and cleared the parking lot, itself. He came to the wide space marked by faded yellow lines painted on the pavement designating where pedestrians would cross. There were a few "go slow" signs mounted on poles at car height in the middle of the spaces.

As he was exposed, the entry door swished open, and three men and two women stepped through, talking animatedly and laughing. Two of the men had what appeared to be some kind of semi-auto AR-type rifles, and one had a scoped, bolt action hunting rifle, and one woman had what appeared to be an AK47 variant.

They were all pushing carts filled with groceries and cases of water and soft drinks, and the weapons were sitting crosswise on top of the carts.

The familiar rage hit him when he realized they were speaking Spanish and he raised the Colt while in the open.

A shout sounded from his right.

JONAS WATCHED VICTOR'S PROGRESS through the binocs, but made sure to periodically scan to the right and left of the storefronts. From time to time, he swept over the cars parked chevron-style, looking for any movement. This parking pattern was only broken up by cart racks scattered over the various rows.

There were many bodies and loose shopping carts on the "aisles" of the lot.

There also were some cars, lorries and vans askew at various points on the parking lot - some having crashed into parked cars, further disrupting the neat parking pattern.

Some of the cars had swerved over to impact on the outside front walls of the store - some having crushed outdoor displays of assorted merchandise. One big, open bed "Ute" - what the Yanks called a "pick-up truck" - had run over a variety of small plants and stacked fertilizer bags on display on the sidewalk, only to crash diagonally into a cage rack filled with small propane tanks.

Luckily, none of the cars were going fast enough to do any real damage.

He heard Janis finish pumping the petrol and returning the hose to its holding rack. He tried to focus back on Victor, but his view was obstructed by the parking lot filled with cars.

He looked for Victor using the lowest power on the binocs to take in a wider field of view. He spotted him, or at least the piece of him that could be glimpsed in-between the cars, at about a 100 or so yards downrange. He was squatting by a gleaming black car and was wiping his forehead with his sleeve. So the iron man was human after all.

Even in the shade of the open roof carrel that housed the petrol station - and with a seemingly perpetual breeze blowing amongst the pumps - he felt the heat. It must be hellacious down there in the burning sun wearing a full suit of combat armour, and the sun reflecting heat waves off the pavement.

He smiled. He could almost feel sorry for the enigmatic Victor.

Janis said, "Do you see anything moving?"

"No... only Victor."

Jonas then swept the binoculars left in a smooth motion, then right, sweeping past Victor. He focused back on Victor as he was standing and moving toward the store entrance. It was a good thing the petrol station was on a slight rise, else he could not have seen anything above the parked cars.

He then spotted Victor's head and shoulders over the cars blocking his view as Victor entered the space between the lot and the store entrance.

Victor had stopped right in the open. He seemed to be staring at something at the front. Jonas placed Victor at the "bottom" view of the binoculars so he could focus on the entrance.

There!

People were coming out with shopping carts filled with groceries. They were laughing and talking animatedly when they heard a shout coming from their left. It sounded like a warning. They looked toward the shout, then snapped back to the front to look at Victor.

Then chaos.

VICTOR RAISED THE COLT INTO FIRING POSITION.

The two women looked shocked, and two of the men looked as if they were seeing an evil spirit. Only one of the men reacted by reaching for the AR on his cart. He was between the other man on his right - who also had an AR - and the two women. The man with the hunting rifle was on their left and trailing behind.

The man never made it to his rifle as Victor fired an 8 round burst that shredded him like bloody rags, organs and blood flying back to fall on the now shattered glass entrance doorway. The metal cart also suffered severe damage, pieces of the cart flying away like shrapnel.

The noise from the Colt Commando was deep throated and deafening. Once again, Victor had not inserted his earplugs. But that was the last thing he was thinking about as he reveled in his rage.

Victor then moved lightening fast to the other AR man, who seemed frozen in time. Another burst shredded him and his cart - and, incidentally, the man's AR - with the armor piercing rounds punching through the metal parts and sending them pin wheeling through the air.

He moved on to the women who appeared frozen - their mouths and eyes wide open, appearing like that famous painting "The Scream." He shot them down using two economical 3-round bursts. The Colt was riding high by then, so he took off the tops of their heads starting at the bridge of their noses; their brains, hair and blood spraying violently behind them.

He had to bring down the Colt's elevation to fire on the man with the hunting rifle, but by that time, the man had snatched the rifle in one hand and was stumbling away crouched and with back turned, trying for cover behind a stone archway at the entrance that held stacked shopping carts.

Victor brought the Colt to bear and fired the last of his magazine. The bullets punched through the man's back - some of the rounds punching deep craters in the stone archway.

Victor dropped the empty mag and reached for a fresh one on his vest. He was about to insert it, when he felt a painful punch on his left side - then another, which knocked the wind out of him and brought him to one knee.

He had been shot, and only the armor had kept him from being mortally injured.

Now shots were cracking sharply over his head. It was only a matter of time before he was hit, fatally. No helmet, no armor on his arms and legs.

He inserted the fresh mag and began firing to his left where he thought the rounds had come from. He saw a car that was positioned parallel to, and at a slight angle out, in front of another storefront about 300 feet away.

He figured the shooter had to be hiding somewhere back there. He heard what he thought was Jonas opening fire - in that same direction.

It was the distinctive sound of an M16 firing at full auto and hitting, somewhat spottily, on the car and mostly on the wall and glass storefront behind it. Not only was it lousy shooting - especially with a 'scope - but apparently Jonas had selected "full auto" against Victor's orders.

For which Victor was now glad, as the shooter was firing back - but not his way. He laid down his own suppressing fire, and got back on his feet, preparing to move to cover. The shooter was just too good for Victor to be out in the open. He only hoped Jonas - and Janis - were keeping their heads down, as he heard the shooter return fire toward the gas station.

He fired off half his clip - the rounds thunking into the back end of the angled car and sending glass and metal flying every which way. That should make the shooter think - if the armor piercing rounds hadn't found him.

Victor stood up to move, when he felt two violent punches on his torso - this time from the right. It felt as though he had taken two kicks to the liver from a very experienced fighter. They dropped him to his back, his body spasming from the violence of the blows, despite the advanced body armor protecting him.

As he fell back, he twisted to the right and saw another man aiming at him with the largest bore AR-type rifle he had ever seen from behind a car that had run over the sidewalk.

Victor squeezed his own trigger, but the rounds completely missed his new attacker, firing uselessly into the car and into the air, and the Colt clicked empty. The man had flinched and ducked his head, but came up grinning as he aimed downward at the fallen Victor once more.

Victor stared at the death coming his way, when he saw the man's head disappear in a pink mist, spraying to the man's left, and the shooter's body drop bonelessly to the ground like a puppet that had its strings suddenly cut.

He then heard a rolling, cracking sound coming from his own left. Jonas?

It did not sound like M16 fire, but that thought was lost in the pain and spasms his own body was going through. Victor struggled to breathe. He couldn't move.

JONAS HAD WATCHED AS VICTOR MOWED DOWN the cart-wielding shoppers. They hadn't stood a chance.

Jonas could only believe they were armed and probably non-English speakers. He knew how the rage took over - at least he hoped Victor had been overcome by that rage and had not killed "innocent" people.

He breathed, "Jesus!"

Janis ignored the blasphemy and asked, "What is happening?"

He saw Victor go down to one knee, as if he was hurt. Simultaneously, he heard firing coming from the left. It was rapid fire, although not fully automatic- crack, crack, crack!

He swept the binocs rapidly to the left and saw a shooter standing up and firing an AR rifle in Victor's direction. Jonas put down the binoculars and raised the M16 to his shoulder, peering down the 'scope. He fired at the man and - missed! He saw the gouge in the stone wall, high above the man.

Crap!

He had to do something to distract the shooter now! He clicked the lever to auto as he heard Janis shout, "What is going on?!!"

His answer was to fire on his target at full auto. He hit all around the man, but had no luck bringing him down.

Distantly, he heard his bullets tearing into the wall, and in the metal body of the car the shooter was standing behind. That got the shooter's attention and drove him down behind the automobile seeking cover.

Jonas grinned and fired the rest of his clip on full auto, punching huge holes in the car, and blowing out the side windows. At least he wasn't shooting at Victor anymore!

But then the shooter appeared over the bonnet of the car where he would be better protected and began firing in Jonas' direction - and hitting uncomfortably close! Jonas shouted an expletive, ducked down and scrabbled for cover.

He yelled, "Janis - get down!"

Bullets thunked into the side panels and windows of the Sheriff's SUV. As both were armored, the rounds only splintered on the side panels and spider webbed against the armored glass.

Jonas realized that he had left the spare magazines for the M16 in the back hatch of the SUV - and he could now not get to them. He was hopelessly pinned down, unless he wanted to enter the SUV through the back doors and try to hump over the seat to get to them. By that time,

Jonas figured, Victor would again receive fire.

Before he could move, however, he heard two loud booms that had a different sound than Victor's weapon. He heard Victor's weapon shooting off what sounded like a full clip. Janis exclaimed, "Oh no! - Victor!!!..."

He turned to look over at her. She was peering over the bonnet and was looking at the front entrance. Jonas asked, urgently, "What is it?!!"

"Victor is down!" she answered.

He was about to stand up to take his own look when he heard a rolling, echoing, cracking sound coming from his left. He heard Janis say, "Oh!" Surprised.

Almost simultaneously, he heard the "crack... crack... crack" of the shooter firing again. This time, none of the rounds hit near the SUV. He was obviously shooting in Victor's direction again.

Desperately, Jonas leaped up to get to the open hatch door and at looked in the shooter's direction.

He was now standing and aiming in Victor's direction.

Before Jonas could turn to the open hatch to retrieve a magazine, he saw a splash of red coming from the shooter's head, then saw the shooter drop to the ground. The phrase "like a sack of potatoes" came to mind.

A split second later he heard the same rolling, echoing, cracking sound coming from his left.

All the noise suddenly stopped.

He looked back over his left shoulder and up, and spotted a figure standing on the overpass of the main highway overlooking the store parking lot - waving a hunting rifle over his head in what appeared to be a very friendly gesture.

VICTOR WAS SITTING UP with his back against the car that he had shredded with his last clip. He had the Colt in his lap, and was examining the body armor on his right hand side. It was ragged, with cracked and jagged ceramic plates. A large slug had punched through to the padded Kevlar lining.

He looked up as he saw the SUV driven by Jonas skid to a stop in front of him. Both Janis and Jonas scrambled out of the car. Janis ran up to him and knelt down exclaiming, "Where are you wounded? Are you bleeding?"

Jonas stood behind hovering with concern.

Victor smiled and shook his head, saying, "I'm not. Vest did its work."

"Oh, thank the Lord!" She said. But then she looked down at the gaping, ragged holes in the armor. "Are you positive?!" Incredulous.

"Yeah," Victor said. "But I'll be very sore tomorrow. Don't think anything's broken, though."

Jonas was also staring at the holes in Victor's armor and said, "What the hell did that, mate? A Howitzer?"

Victor chuckled and winced. "Dunno. Looks like a modified AR. It's over there."

Jonas and Janis looked over at the weapon lying beside the headless body.

Janis gasped at the sight of the bloody corpse, and Jonas exclaimed softly, "Bloody hell!"

"Nice shooting, by the way," Victor said, nodding to the M16 Jonas was holding in one hand. He jerked as if shocked and looked at the rifle as if realizing it was there for the first time.

He said, "Oh, not me, mate. I missed with every bloody shot!"

"Then, who...?"

They all looked up as a figure was striding, almost casually down the center aisle of the parking lot. He was a rugged looking man, about in his mid forties, dressed in jeans, cowboy boots and a camo t-shirt. His arms bulged with farm-worked, honestly earned (not gym-enhanced) muscles.

He was carrying a civilian bolt-action hunting rifle with a beautiful walnut stock. The 'scope on it was a garden-variety big-box store type. He also wore what looked to be a .45 automatic on a belt holster.

He looked Hispanic, so Victor casually placed his hand on his sidearm, getting ready.

Jonas saw the move and said, quietly, "Hold on, mate! I think he's a friend. Took out my shooter - and looks like he took yours, too, with bloody impressive head shots from way over on the highway overhang!"

The guy stopped just short of them. Janis was looking up over her shoulder at him. He nodded his head, politely and greeted her, saying, "Ma'am." Janis nodded slowly back. He nodded to Jonas, and then looked at Victor and said, "Sir. Are you hurt?"

Victor relaxed and smiled at him and said, "No. I'm okay... I think thanks to you... uh... soldier?" He guessed, with all the "sirs."

"Marine, sir," seeming slightly offended.

Victor, groaning, stood up - Janis trying to help by supporting his elbow - and reached out his hand to shake, smiling. "Shoulda known it takes a Marine to save the day. Thank you, and nice shooting."

"No thanks necessary... uh... general?" he ventured, looking at the black stars on Victor's collar.

Victor shook his head and said, "No, my rank is captain and I'm the commander of a special Texas Bexar County Sheriff's Unit. Apparently, like the Navy, the sheriff department screws up its rank and insignia.

"This is Janis and he's Jonas," he said, "and I'm Victor."

"Lance Corporal Tim McCoy, out of Quantico Advanced Sniper Training by way of Hallysberg, Tennessee, Cap'n." he said, shakings hands with them. "Pleased to meet you, Ma'am - Sir," nodding to Jonas, last.

He then looked over at the weapon the now headless shooter was using.

He whistled, "That there is a SOCOM .458 - it's made to take out charging boar hogs with a very big, slow moving slug. You're mighty lucky to be wearin' that Dragon Skin, sir. It looks the worse for wear."

Victor barked out a laugh, already feeling better. "What say we continue this inside out of the heat?"

"You mind if I pick up one of those ARs, sir, just in case?" Tim asked.

"Good idea," Victor said, "but one of 'ems shot all to hell."

The Marine scooped up the intact AR15 in his free hand. They all followed him into the store with the air conditioning wafting at them through the shattered entryway.

They found a sitting area just behind the registers in an alcove that provided a banking center within the store. It was an all service "superstore'" apparently.

They all sat, except for Janis, who said, "Pardon me, but I saw a ladies room by the entrance." She went back in that direction.

Victor sighed, sat back and said, "So, corporal, what's your story?"

He started to answer when Janis showed up looking flustered. They looked at her in concern, and the stranger stood up. She said, "There is a dead woman in one of the stalls."

"I'll take care of it, ma'am," the Marine said, standing quickly.

"No, you sit, corporal. Let Jonas handle it."

Jonas looked at Victor sourly, stood and said, "Right-o, Mate. At 'yer beck n' call," and marched off.

"He's just a little testy from the heat," Victor said, noticing the Marine's discomfort. "Sit down."

"Yes, sir." He complied. "Sounds like an Aussie to me."

"That he is, corporal," Victor acknowledged. "That young black man was a 50-something White Australian engineer - and this beautiful young woman," he nodded toward the trim blonde, "was an 84 year old, African, black female professor of agriculture... or some such thing."

Janis smiled. "Close enough," she said sweetly, staring daggers at Victor.

Victor went on, "And I made friends with a young computer nerd guy who now looks like a stunningly beautiful Indian or Pakistani girl." Victor smiled at the man's startled look. "Yes, it's rather uncomfortable for him - uh - her."

The Marine looked at him, and asked, "And you, sir?"

Victor smiled, grimly, "Let's just say I was old enough to have fought in Viet Nam. I assume, corporal, that you were not as you seem, now?"

Janis noticed a distinct change in Victor's tone and phrasing - more formal and slightly avuncular. He had taken on the tone of "officer speaking to enlisted ranks" that was so common in British society. It rather rankled her.

At that moment, Jonas returned and nodded to Janis, "All clear."

"Thank you, my dear Jonas," she said, and hurried off in the direction of the bathroom.

"You were saying, corporal?" Victor prompted.

"Um... no, sir. I'm 22 years old and from good Tennessee Scots-Irish stock. This here fella's named Greg Martinez and he's 42 by his driver's license. I... uh... checked."

"Have you encountered... others, Tim?" Jonas asked.

"Yeah," He answered. "I was in this small town and ran into some folks as confused as me... and we saw all the dead, too."

"And where are they, now, corporal?" Victor asked.

"All dead, sir. We ran into other... groups." He answered.

"Spanish-speakers, I'm guessing." Janis, rejoining them as he said this.

"Yes, Ma'am, but... Look, I'm from Tennessee, but I'm no bigot. I've served with a lot of Mexican-Americans. They've all been good Marines - and patriotic. Some of them speak better English than... well, you know... me. Hell, my captain is Mexican and he graduated from the Academy.

But, when I heard those other folks speak... another language... I saw red, sir!"

Victor said, "I don't think this has anything to do with ethnicity, corporal, or just hearing Spanish...

Look, do you have any buddies that came home from deployment with TBI?"

"Yes, sir," he answered slowly, wondering where this was going. Jonas looked quizzical, so Victor translated, "TBI - Traumatic Brain Injury."

Jonas nodded his understanding and silently mouthed, "Ah…"

"Anyway, corporal, I'll bet some of them suffered from aphasia of some kind - difficulty in speaking," Victor went on.

"Yes, sir. I had a buddy that had to learn to talk all over again," he said. "He never got really good, again."

"Well, I imagine he was frustrated and sometimes became very angry,"

The Marine nodded slowly, remembering.

Jonas stared at Victor as if learning something new. Janis looked at him with dawning understanding.

"Well, corporal, it's something like that." He paused… "Tell me, what do you think's happened to us? I mean, to everybody?"

"Well…" he replied slowly, "we all talked about it - especially after we ran into other… folks."

"And…?"

"Well, we all knew we were not in our own bodies… and not in our own… locations… after… uh… the event.

One of the fellas called it a 'Freaky Friday' event… you know the movie where Lindsey Lohan and that older woman that comes out in those yogurt commercials traded bodies?" He looked at them.

Victor nodded and smiled.

Janis and Jonas probably didn't know the commercial, but Jonas - if not Janis - probably knew about the movie.

"Well, none of us knew what had caused it… but we knew what we all went through with the seizures and all…" He looked around at them. "And we figured… you know… most people died from them… and in accidents, and stuff.

But the… way we reacted to hearing Spanish… and those people hearing us speaking English…" he trailed off.

Victor said, "Well, what we all went through, I think, damaged these bodies' - our new bodies' - brains like TBI.

I figure it caused a type of aphasia where you can only speak your own 'hard-wired' native language - IF it matches the 'receiving' body's own native language. And hearing another language spoken sets off a killing rage."

Jonas spoke up and asked, quietly, "But why?"

Victor looked at him, paused, and said, "In my other life, I… suffered… from TBI.

I had total aphasia - I couldn't speak, nor even THINK about, words. It was pretty horrible. I could THINK and FEEL, but - I can't explain to you how it was.

Anyway, as I started to recover, I began to slowly remember words, and I practiced how to say them. One word at a time, over several months.

The funny thing was that - even though I spoke - and could read - three other languages, the only language that came back to me was my own English. As I practiced these words, if someone were to speak something in another language, I would get furious!

When I told my speech therapist about this, she explained that it was not unusual - especially with TBI and some associated brain damage.

It seems the brain has something called "the RAGE center" that trips with perceived threats and frustrations - sometimes mixing up frustration with a threat, and that triggers rage."

He paused here, looking around at them and seeing that he had their attention.

"I... think..." he continued, speaking slowly, "that something like that is at work, here.

Hearing another language sets up frustration at trying to process it through the hearing and speech centers - and the brain interprets that as uncontrollable rage.

Makes sense, since we can't read foreign words, now - we're made uncomfortable and antsy, but not angry. That could be because visual input is not processed the same way."

"OH!" Janis exclaimed, "I've always wondered..." She stopped when she noticed them looking at her in surprise.

Jonas said, "ALWAYS wondered what? Janis, this just happened."

"Not quite true, my dear Jonas. The Bible tells us - oh, Jonas, do stop rolling your eyes and listen - the Bible tells that at one time 'the whole world had one language and a common speech.'

It goes on to say that Man became so full of hubris that they thought nothing was beyond them, so they had a massive project to 'build a city, with a tower that reaches to the heavens.'

God decided that they needed humbling so he said:

'Come, let us go down and confuse their language so they will not understand each other. That is why it was called Babel - because there the LORD confused the language of the whole world. From there the LORD scattered them over the face of the whole earth.'

Don't you see - that is what is happening again!"

Jonas snorted. "Pfffft, that fairy tale doesn't even compare!"

"Despite what you think you know, Jonas," Janis said, evenly, "It is NOT a fairy tale!

And that is just the kind of hubris that has plagued mankind before - and is now plaguing it again."

The Marine said, "No. The lady's right.

Think about it. Why didn't the people in that Bible story not just stick around and make do - teach each other the new languages - even use sign language - to cooperate?" He looked around to the others.

"I think they mighta gone through this very thing. Else, why 'scatter' over the face of the earth?

Maybe they had to separate to keep themselves from killin' each other - and they gathered in groups - or tribes - to help them survive. Just like we're doin'."

They were silent, for a while. Victor said, "Well... It kinda makes sense, in a way."

Jonas looked at him with a skeptical frown.

"No... listen," Victor said. "We may be a polyglot world now - and despite all the troubles we have plaguing civilization - we've managed to invent a new way to communicate and share knowledge instantly - the internet. We have machines to translate for us. And calculate for us.

Think of the advances in genome sequencing, cloning, supercolliders, the discovery of 'the God particle'. We're on the verge of discovering ways to go beyond our solar system... nothing seems beyond our grasp."

Jonas snorted, "I would think super space aliens would be more afraid of us rather than some mythical omnipotent God!"

Victor laughed and said, "So 'super space aliens' are more real to you?"

He stood up and stretched his aching body. "Well... no use speculating on the unknowable. We have other fish to fry.

But first..." he paused.

"Lance Corporal McCoy - I am here-by promoting you to Gunnery Sergeant by the powers vested in me by the County of Bexar in the great Republic of Texas, USA."

"Is that legal, sir?" He asked. "And why Gunnery Sergeant?"

"In the words of that great actor, Sylvester Stallone, 'I AM the Law!'

And it's much easier to call you 'Gunny' rather than 'Lance Corporal'' all the time," and laughed.

And so "Gunny" it was.

VICTOR TOLD THE NEWLY-CHRISTENED "Gunny" the plan they had made, earlier. They then explored the store, found the mini-warehouse, and discovered forklifts and hand trucks.

They also found a refrigerated truck at the dock, loaded it halfway full of supplies, at Victor's insistence. He felt the need to reserve the other half to strip the Bass Pro Shops of most of their stocks of guns and ammo.

Jonas claimed he could drive a semi, "Anything with a motor, mate!"

After policing up the enemies' dropped weapons, they headed to Bass Pro to take care of business (no trouble, no fighting - but the stink had gotten worse inside the store) and then went on to Gore's Folly, where Sam was waiting with news.

XI. SAM's LOG

I WAS THINKING ABOUT HOW Victor would react to the news that we had company coming.

Even if Floozer left Montreal right away, it was still 2000 miles away - about 31 hours at 60 MPH, if he drove straight through. That wouldn't be possible, given that he would have to pick his way around wrecks, wildfires and hostiles (if any.)

I figured they - Floozer had mentioned that there were currently six of them - would be here, if they actually made it, in about a week, or so. Maybe more, if they ran into trouble. He also said they would try to gather up other "anglo-phones" along the way - especially those people who were on their route or agreed to meet them on their route - that had responded to the social media threads.

I told him to prepare for the worst, and that they should arm themselves as heavily as possible. I told him about the SWAT vehicle we hadn't yet broken into, and that maybe they should look for a "Frenchie SWAT-mobile."

I had said it as a joke, but Floozer had gotten a real gleam in his eye and said, "Yeahhh!... Great ideaaa!"

He said he that would pick up a U.S. cell phone when he crossed over and asked for my number. I gave him the number of the phone Victor had given me, then I said, "Wait... what? There ARE cell phones in Canada. And the last time I checked, they COULD call the U.S."

I chuckled, "You afraid of being billed too much or going over your minutes?"

He said, soberly, "No, dude! These phones are in FRENCH! Even the icons are labeled in French. The numbers on the dial pad are just numbers, but getting past the French is a bitch! It gives us raging headaches - and it causes us to lose focus.

Luckily I found a laptop that was in English to get us on to Twitter and Skype. No such luck with any phones we found."

I hadn't considered that.

Since I really hadn't tried to read anything other than English, (the logins in foreign languages I had ignored) I had to take his word for it. I believe Victor had said something about reacting weirdly to written foreign words.

After we signed off, (Floozer said he'd call when he crossed over to the USA and "borrowed" a phone) I sat and thought about what they would have to go through to get here. I could probably "be their eyes" and plan a route for them using my "spy-eye" system, but I decided not to call him back until I talked it over with Victor.

I also sat thinking about the stuff Floozer had mentioned about the long-term effects of such a radical de-population. When I had reacted with so much enthusiasm to Victor's revelation that he was in the AGT Complex, I had just those thoughts in mind.

I knew that I had to prepare a list for Victor so that he could understand what we would be facing - especially over the long haul. I decided to base this on the bottom of Maslow's hierarchy of needs, which is normally shown as a graphic pyramid. The bottom is where we needed to concentrate our list, because the top of the pyramid is based on more... civilized concerns.

For those of you that weren't paying attention in class, (Yes, I mean you, you jocks!) here is that graphic.

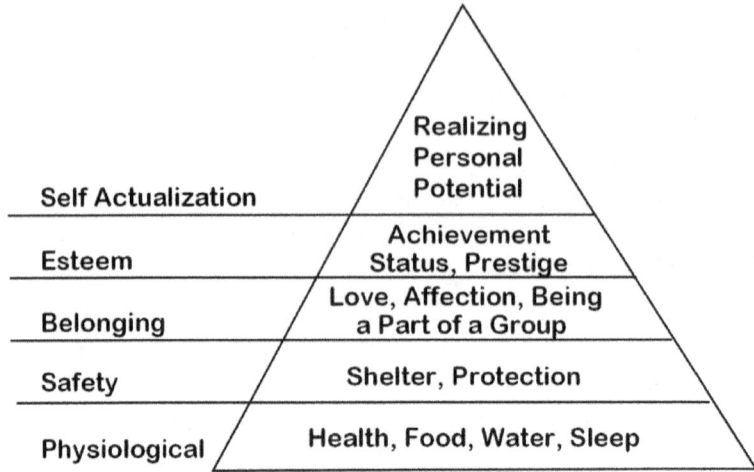

Forget all that Love, Esteem and Self-actualization malarkey.

That was all good when you weren't worried about where your next meal was going to come from - or that YOU would be the next meal for some beastie!

No. The TOP concerns for us would be basic SURVIVAL! Both short term and long term.

Food, water, shelter and sanitation were essential for meeting the Physiological needs. Safety needs should be met with shelter (fortification); weapons (self protection and hunting) and medical care.

I tried to mind-map the needs so that we could organize them into manageable chunks, both short and long term. I figured this was necessary so that Victor could see how the AGT Complex itself could meet those needs.

I had thought it was a good idea to try it when I first started, but it got too convoluted, too fast.

For example, the branch that reads "Security and safety" tees out to "Information" which, in turn, leads to "Dependant on Energy Grid". It would have to loop back around to the base branch reading "Energy and production."

Same way that, let's say, "Weapons" would have to branch back to the base branch of "Tools and Production."

It would get messy right away with all kinds of loops and cross backs. Knowing Victor, I could rapidly lose his attention.

So, I decided to make it simple by providing a simple linear LIST.

The list headings should be "Long Term" and "Short Term" needs.

I needed Victor to understand that the AGT Complex would solve most of our Short Term needs - say 3 to 5 years out. But in the longer term, we would have to begin the process of building a new, independent infrastructure that would lend itself to a larger community.

And that would take lots of planning and a lot of work and a lot of resources - both material and intellectual.

Little did I know that this "simple" LIST would become my life's work and end up being our veritable "Bible of Survival" - our own "Book of Lists."

BOOK THREE: ENEMIES

*See, the Lord is going to lay waste the earth and devastate it;
he will ruin its face and scatter its inhabitants*
(Isaiah 24:1)

SIX MONTHS AFTER THE EVENT

I. RIVERA

I WATCHED AS MY PEOPLE looked at me wanting words of wisdom, as if from on high.

I felt like a fraud.

Prior to "the event," I was just another Division Manager of Accountancy at Cote–Horvath and Associates in Buenos Aires, Argentina.

I headed my own Division, and was paid very well to manage accounts, globally.

I had the satisfaction of raising my two daughters to be successful in their own right.

My wife, their mother, was deceased. I knew she would have been proud to see the eldest become THE leading female pediatrician in all of Argentina, and the other a successful professor of Cultural Studies at the University of Buenos Aires.

I was looking forward to having my daughters provide me with grandchildren to spoil - but now, that was never to be.

I knew not what happened to my own daughters - if they, too, found themselves translated to another body and another life - but I thought not. My training in statistical and risk analysis told me - through observation - that the probabilities were just too low for that.

I saw the many dead - and those killed by others - and also, God forgive me, by my hand.

I thought it best they not suffer this hell. That they not experience the utter rage that consumed us at hearing another language than our own native Spanish.

For that was what was happening in this obviously God-forsaken world.

After the event, I found myself just across the American Border in Nuevo Laredo, Mexico, although I did not realize it at the time.

I had been translated into a much younger man than I, and - as it turned out - a much more dynamic man than I ever could be.

He was tall, handsome and very European-Spanish looking, with bright blue eyes and dusty blonde hair.

I, too, came from very European stock - the usual Argentinean mixture of Italian, German, and Spanish.

In my case I had always more resembled a jolly, plump German Merchant than a Spanish aristocrat.

This gentleman I now inhabited was very aristocratic-looking with a deep mellifluous voice that was capable of persuading others just by the rolling sound of his voice.

I have never been comfortable speaking in public - other than in business meetings - and then only to provide facts and analyses. I now find myself able to do things and say things of which I never felt capable.

This man I became was really not an orator - only when the moment called for it. He was more of a man of action, as I came to find out. But he ("I") became very persuasive in our melding.

He had been here, Nuevo Laredo, at the behest of the Mexican Government to help them in their fight against the ever more dangerous drug cartels that plague Central America.

Alberto Álvarez y Ribacoba, as commanding officer of The "Grupo Especial de Operaciones" (GEO), headed the Special Operations Forces of the "Cuerpo Nacional de Policía" in Spain. The GEO had rapid response capabilities and was responsible for Political protection duties, as well as countering and responding to terrorism.

The Grupo was organized along the lines of many other special counter-terrorism units throughout Europe and was focused on dealing with terrorist attacks, including aircraft hijackings and hostage taking, which

Mexico - and the United States along its border - was facing more and more as the Twenty-first century rolled along.

I found this out when I read the text of his speech that he was, apparently, to give in this place.

So when I, the "old me," Ulrich Schmidl-Rivera, was dining at my usual hour of 9 o'clock in the evening, and drinking my one glass of a fine Argentinean Red allowed me by my medico, Señor Álvarez was, no doubt, regaling the senior officers of the Special Operations Group of the Federal Police of Mexico with countless tales of derring-do at his own dinner celebration.

I deduce this from the spilt drinks and multiple smoldering cigars I found "myself" among at the head of the table surrounded by uniformed and very high ranking Federales - all dead, of course.

That is, I noticed this when I was able to recover from the pain and seizures caused by the event.

I, too, went through the usual discovery process and the coming to grips that I imagine all survivors went through. It was remarkable that I did not go mad at that time. Or perhaps I did, and all of this is just the product of a fevered brain.

Alas, I think not.

One of the things I have trouble understanding, is why - having never handled a firearm in my life - I felt compelled to arm myself with one of those machine guns that were manufactured and provided by the Americans to the Mexican government.

It was one of those efficient-looking black automatic rifles that all the uniformed Federales seemed to carry about.

In my Argentina, the National Police and the local gendarmes all carried those little sub-compact machine guns - or machine pistols - on a sling. My own bodyguard carried one of those with a folded up handle under his suit coat.

Yes, I had a bodyguard. Those of us in top managerial positions all had one or two.

I suppose that says something about the sad state of affairs, these days, when we needed guards against not only the criminals - but against the corrupt police. It mortified me for my fatherland.

I have never had to handle a firearm, nor did I ever wish to. But now, after coming to grips with the changes wrought in me by the event, I automatically picked up a weapon and checked its firing capability, as though I knew how to.

It was ludicrous.

Here I was, a mild mannered accountancy director for one of the biggest firms in Argentina, ejecting the magazine, checking the weapon, and cocking it for ready fire as though I was a South American Rambo!

My hands moved steadily and with great skill and assurance.

This was my first hint that I was as transformed by the body I now inhabited as I had transformed it. I had skill of hands and body that did not require thought. Only action.

The first few days were spent in exploring this... city... which can only be described as a fourth-world village aspiring to become a third-world greatly impoverished town. There were signs (and graffiti) everywhere in Spanish, naturally, but intermixed with English here and there.

I could not read them - the English signs, that is - since the event. I had been fluent in Italian, German and English in addition to my own native Spanish - but no longer.

I saw death all around the crowded streets. The building I had found "myself" in was the Crowne Plaza Hotel. Not a very luxurious hotel, by any normal standards, but probably the best place in this feces-receptacle of a town.

In addition to the dead I awoke to in that private banquet room, the hotel itself was filled with the dead. The crowded streets were, as well.

Naturally, I encountered some individuals that had survived the experience as had I.

All (with few exceptions) were Spanish speakers that seemed of a like. All were relatively young, very fit and healthy (at least their "new" bodies were) - and all struggling to understand what was happening to them and why.

Now, I must confess something that my daughters would be horrified had they known. Oh, they must have suspected, but could not have direct knowledge of this fact.

I am - I was - somewhat of a bigot.

Oh, not as the Americans understand their own "hidden" bigotry to be (and are liberally ashamed of).

There, the bigotry was reserved mainly for differences on race. Although lately, mainly by the efforts of their cultural propagandists (the intelligentsia, Hollywood, and other forces of liberal thinking) they were including - in their guilty feelings - those having perverted sexual practices, as well. They had become very accepting of these persons, and even celebrated "inclusion."

Laughable.

No, my "bigotry" was reserved MAINLY for the countries and peoples that produced perverted Spanish dialects that verged on the moronic.

I will admit that the Spanish spoken in these lands were mainly populated by intermixing of the purity of the European genes with various indigenous peoples, and with those Negro slaves brought to work the fields where the indigenous peoples did not survive.

For example Cuba, the Dominican Republic, Puerto Rico - the Caribbean Islands mainly - that have so perverted the Spanish Language as to make it virtually incomprehensible to educated ears.

Much like the English spoken in the black American ghettos my American friends were always complaining about.

That "Spanish" grates on my nerves, and I cannot bear to listen to it for very long.

Almost as bad were the intonations with which the Indio-Mestizos - those persons of mixed European and American Indian ancestry - brought to bear on our beautiful language.

Mexico is racially composed of mainly the Indio-Mestizo, not really having had the opportunity to preserve the purity of European genetics as well as we in Argentina.

I once heard Argentina described as "the whitest country in South America."

Oh, there are some in Mexico that have kept their racial mixing down to an acceptable level - and those were generally the ruling class.

Blondes, redheads and blue and green eyes are the norm in the upper strata of Mexican society - but here in the borderlands - the frontier as it is known in Mexico - this is not the case.

Here I found myself amongst mainly brown faces.

However, since the "transition" of the souls into their new bodies happened randomly, one could hear the Negro-based dialect of the Dominican coming from a very European looking person, and just as easily hear the cultured, educated syntax of Spain coming from a very Indio brown face.

It was virtually the luck of the draw.

Hence, I stopped judging the books by their covers.

The mantle of leadership seemed to fall on me quite easily and naturally. My new looks, my new skills, and my own native intelligence was coupled with an emerging decisiveness and charisma I am at a loss to explain.

It just... happened.

As I explored the hotel I was in, I first encountered two other people that had been translated and survived. There was obvious concern and confusion on their part, and questioning what was real and what was not.

One of these people was bloody, with scratches on his head, face, hands and arms.

It seems that he had gone into a blind rage upon hearing a woman - who was in the same room with him - exclaim aloud in what he recognized as English. He could not understand her - obviously, in retrospect. But the mere sound of that English so enraged as to cause them both to violently react.

He strangled her to death.

This was the first inkling we had of this phenomenon we began calling "la lenqua de odio" - the language of hate.

Please understand, the "syndrome" was very rarely encountered on this side of the border, as most of the 700,000 residents were Spanish-speakers, with VERY few visiting other-language people. Mexico was not deemed "safe to visit" by other countries - especially the United States - AND especially to this violent border town.

So the odds of ANY survivors emerging other than Spanish speakers would be very low. Yet, it did happen enough that we became aware of the phenomenon. It just wasn't germane (as it would become later) to our current situation.

In any case, as we explored this city of the dead, we encountered other groups that were trying to make sense of what had happened to us. There were many theories, of course, but again, not very relevant to our current situation.

As it was getting dark, we had gathered about 15 others from the streets. They were coming together and talking in their various Spanish dialects trying to make sense of what was happening, and talking at cross purposes, and over one another. It was very irritating, especially as I listened to some Caribbean accents mangling and "swallowing" their "eses."

I raised the menacing-looking black assault rifle high over my head. As I was much taller than anyone else, that was very high, indeed. They, one at a time, stopped speaking at looked at me as I stood silently.

Once I knew I had their full attention I began to speak.

I told them what we needed to do that night, and what we would do in the morning light. They listened to me, silently and nodded, all agreeing that what I said made sense.

That night, I became the de facto leader of the group - and that group would grow into the thousands. And would continue to grow as we crossed the border and beyond.

II. AT GORE'S FOLLY

JANIS SET THE BUCKET DOWN and looked in satisfaction at the rows of prepared soil at the top of Gore's Folly, ready to receive both fall vegetable plants, as well as the midsummer plantings that Sam had talked her into.

Sam had told her, "This is TEXAS! There IS no autumn. Forget your 'book-learning,' lady!", and laughed.

Over the last six months, Janis had grown quite fond of Sam - that poor genius boy in a girl's body, trying so hard not to give in to the physical changes wrought on the inhabiting minds by the inhabited bodies.

She tried so hard to deny her attractiveness - going to great lengths to dress sloppily and hide that lush, perfect figure - and completely failing.

Other schemes - such as not bathing or washing her luxuriant black hair were complete disasters.

After a few weeks of this, Janis saw Victor take Sam aside and have a quiet, but firm, talk.

Janis tried not to eavesdrop, but she caught the words "pheromones" and "the opposite effect on dudes" from the obviously adamant Victor. Sam looked abashed, her tan face taking on the color of embarrassment.

The poor dear.

The next day, Sam had shown up to work and Janis noticed the scent of fresh soap. But then she noticed Sam's latest attempt - and tried not to laugh.

Sam had hacked off that great fall of hair - in an obvious attempt to diminish the exotic effect of that black, cascade of luxuriousness. But she had only succeeded in making herself look like a pixie - a cute, sexy pixie. Sam could not win this battle.

But now, some five and a half months later, Janis was standing on the flattened hilltop and surveying the fruits of her labour. This was how it came about.

There was no denying the genius of little Sam. Janis began to work with her on projects almost upon first meeting.

In that first meeting, Sam had explained the conclusions both she and the unknown "Floozer," (what an odd name) with whom she had been in contact over something called "Skype" (another odd name) had drawn.

She had talked about the "Book of Lists" she had drawn up that included both short and long-term needs.

Victor had listened very intently, nodding, but not interrupting, and then drew his own conclusions about what needed to be done (thus, showing his own genius.)

Victor - always the man of action, Janis thought with a moue of slight distaste.

He had assigned Jonas to work on the immediate - that is, to fully understand the building's capabilities and what could be found elsewhere in the city to augment those capabilities. He also needed an assessment of space requirements and power consumption limits to gauge how many people could be housed here.

He said, "According to Sam's projections, about 30 thousand or so English speakers may have survived in the metro area alone. No telling how many will survive the following days ahead, and whether they will have the skills to find us."

He looked at Sam severely, "And this 'Floozer' apparently is coming here from Canada with a few others, and he will be playing 'the Pied Piper' all along the way.

So we need to ferret out skills and abilities we will require and to make sure the resources of 'Gore's Folly' can sustain us. Else... we will need to make some... tough decisions."

Janis, he had assigned to planning for future capabilities when foodstuffs ran out. What was needed for agriculture and animal husbandry and what skill sets or knowledge would be required.

When Sam objected that they needn't look into that now - that they had an entire city, and cities beyond, to scavenge for foodstuffs, Victor told her, "Sam, think about it - there's a limited shelf life on all goods." He also mentioned the need for fresh foods and meats, milk, etc.

Janis nodded her agreement, but was not hopeful that they would be able to pull off more than a mere "truck garden" without the requisite skills and knowledge - as well as modern farming equipment and seed stocks.

He assigned Sam to work on researching what knowledge or skills were needed to survive long-term - medicine, chemistry, agriculture, engineering, electronics and so on.

He wanted a plan to "download" the needed information to the building's storage servers, and, if need be, to scavenge for other server equipment, for when, not if, the Internet "went down".

He also wanted Sam to poll the electronic social media community to build résumés of skill sets and experiential knowledge in order to recruit and give priority.

Also, he wanted her to find a way to continue communications with other, isolated communities that would undoubtedly form across the nation, when the electrical grid failed, thus ending modern-day communications.

"Look into short-wave radio and CB's for when the time comes," he said.

Sam had nodded, but Janis noticed her puzzled squint at the term, "CB."

So young! Janis smiled.

Victor turned to Jonas and said, "I want you to put your engineering hat on and look at the capabilities we have in-house with the custom-car machine shop and the Gun-Smithing business."

Jonas said, "I can give you an assessment of what the machine shop brings to the table, Mate, but haven't the foggiest notion of how to assess the gun stuff."

"I'm not asking you to assess 'the gun stuff' - Gunny and I will do that," an acknowledgement nod from "Gunny," who had remained silent, throughout, "but I want you to assess the machining and custom fabrication capabilities. These custom gun manufacturers have some pretty sophisticated stuff - water jets, computer-controlled fabbing and such." Jonas nodded his understanding.

"Gunny," he said to the older gentleman (who, in truth was just a 22 year-old Marine corporal, inside), "You and I need to discuss a security plan." Gunny nodded.

"But for now, we've got two things to take care of before I invite you all to 'my' gym to get some much needed rest." Victor continued.

"We've got some couches up there, and some mats to lie on. The gym also has full restroom and shower facilities."

"But..." he said, "we now have some guns, ammo and food to unload from the truck.

Sam, you'll be glad to hear we brought changes of clothes from the mall - Janis was kind enough to 'shop' for you based on my description - and you'll be glad to know we also brought toiletries."

He went on, "If you can confirm that the freezers and refrigeration units are working in the Restaurant Supply House..." He paused as Sam nodded and silently mouthed, "They are."

"...Then we can off-load the groceries and put them up there in the Supply House. The guns and ammo we can keep in here for the moment." He paused again. "The second thing we need to do is police up the dead.

Sam, if that Bio-Mass system works like you think it does, I suggest a couple of us use some hand trucks to pick them up, and to deposit them in the... converter."

"I'll do it," said Gunny.

"Okay, Gunny," Victor said. "You and me. I know where most of the bodies are, anyway. We all can start on the weapons cache, and then you three," nodding to the others, "can finish up with the supplies. When you're all up there, take a look at the gym, since it's on the same floor."

They all nodded.

"Oh!" said Victor, as if just remembering something. "We've got a messy deader on that floor and there might be others. Sam did you see any bodies on the 'cams?"

Sam nodded and grimaced, "Yeah. None in the Supply House, but few on the next floor in the Gun Smith Shop. And you already know about the others..."

"Okay," Victor said, "So we'll start unloading the weapons, secure them in here, and you guys can start on the supplies while Gunny and I take out the deaders." He looked around seeing their morose faces, only Gunny appearing placid.

He grinned, "Hey! Look at the bright side... at least no one's trying to shoot you!"

There was that.

Jonas sighed, slapped his knee and said, "Okay, mates. Let's have at it!" and stood.

Janis followed suit and quoted, "... 'and miles to go before we sleep'..."

It didn't take them miles, but it took a couple of hours to do what they needed to do that night.

OVER THE NEXT FEW DAYS, Gunny and Victor were out reconnoitering, while the three others were conducting their own research and exchanging ideas and information.

Sam first helped Janis navigate through web-based systems to conduct research... and Janis caught on quickly "for an old lady."

She was in her element anyway, even if the books WERE virtual, rather than paper.

The familiarity of searching and seeking branching information was nothing new - but this occurred virtually at the speed of light with fantastic indexing and cross-referencing. Janis thought she could get used to the ease of using computers - but she didn't like to admit it.

It was hard for Sam to picture the old African lady in this young, trim, good looking, green-eyed blonde. But once in a while Janis would clap delightedly at something she found, and Sam could catch a glimmer. Sam became very fond of this lady.

Jonas, for his part, was himself delightedly exploring all the mechanical systems - carrying a computer tablet to take notes and capture pictures. He, also, was in his element, and had to be reminded by Janis to take a break to eat.

Every day, Victor and Gunny would return from their explorations, having reconnoitered up and down IH-10. Each day, it seemed, they were bringing more and more survivors to Gore's Folly. The first week, they had come back with sixteen survivors in total.

Sam was introduced to them to "index" their knowledge and skill sets. If they had no particular skills, they were assigned "grunt work" by Gunny.

In the second week, they ran across a group of eleven survivors. They had lost thirteen others having to fight their way from downtown San Antonio north across the city.

One of this group of eleven was a young lady named Gwen Philpot.

She had been Welsh, from the capital city of Cardiff, and she had retired from the South Wales Constabulary as Deputy Chief Constable.

Her body, however, now was that of a 20-something Mexican-American girl who had been a dancer for a folk-dancing troupe on the San Antonio Riverwalk. The Event had occurred in the middle of a performance. Needless to say this Welsh lady was not prepared for having to fight across a foreign city dressed in a colorful Mexican dancer's costume.

But, Gwen's experience with firearms and her now youthful and athletic body had proved essential in getting the group safely to the point where Victor and Gunny first encountered them, 15 miles south of Gore's Folly.

Gwen had joined the Metropolitan Police Service (MPS) after graduating from police academy, and first walked a beat in Edmonton, North London.

She soon progressed into the Criminal Investigation Division and spent a large part of her career as an operational detective, including work within the Vice Unit, Murder Squad, and the Race and Violent Crime Task Force.

She had been appointed as the Detective Superintendent of the MPS Anti-Terrorist Branch and set up the MPS War Crimes Unit and the Counter Terrorist Intelligence Cell. She had also acted as the Senior Investigating Officer in a number of terrorist investigations.

Gwen went on to hold responsibility for all operational strategy in the MPS before joining South Wales Police as an Assistant Chief Constable in 2008, responsible for Protective Services, Serious & Organised Crime,

Counter Terrorism, Firearms, Roads Policing and other operational policing specialties.

She retired at age 55, two weeks before the Event.

GWEN WAS VICTOR'S CUP OF TEA: a female Victor.

She had begun to accompany Victor and Gunny on their recon missions, but then was assigned by Victor to lead the now necessary foraging parties as Gore's Folly found and recruited more and more survivors - as well as growth from the social media people Sam had "invited" to join them.

There was a steady trickle of people arriving daily - guided by GPS directions.

This eventually slowed, then stopped, with the failure of the electric grid - and hence the internet and GPS services - in vast swathes of the Americas.

Getting supplies and materials was essential for the ever-growing population of Gore's Folly, but had also proven very dangerous, with competing bands of foreign adversaries threatening the foraging parties' safety. Just as important was the clean-up effort of clearing the streets (and selected buildings) of the dead.

This also required protection as they ran into other foreign groups.

Gwen's group was charged with obtaining foodstuffs and clothing and toiletries. Jonas had worked out what was needed to sustain a growing population over time, and this list had priority.

One simple example was toilets.

While Gore's Folly had 26 toilet facilities, they were not readily accessible. They were not in the spaces designated to be "residential quarters."

God knows there was plenty of space in the building.

The top floor was completely empty and had been sub-divided to accommodate large offices. These had separate temperature controls and lighting, so they could easily be set up as large dormitories. All of them could be further sub-divided to give some privacy as needed.

The back of each space had some pre-fabbed walls in storage that could interlock with each other within the tracks laid on the floor and giant ceilings. Like Lego Blocks, they fit neatly and logically, even providing pre-wired conduit for electrical and Ethernet.

And, even though each large division had pre-plumbing built into the walls and floors capped for easy access - they had no fixtures. None.

No toilets, no sinks, and no pipes or connections.

Hence, the foraging for materials. Especially as in about the third month after the event, they had upwards of 670 people housed at Gore's Folly. That number was expected to quadruple in the next six months.

JONAS HAD GONE TO GWEN with a list of materials.

Gwen had looked at the list and asked, in her very Cardiff accent, "So... Have you estimated the TOE requirements of these?" By which she meant what guidance could Jonas provide as to the number of trucks, the size of the work gangs, hand trucks or dollies required to "complete the mission."

She needed to know how many people to take along and how many guns she'd have to have riding along on protection duty.

So guns - and those trained and ready to use them - became as necessary as food. And someone experienced in leading such an armed force - whether law or military - was an important skill set.

Hence: Gwen.

Another new addition came in the form of Staff Sgt. Lori Ann Chester.

She had been a Tennessee National Guard soldier and was the second woman ever awarded the Silver Star for courage under fire in the war on terror. Her convoy had come under attack outside Baghdad. She was cited for killing several insurgents and saving the lives of numerous convoy members.

She was now in the uncomfortable position of having been translated into a rather large black man. It was easier to call Lori "Sarge."

Lori became fast friends with Sam, as they shared the irritating and often embarrassing experience of getting used to the new, or missing, parts of their bodies.

That convoy protection experience was invaluable as the Gore's Folly community grew, and more foraging parties had to be sent to replace food stocks and other items. So naturally Lori - "Sarge" - had been recruited by Gwen for the task.

These missions called for both arms and protection - and grunt workers.

Arms and ammo were basically no problem (yet.)

Victor and Gunny had managed to cut the lock off the SWAT van that first night in Gore's Folly, yielding a treasure trove that made what had been found in Victor's trunk pale by comparison.

The SWAT unit was equipped with specialized firearms including six MP5 submachine guns; eight M16A4 assault rifles; three shotguns; two 7.62×51mm M40 sniper rifles (which made Gunny smile dreamily), riot control agents, and boxes of stun grenades, as well as two M32 grenade launchers and a bunch of High Explosive (HE) rounds.

It also contained eight sets of heavy (Advanced Dragon Skin) body armor; helmets; knee and elbow pads; three ballistic shields; various entry tools; eight sets of advanced night vision optics and two sets of motion detectors.

Naturally, Gunny laid claim to one of the M40's as his own possession, and took one of the M16's as his backup weapon. He also equipped himself with a full set of body armor.

Victor had replaced his own torso armor as his had been breached and damaged by the .458 SOCOM.

They outfitted Gwen's troops with the remaining armor and let them choose their preference of armament - with some guidance from Gwen and "Sarge."

Beside the weapons and ammo they had boosted from the Bass Pro Shops (they had enough to supply a small division with a variety of weapons - pistols of all calibers, "assault rifles" - albeit single shot civilian models - shotguns and hunting and sport-shooting rifles) what they discovered in the gunsmith shop made their jaws drop.

They had entered the shop that first night and what they saw made them stop dead in their tracks. Gunny whistled in either admiration or surprise - or maybe both.

Beside the usual displays of peg-mounted weapons of various types (ARs, AKs, FNs, civilian-type MP5s) behind the glass counter display of pistols and ammo, there was a display that caught the eye immediately.

There, sitting on a pedestal-mount, was an M60 machine gun!

Generally, it's operated by a team of two or three. It fires the 7.62×51mm NATO round at a rate of fire of 500–650 rounds per minute with an effective range of 1,200 yards.

And to its immediate right, at the opposite end of the counter, was its bigger brother - a Twin Mount M2HB .50 caliber machine gun.

Gunny said that the ammunition it fired along with the M903 Saboted Light Armor Penetrator Round could punch through 11/2 inches of hardened steel plate at 550 yards.

Crazy! They were real war machines.

"Do you think they work?" Gunny whispered, as though in church.

"You kidding, man?" Victor said with a grin splitting his face ear to ear, "This is TEXAS! Of COURSE they do!"

They had also uncovered a cache of customized rifles (all types); customized combat shotguns - many in AK-type frames - fully automatic ARs and AKs, full auto MP4's and MP5's; all manner of Belgian-Made weapons; automatic pistols; revolvers; hunting rifles; scopes and optics of all kinds; and parts of all kinds.

Also Kevlar vests - not quite up to Dragon Skin but useful, nonetheless.

The shop had full reloading capability; brass stamping equipment; propellant manufacturing equipment and specialized tools to build, fix or fabricate whatever was needed.

It was mind-blowing.

They grinned at each other like nerds getting lucky with costumed girls at Comic Con.

They figured they had all the armaments they would ever need.

They were wrong.

ONE OF THE SIDE OUTCOMES OF THE FORAGING EXPEDITIONS was that roads had to be cleared of wrecked cars and bodies because it made for easier passage for the trucks and personnel going to and from these expeditions.

In addition, there was major concern for basic sanitation and disease control. When the Texas summer drought ended, and the rainy fall season began, there was concern that rotting bits of corpse could enter the water table.

Under "normal" circumstances, the occasional deer or skunk carcass on the road would be taken care of by Mother Nature. Vultures, coyotes and other carrion eaters were very proficient at disposing of this problem, but the entire population of these were unable to put even a dent in the million or two bodies that lay baking in the sun.

Sam had estimated that there were at least 1/2 million bodies in wrecked vehicles, and an unfathomable number of dead in homes, businesses and apartments. These would not be a problem for the Gore's Folly community, except for the bodies in the stores they had targeted for foraging.

These businesses had to be cleared out in order to make gathering possible and acceptable for the foraging parties.

Gwen in her efficient way (with Sam's help), came up with a plan.

First: to clear the road ways, they would use tow trucks and flatbeds to move the wrecked vehicles aside or place them in open lots and parking spaces.

Second: crews working alongside the tow trucks would clear the bodies (or the parts left over) from the streets, sidewalks and parking lots, by loading them on dump trucks. These dump trucks would then drive to the Gore's Folly Bio-Mass loading dock and disgorge the "cargo" for processing.

Since the dump trucks ran on diesel fuel, the Converter would produce biomass diesel fuel and the truck could refuel with the output. Corpses in, fuel to transport the corpses, out. It was a virtual "perpetual motion machine."

Very little was wasted as the bodies - in addition to the animal fat that produced the fuel - produced water (which was purified and treated for return to the environment); methane gas for energy production; and a whole host of useable minerals, metals and chemicals and nitrogen-enriched liquid fertilizer.

Third: foraging parties would go out as required.

All that this needed was: 1. Qualified truck drivers; 2. Working Crews; and 3. Trained armed escorts.

The first part they had - or could train. After all, safe highway driving in traffic was not a real problem.

The third requirement was a bit problematic as, surprisingly, they had few experienced or trained professionals. This was surprising, as most of the survivors had had run-ins with hostile groups. But they had mostly adapted and could be trained on the rudiments of squad tactics and protection oversight.

The second requirement, however, was a doozey.

NOBODY wanted to be on the work crews - especially on the body removal detail.

Not only did the work require physical exertion in the stifling Texas heat, but to prevent disease and contamination (not to mention not passing out from the smell) the work parties would have to wear respirators and light-weight "hazmat" suits. That made it intolerable for any period of time.

So Gunny was forced to "volunteer" people, based on their skills, or lack thereof, to be on the appropriate work crews. Some people objected, but Gunny was nothing if not persuasive.

After a few successful runs, however, Gunny was forced to stop the work details because of a lack of cooperation. He went to Gwen who, upon speaking with three of the self appointed "representatives" of the objecting parties, decided to defer to Victor.

She had Gunny accompany the objecting representatives up to the gym where Victor was having a planning discussion with Sam, Jonas, and Janis.

They were discussing what to do with the excess material being produced by the biomass system since it had so much material to work with, now that the carcasses were being introduced in such large quantities and at such a rapid rate.

Jonas was saying, "Normally, this would not be a problem, as the methane gas," he pronounced it MEE-THANE, "would be used to power the turbines to generate electricity. Any excess energy production would be passed on to the commercial grid. However, since there is no demand from the grid... it is wasted."

Victor frowned and said, "And so...?"

"Well," Jonas replied, "it's not just a matter of waste. There're two other issues. One is the running of the turbines continually JUST to get rid of the methane. Not only wasteful, but it will have an effect on the turbine useable life."

Victor nodded, "I can see how that wouldn't be good. We can't just run down to 'Turbines R Us' to get parts."

"Exactly," Jonas agreed, "but there's a more serious problem."

Victor raised his eyebrows in askance.

Jonas said, "I'll have Janis take over here," and he looked toward Janis, who nodded.

She cleared her throat. She said, "Well. There's the matter of methane oversaturation of the water extracted from the process. The system is built to purify and filter that water and return it to the aquifer. A nice, open system.

But that is compromised by the over-production of the methane. It can - it will - over-saturate the water over time and contaminate our drinking supply.

Burning it off into the atmosphere is not the answer. The heat alone proves problematic.

We can bottle and pressurize some of it to run machinery - vehicles, lorries and the like - but we do not have the capacity to do much of that."

Victor said, "Yeaaaah...?" The equivalent of looking at his watch.

Janis went on, "It seems that by combining atmospheric nitrogen with hydrogen - which is usually derived from methane - we can easily produce vast quantities of ammonium nitrate and ammonium sulfate in order to produce - fertilizer!"

"Hmmm..." Victor said, "so... problem not solved?"

Jonas took over, "Well, not quite. While we can produce the fertilizer, there's the small matter of storing it. God knows we've plenty of room for storage, but... do we really want to sit on the equivalent explosive power of a small nuke, mate?"

Visions of Timothy McVey and the bomb that took down the building in Oklahoma danced in Victor's mind. He sighed and said, "Quit messing around and just give the answer you guys have come up with. I don't need all this hoopla."

Sam piped up and said, "We can produce LIQUID fertilizer to pump up to the top of the hill to produce crops for Janis' agricultural plans.

Before you say, 'Just DO it,' Jonas will need materials to modify the system which requires a change in foraging priorities."

Victor sighed mightily and said, "So just do it!"

Gunny chose just that time to walk in with the protestors.

VICTOR WAS SITTING ON THE EDGE OF THE DESKTOP, facing the trio, while Gunny explained the situation. He looked at Gunny with a frown and lowered eyebrows as if to say, "So you couldn't handle this?" Gunny looked at him and shrugged.

"Okay," Victor said, "So, let me get this straight. You feel the work detail is beneath you? Is that correct?"

The woman of the trio shook her head, frowning, and said in a condescending manner, as though speaking to one of inferior intellect, "We just feel we are not given a democratic voice in what needs to be done and by whom."

Victor leaned forward and asked, "What gave you the idea that this is a democracy? That you have ANY voice in the matter?"

They looked shocked. The woman huffed and said, "We have basic human rights!"

"Who said?" Victor questioned.

The trio were left with their mouths open.

Victor leaned in and sighed. He said, speaking reasonably, "Look: let me explain just this once for you why these work crews are so essential for our survival..."

The woman interrupted, saying, "Who says?" sneering triumphantly.

Victor looked at her and said quietly, "Who were you, exactly? What skills do you bring?"

She looked offended and said, "If you must know, I am - I was - Osma Baader-Shadd. I was Director, Office of Equity, Diversity, and Human Rights, for the City of Toronto.

I am - was - a community-based researcher, advocate, and an activist. I served as the Executive Director of Council of Agencies serving on issues of race, erosion of civil liberties, and critical multiculturalism. I have been an advocate, an organizer/facilitator, a writer, and a lecturer on diverse issues facing racialised communities," She paused, proudly.

Victor said, blandly, "In other words - no skills."

The trio looked shocked and offended. Sam snickered.

"Just leave." Victor turned around, dismissively. "Gunny, get these people back to work."

"Yes sir." He grabbed the woman's arm and said, "You heard the Captain. Let's go."

The woman shook off Gunny's grasp and yelled, "I will NOT!"

Victor turned around slowly to look at her.

She said, "I will not work for you."

"So... get out," Victor said.

"We will NOT! We have every right to be here! Just as much right as you!" She said. "If you insist on treating us this way, I will organise all the others to defy your tyrannical orders!"

The two with her were smiling. They must have thought they were dealing with a city council or some other political body.

Victor smiled slightly, cocked his head quizzically, and said softly, "Okay... so, tell me, lady... Can you make coffee?"

She sneered and said forcibly, "I am NOT a domestic!"

"So what damn good are you?" Victor drew his sidearm and shot her.

JANIS WAS LOOKING OVER THE HILLTOP where they would be planting crops, soon.

Freshly fertilized fields gleamed with the moisture of the liquefied fertilizer that had been sprayed from the bio-mass converter tanks modified by Jonas with scavenged materials.

Now numbering at 2,700 souls, Gore's Folly could well use it.

And they had no more difficulty with getting volunteers for work details.

None.

III. RIVERA

CROSSING THE BORDER BECAME a necessity as the power failed throughout Nuevo Laredo.

I despised this frontier Mexican city. But this purportedly "best hotel in town" was not so bad. It was surrounded by greenery and tree-lined streets. Surprising.

At least it had air conditioning, plenty of beds, a "restaurant-quality" kitchen and a larder.

As a high-rise, it was the perfect place to attract and house the survivors of the event. As they straggled in, they were greeted as "guests" - their former names written down, along with their "new body" identification, if they had it, and their previous experience and profession.

That first night, I had "bonded" with three individuals.

In truth - I didn't care for them in any emotional sense, but they had the skills or presence to help me accomplish what I needed. Now, they formed the core of what I considered "my" group - those housed in the Crowne Plaza hotel on Paseo Colón.

One of these was a heavily muscled, tattooed individual named "Abdul Oyala" in his former life. He was from the Republic of Equatorial Guinea somewhere in Africa. I hadn't known about that as a Spanish language country, and I had considered myself well traveled. But, there you are.

This Abdul turned out to be a very useful fellow. He had apparently worked for the less than democratic government of Equatorial Guinea as an… operative, I guess you could say. I would guess that his job was "law enforcement" - or what passes for laws in those Third World areas.

He was now housed in the body of what gave the appearance of being a long-term gangster and hardened criminal. Prison and gang tattoos lined his face, neck, arms and body.

He seemed not bothered by this, as this was probably a close approximation of what he had been, before. But he was a follower - not a leader. So, he naturally gravitated to me and became my good right arm. I treated him carefully and gave the appearance of treating him as a trusted equal. With his low - but cunning - intelligence this served to gain his absolute loyalty.

He could, as the Americans have it, play "bad cop" to my "good cop." I just had to grit my teeth and bear his atrocious dialect. Fah!

Next was a young woman - now housed in a burly 40-ish man of indeterminate race. She had been a recently graduated neurosurgeon working in Mexico City. She had the surgeon's detachment, and had assessed her - now "his" - own experience with the acceptance of an observing scientist. He was the greatest provider of information about - from the neurological sense - what we had all experienced.

He (formerly "she") provided a scientific detachment, and could provide me with an assessment of whatever I was planning. He had a broad knowledge of all things technical, and seemed just a step ahead of anybody else, looking out long term as to the consequences of the new world.

She had been named Joséfina, but now went by the name "José," due to the transformation to the masculine.

The final person of my leadership trio was a young man that insisted he be called "Penzo," although that was not a name I have ever been exposed to.

I could not place his accent. It seemed to reflect the dialect patterns of what to us - the Spanish speaking world - was the neutral newscaster accent of an educated Central American. Much as, in the United States, the neutral accent of the American Midwest was the mainstay, or the educated Londoner was to the Brits.

He told us nothing about his previous life and, when asked, he simply stared at the inquisitor in dead silence. Uncomfortable, to say the least.

He was a quietly observant man. He always appeared to be watching in total detachment - hardly reacting to any startling event.

I noticed this when we - while standing in the street that first night - were shot at.

Everyone - even Abdul - reacted by flinching and ducking. Everyone, that is, but Penzo. He merely kept standing and peered around him until he spotted the flashes from the discharging weapon. Everyone else was confused by the echoing sounds and looked wildly around. He merely pointed and said, "There! The shooting is coming from there."

Those of us that were armed shot and concentrated our fire on the now obvious target.

Needless to say we were successful in killing the attacker. But Penzo just stood there, while we did.

Later I found him to be of equal intelligence as our erstwhile neurosurgeon. Or perhaps superior to.

I was grateful that he seemed not to have leadership aspirations. Else, I would have had to turn Abdul's attention to him. But he seemed not at all cowed by Abdul, which, thankfully, only puzzled Abdul, rather than enraging him.

A very useful man to have around, our Penzo was.

There were other groups that had gathered around this surprisingly large community. We did our best not to clash with any of them, and they reciprocated, realizing that the greater enemies were those that did not speak our mother tongue.

Admittedly, those were few. But these few turned out to be tenacious and very, very dangerous, when they realized they were vastly outnumbered in this land. They had managed to arm themselves well, and apparently had the skills to use those arms.

Since only the fit and athletic seemed to have survived the transition, Penzo thought (and I agreed) that, if they were in this country from an English-speaking world, then they were probably not tourists, but rather some kind of military, law enforcement or other kinds of agents. This gave their bodies "muscle memory" skills, but not necessarily the violent mindset to carry out a skillful attack. But the "rage" might have enhanced their abilities. José, our nuero-scientist, thought that might be the case.

In any case, they were too few in number to be worrisome. I was more concerned with the future and my place in it.

I really hadn't truly formulated for myself what I had in mind - although I had a growing sense that this was a new beginning - a brand new life I could lead as a truly different person. It was... exhilarating!

So, after a few months of organizing group life and coming to terms with what would be required to survive and thrive, I had gathered my people around me and said, "As you know, our world has changed in ways that we cannot imagine."

I looked at the faces around me and saw that I had their attention. They wanted - they NEEDED - answers, or just a direction that APPEARED to answer their fear, loss and confusion.

I went on to tell them that we needed to build a new society - a better society - from the ashes of the old.

I said, "But, my friends, we would be better off building a new society from the RICHES of the old."

I smiled and they smiled along with me.

"Frankly, my friends, these 'ashes' around us cannot compare to what we can build upon the riches across the northern border in the 'Estados Unidos!'."

IV. VICTOR

I OPENED THE DOOR, expecting the usual stench of decomposition, but only getting the stale smell that accompanies any closed-in stuffy room that's been sitting over a long period of time.

It appears as though "I" had been living single - which didn't surprise me at all, given what I've learned about the person - this "Victor" - I was now inhabiting.

After the stifling summer we had just gone through, it was a relief to have a cool 75 degree day to go out in. The apartment - "my" apartment - was not as hot as I had expected it to be, even though the power had gone out in this area over two months ago.

I don't really know why I had Gunny drop me off here as we were going through the area on an exploratory recon. Just curiosity, I guess, about what Victor's life had been like before I... took over. I had recognized the street address from the ID I carried - and Gunny was well able to handle a simple scouting mission without me.

I told him to pick me up on the way back.

Truth to tell, I was just out to get away from Gore's Folly. Since we had grown in population over the past few months, I found myself growling with impatience at folks. I saw the wary looks that people gave me - part fear, part tension - as though at any moment I might snap. That was all right with me. Since shooting that annoying woman, no one questioned my orders, and generally left me alone.

Well, except for my "friends." Sam, certainly, but now she treated me like a dog that's shit the floor too many times. Exasperated anger, I'd call it.

Jonas - and especially Janis - were both angered and disappointed in me, I'd say.

Gunny showed nothing.

Anyway, that lady had been really annoying. When I had said so, Jonas said, "Being annoying is not a capital offense, mate."

I smiled thinly, play acting the menace a bit, and said, "It is, now."

He looked faintly disgusted.

I couldn't tell them that I had acted on impulse.

No. That wasn't quite right.

I had acted for a reason - even though the reason hadn't come to me until later. The real reason I had acted so "impulsively" is that I couldn't allow dissention to work its way into our community. We needed people to do their jobs, or they were just a waste of water.

I remembered reading "Dune," the old science-fiction book, for the first time as a kid. If you don't know the story, look it up on Sam's library servers. (Don't bother with the movies - they're just poorly made.)

The major characters were part of a desert society on a virtually waterless planet, where even the moisture of one's breath was precious and should not be wasted. They rendered their dead - and their enemies - for the "water of life." This seemed both sensible and poetic to my young mind at the time.

These people - the "Fremen" - I guess it was a play on "free men" - were ruthless to those that threatened them and their clans, and equally ruthless with themselves in order to survive.

I needed to be equally ruthless in my application of discipline and order. The perfect application of violence is that which completes the mission: "when you move, move with a sense of purpose and aggression, and the intent of finishing the enemy."

Our mission at Gore's Folly was to survive and thrive. Our enemies were not just foreign speakers. They were also disease, starvation, wild animals and inertia.

We couldn't survive with the threat of disorder and dissention. Examples had to be made.

I did that by acting swiftly and without mercy, as I dispatched that woman. A "community organizer" was a waste of water, anyway.

I sent a message also by having Gunny publically kneecap the other two guys and throw them out the gate, where they eventually became buzzard food.

Object lessons.

No one went to their aid. Nor, did anyone leave.

End of story.

ANYWAY, NOTHING SEEMED FAMILIAR about this apartment. Although, how could it have? I had none of the memories associated with the body I now inhabited. Well, except for "muscle memory" of actions repeated over time.

But this place was sterile. No pictures on the walls, nothing on shelves, nothing to give a clue as to "my" personality.

I sat down on the plain brown generic "leather" couch that had no personality and put my boots on the equally generic coffee table. I looked at the only thing that looked like Victor had taken the time to think about - the latest, flat screen monstrosity that was, no doubt, a "Smart" TV.

I could see "myself" reflected in the black surface of the TV - both literally and figuratively.

I put my head back while slouching on the couch and thought of what my life had become. What I had become.

I rested my head on the sofa back and looked up at the ceiling. I was enjoying the quiet of the apartment, if not the ambience.

I had left the door open, hoping a stray breeze would waft through, and the stillness outside was a cementing punctuation of how the world had completely changed. No vehicle noise, no planes flying overhead, no people laughing, talking or arguing, no TV or radio playing. It was... peaceful.

I heard a loud "thump!" coming from overhead. I sat up, stiffened and cocked my head to see if the sound would be repeated. Tingling adrenalin surged through my body and I had to tamp it down and slow my breathing.

I didn't hear anything now.

I slowly and quietly stood up, making sure that I would not make any noise, myself. I had my hand on my sidearm by reflex.

I had let Gunny have my FN Five-seveN - he had admired it so much - and truth to tell, I didn't really care for it. The bullets were too weird, and I didn't care for the extra heavy magazine, so I let him have it.

A good old 1911 was good enough for me. But Gunny wouldn't hear of it. He talked me into a Mk23 (Mark 23) chambered for .45. It was heavy, but well suited to my new frame and big hands. So I took it, and that's what I was carrying. I also was carrying the Colt Commando on a chest sling.

The apartment was on the ground floor, so the thump I heard had to have been from the apartment directly above me. I brought the Colt up to my shoulder in the ready position and eased my way through the open doorway.

THE STAIRCASE WAS THREE APARTMENTS down and was inset along a perpendicular hallway that had more apartments lining it. I moved slowly down the sidewalk passing the other ground floor apartments leading to the hall and the stairway.

There was an overhang that made up an "open" hallway leading to the second story apartments facing the same way as mine. There was no way I could see what was up there without stepping out into the parking lot that faced the apartment fronts and look up. So I opted to make as little noise as possible.

Once again, I was grateful for the "soundless" boots I wore. That made it much easier.

The ascent up the stairs and the trip back towards the apartment sitting right over "mine" was tense but uneventful.

I got to the doorway - the main window overlooking the parking lot was thankfully beyond the door, so I didn't have to cross it where I could be seen from inside.

The door was open - apparently the person inside was hoping to catch a breeze, as I had been. That was probably met with more success on this top floor, which was a good idea now that electric power, and therefore, air conditioning had failed in this area.

I sidled up to the door and looked in. A man was in the kitchen putting some cans of food away. That's probably what he had dropped, making the thumping noise. The kitchen area was open to the living room, so nothing was really in between us.

I went in behind him.

I noticed a pistol on the countertop. I pointed the Colt Commando and yelled, "Freeze!"

He jumped up, startled, and quickly turned half way around and promptly fell on his ass while emitting a scared scream. He looked very frightened, but didn't seem to react to my English with rage.

His mouth kept opening up like a fish and he gurgled something. That something wasn't a language, so my body did not go into flight or fight mode.

I said, "Who are you? Answer me!"

He kept mouthing something, but there was no sense to the grunting noises he produced.

"Can you hear me? Are you deaf?"

He didn't nod, or shake his head, or gesture towards his ears, or his mouth like some deaf people might. He just looked scared and uncomprehending.

"God," I thought, "this guy's a Mutie!"

For the last few months our people, and the folks we were in contact with online, were reporting encounters with survivors they called "Muties," or sometimes "Morlocks."

These were not actually mutes - nor were they deaf. They just didn't understand and couldn't speak ANY language. Their speech processing centers were apparently burned out by the event. They were totally aphasic, which meant they couldn't even THINK of a word, much less understand it.

Even their symbol-processing capabilities were completely burned out, so that they couldn't process pictures, signs or gestures.

Unlike people that suffer from Aspergers syndrome, they could read facial cues such as anger, hate, rage and fear. But - according to a neurologist that posted on Sam's social media forum (before it all went down) - they appeared to suffer from a form of "visual agnosia," which blocked their ability to process any symbols, drawings, pictures, written words... just about ANY form of communication.

Coupled with complete aphasia, this meant they could not communicate at all. With anybody.

Think about this a minute:

Even Helen Keller, who was both deaf AND blind, had learned to read Braille (symbols) and could "listen" to a person signing language symbols into her palms. She was made "not alone" by her care-taker teaching these things and communicating with her.

THESE people did not have even that capability.

They were still intelligent and could reason well, still felt all the emotions, still saw, still heard and still feared. But they couldn't learn from others verbally, they could not follow directions, they could not process even stick figure drawings to have something explained to them, and they could not say a thing to anybody.

They could be in a crowd - even another crowd of Muties - and they would be forever cutoff and alone.

They could not cooperate or be of benefit to anyone since they could not process orders, gestures, words, or anything. Even dogs could communicate and be given tasks by others.

But not these people.

They would never be a collective danger - only a solitary one.

They didn't react from rage like we did with foreigners, but they were intelligent, could make plans, had a sense of self preservation and could use tools - like that pistol on the counter.

I had no doubt that if I let him get to that gun, he would try to kill me.

Not out of hate - but out of self interest.

Other groups around the country had tried working with them in order to organize them into working parties. These experiments had been met with utter failure.

Sometimes, they would "escape" (individually, of course), and sometimes they would kill. They were at the same time "un-trainable," not able to work even under direction, and downright dangerous when threatened.

Left alone, they would generally do the smart thing and not seek trouble, especially from groups.

Forever individuals, forever alone, and, perhaps, forever not understanding what had happened to them or their world.

Think of the loneliness.

I squatted down beside this individual and looked him in the eyes. They were full of intelligence - aware, and bright. Who had he been? What did he think had happened to him?

I cocked my head, wondering at how resourceful and intelligent this person had to be to survive - alone - in this new world. People had gathered in groups to accomplish just that. But here was a guy that had faced communities full of dangerous hostiles and even wild animals that wandered the city streets hunting in packs. Feral dogs and wild pigs were an ever-increasing danger.

It took groups, using weapons, to guard against these.

Yet this guy had managed to survive all alone against these odds.

I had to admire his skill and intelligence. I wish we had a person like that in our community. But, since he couldn't even understand the simplest directions or commands, this made him useless to group efforts. And group effort was what was keeping us alive.

It was a shame.

The look in his eyes turned from fear into puzzlement. He was wondering what I would do with him. I was no longer pointing the Colt Commando, but had let it come down, barrel down, hanging on its sling over my chest.

I reached out a gloved hand to touch his shoulder reassuringly.

He moved suddenly, violently snatching at my hand and was coming up to stand, but I immediately blocked his movement, grasped his shirt at the collarbone, leaned all my weight forward on him, put my forearm on his throat, and thrust him back down, pinning him to immobility. I had also drawn my sidearm and thrust the hard barrel into his breast bone, winding him.

I did all of this automatically.

I hadn't relied on just "muscle memory" to keep up Victor's skills in the martial arts. Every day for the past few months I had grappled and sparred with anybody that had expressed experience or interest in the fight game. Apparently, I was pretty good, as none had beaten me so far. I had also taught combatives classes for the crew, drawing on my old experience and bolstered by Victor's "muscle memory."

I "just knew" how to execute a triangle choke, for example - never having done one before. I'd seen plenty of UFC matches, though, and with my own martial arts background I pretty well followed the techniques and used "Victor's" automatic reflexes. This kept my own reflexes up to snuff.

I smiled into his face up close and shook my head as though to say, "no, nooo..."

I knew that even the so-called "universal" head shake he would not be able to process. But the hard barrel of the pistol could not be mistaken for a kiss.

I waited for him to get it. I stared into his eyes until I felt the resistance disappear. Then I smiled, let go of him, and went back on my haunches. I didn't holster the gun, but held it casually, my wrist over my knee.

I decided to try something. I hoped that I would get through to him.

With my empty left hand, I snapped my fingers. That drew his eyes to my hand. I then extended it and pointed to the can he had dropped. He saw what I was pointing to, and he furrowed his brows.

He turned his gaze back to my eyes and gave me an angry glare. Ah! He understood.

Good. But, although he understood I was telling him to pick up the can, he just looked at me steadily and angrily. He didn't shake his head in negation as that gesture - any gesture - was probably beyond his ability.

I snapped my fingers louder and pointed to the can again. I didn't bother to animate my pointing finger, as that was a gesture. He looked over and snapped his eyes back to mine and gave me an angry scowl. He was now breathing heavily and angrily.

I slowly brought my gun up for him to see the weapon; I then casually replaced it on my knee.

He started breathing angrily through his nose, almost snorting. His eyes teared up, but he continued to stare daggers at me.

He slowly and carefully raised his hand up shoulder height, looked to the can and leaned his body to the side in order to reach it. He grasped the can in his hand and slowly brought it up to show me.

He emitted a grunting sound to bring my eyes to his face. He quickly smashed my head in with the heavy can.

At least, that was his intention. When I sensed movement my Victor reflexes took over and I ducked the hand, deflected it, and wrapped his arm in a painful shoulder lock. This time I brought the .45 up under his chin and pressed painfully against the soft underside.

Once again he snorted, and real tears - angry, humiliated tears - formed in his eyes.

At that moment I saw the real person behind this uncommunicative man.

I saw the raw pain, the humiliation, the fear, the anger - and the dignity in him.

And the loneliness. Forever alone. Forever apart.

Forever.

My eyes stung wetly in response.

I WAITED FOR GUNNY OUT BY THE GATE.

There was a shade tree right by the fence, draping over the sidewalk. I decided to sit under that, right on the grassy bumper. I didn't have to wait long.

I heard Gunny's armored van coming around the corner. He pulled up to the sidewalk where I was seated lost in my own thoughts. I stood up, and he slid down the passenger window and said loudly above the engine noise, "Wanna drive, Captain?"

I just shook my head, opened the passenger door and slid in, looking straight ahead.

Gunny didn't pull out immediately. He said, "Uh… Captain?"

I looked at him.

"Ummm… you've got blood on your face."

I said, "Do I?" and looked in the rearview mirror.

I wiped my cheek and said, "Let's go, Gunny."

We drove away in silence.

V. RIVERA

CROSSING THE BORDER WAS A LETDOWN. I don't know what I expected, but certainly not what I saw.

Maybe this part of Laredo, Texas, just over the border, was the only shabby part.

It did not compare favorably to Nuevo Laredo, especially where we had stayed at the Crowne Plaza. It seemed to me that the streets we drove on in Nuevo Laredo to get to the border crossing were broader, cleaner and more modern than the seediness we encountered in this Texas city.

Crossing the border proved more difficult than we had imagined. Other groups that had formed nearer the border joined us as we neared their positions. The largest group had formed in and around the IMSS General Hospital near the border just off the Juarez-Lincoln International Bridge.

They had contended with the bodies of U.S. Customs and Border Patrol agents that had "awakened" with new English-speaking minds (even among those bodies of Mexican-American descent.) As agents, they had been, for the main, physically fit and heavily armed - even if their occupying minds were untrained or inexperienced.

Amidst the struggle of coming to grips with the event, extreme deadly violence had broken out almost immediately.

Armed Federalés were on this side of the border. All of those bodies were native Spanish-speakers, and if the transitioned minds weren't Spanish-speaking, they died from the convulsions brought on by the event.

There were the odd exceptions, of course, on both sides.

That was the case for the "Múdos" - the muted ones that could not communicate in any way. Our neurosurgeon theorized about how this came to be. I paid little attention to the science - it not being my interest - but thought about how useful a workforce totally dependent upon the largesse of the group collective would be.

Alas, that turned out to be a pipe dream.

They could not be directed in any way, were useless as workers - and sometimes dangerous. So like the scorpion, we stepped on them when underfoot, but did not go out of our way to hunt them down.

It was for the best.

In any case, when we joined the group housed at the hospital, we had already been in contact with scattered groups around the city before the electricity finally failed along with both telephone and mobile phone services. We had gathered up and made our way to the border crossing in cars, vans, trucks and buses.

This was no easy task as, at this point, we were at least 4,000 strong. Getting coordination and control over this many people required much planning and division of labor.

Clearing the way to the border, even if it was a mere 10 miles, was problematic. Our group had cleared an area of about 5 miles radius around "our" hotel to aid with sanitation and with movement to forage for food and supplies.

The bodies had been stacked into a construction site hole (apparently planned for building an underground parking garage for a new hotel along Paseo Colón.) The dead, rotting bodies were doused in a mixture of diesel fuel and gasoline and burned.

The smoke was atrocious - black and oily, smelling of rendered fat like cooking pork. But at least the flies were kept at a minimum - even at the expense of our lungs.

The cars and trucks clogging the streets were merely pushed or driven aside to make room for our vehicles. This worked well for us and made foraging more tolerable.

But when the electric grid failed - and lights and air conditioning became a mere memory - we decided to move across the border at once.

We knew that the best course was to clear the vehicles along the way as we had been doing, but to not bother with body disposal. We used several bulldozers from the construction site, and the bulldozers would merely scoop the bodies out of the streets and on to the sidewalks.

We had been in contact with other parts of the city - and in Laredo, Texas - by cellular phone service, but now we used police and taxi-cab radios. We had known that mobile phone service was fragile and had prepared.

The people across the border reported fierce fighting initially with a very small group of transitioned English Speakers. Since Laredo, Texas had a 90% Spanish language population, the small number of opposing groups were soon wiped out.

That did not totally make the city safe, as different factions were surviving in different locations. And they each thought to have precedence for the foraging of goods and materials. Such is the human race.

Now, as we were preparing to cross the border, we came to the General Hospital, where we were hoping to get a fairly warm reception. They, of course, were content to stay where they were, as they had backup generators for electricity, a cooking and storage facility with power, lights and gas, and - of course - plenty of beds.

But, we expected some of their number would want to join us, especially as we pointed out some of the long term implications of depending on foraging for dwindling resources without having the capacity of building a self sustaining infrastructure.

Instead, we were confronted with an armed force, and told to stay away or risk being fired upon.

I decided that diplomacy was the best course. I asked to speak to their head man.

After eyeing each other over drawn weapons, my request was granted, and the opposing group parted to let a short, swarthy man approach our position. At first, he appeared to be a typical specimen of this border town. But I have learned not to judge people by appearance alone.

He strode up calmly and looked us over. He - as I - was unarmed. He saw me standing by my core group and picked me out as leader.

Oh, not just by my European appearance, but we both recognized the authority in the other.

He looked at me and smiled, saying, "My name is Peter Gomez. Pardon the chilly reception. My people are worried that they will be forced to join your group."

Peter? Odd name. And a very odd accent, as well.

I said, "My name is Ulrich Schmidl-Rivera. And I assure you we have no evil intent."

"Ulrich? German?..."

"Argentinean, actually," I said. "Yours, I take it, is... American? British?"

"American - born and bred. First generation - as my parents were from Peru. Even though I learned to speak unaccented American English very early in school, my natal language was Spanish - learned at my mother's knee."

He smiled and went on, "I had forgotten, or so I thought, all my Spanish, as my parents sought to have me assimilate by allowing me and my siblings to speak only English, even at home. But apparently the brain retains what is drawn from mother's milk."

José, our learned neurosurgeon, was nodding his agreement.

I said, "Interesting accent. I don't recognize it as Peruvian."

"I'm told," he said, "that I speak Spanish like a gringo."

I barked a laugh, "Yes! That's it!"

He smiled quietly, once again. He said, "And what is it that you want from us?"

I spread my hands and said expansively, "Why, only to offer you the chance to join us in crossing to the U.S. and expanding our access to resources and survival!"

He looked at me quietly and said, "Why don't you - and your companions - join me for a little coffee and some refreshments inside. You are quite safe, I assure you, since you obviously outnumber us." He smiled.

I said, "Why not?"

I gave quiet instructions to Abdul to wait with the main body of our "troops" and to wait one hour. If we did not return, then he was to storm the hospital and kill everything inside. Abdul smiled and said, "One hour."

I patted his shoulder and turned to our host.

HE ESCORTED JOSÉ, PENZO and me into the brightly lit interior of the main Hospital entrance and on to a waiting conference room. There was coffee service waiting and small pastries. I had to wonder how they got those pastries so many months after the event. But perhaps they had a skilled pastry chef in their number.

There were other "leaders" in the room, but, other than acknowledging them with a smile when introduced, I ignored them and concentrated on Señor Gomez.

When we were seated and coffee served, I turned to Gomez and laid out our rationale for going to the U.S.

What I told him was this:

The United States had a denser technological infrastructure - electric generation and transmission, communications, medical facilities and agriculture. Since the Mexican side had already experienced electrical outages, with little chance of having the requisite skill sets to rebuild or maintain that infrastructure, then we had to look elsewhere for resources - hence the U.S.

I told him that his hospital infrastructure could be maintained for a time by using backup generators, but that it would have diminishing returns when they had siphoned off all the available fuel from storage tanks and vehicles. They would then have to venture further into the Mexican interior - which had sparse resources before getting to the more populous zones. Even then, they must realize that gasoline had a limited shelf life.

"Señor Gomez, we have no choice but to go across the border and take what we need for our Spanish community. If we have to fight the gringos, then we must do what we must," I told him.

He took a small sip of his coffee and looked at me over his cup. I could see his eyes crinkle in amusement. He sat the cup down in its saucer and leaned back.

He sighed and said, "Much of what you said is true. Some of it… is mistaken."

I raised my eyebrows in puzzlement and looked at him in askance.

He went on, smiling. "First, I must insist that you call me Peter." I nodded.

"I must also remind you that I am… WAS… a 'gringo.' But those appellations are meaningless now… just as the make-up of these bodies… these ethnicities… are even more meaningless."

I sat back, frowning. I didn't quite cross my arms - barely. "And just where… Peter… am I… mistaken?"

"Well, let's begin with your assumption that merely crossing the border will provide us access to vast resources," he said.

I began to argue that wasn't my assumption, but decided that listening was the better use of our time - which was short, given my instructions to Abdul. I said, "Please, go on."

"Thank you," he said, and went on.

"As I told you, I was born and raised in America. I served as an officer in the U.S. Air Force. In fact, I graduated from the Air Force Academy, and I served around the globe.

My latest command, coincidentally, was just a few miles northwest of here at the Flight Training Command at Laughlin Air Force Base in Del Rio, Texas.

At the 'event' that so transformed us, I was serving as a colonel in charge of the T-1A Jayhawk Flight School. I have also served at the major bases in San Antonio, Colorado and Wyoming - as well as overseas - Japan, the Middle East, and so on. I am well traveled in the U.S. and have some 'not-very-public-information' about what resources are available there."

He paused, seemingly gathering his thoughts.

"I agree with everything you say about the... what did you call it... yes - 'diminishing returns' - on foraging for finite resources without having the means or the infrastructure to replenish them. However, I'm afraid you are going to be disappointed by what you find across the border."

I frowned and asked, "How so?"

I noticed Penzo looking at Gomez quite intensely. Penzo has always proven to have incredible insight, so I would ask him for his thoughts, later.

Gomez continued, "I'm afraid what you will find that, across the border, is just more of the same. Truth to tell, I find Laredo, Texas to be a very primitive 'city' compared to Houston, San Antonio, Dallas... and even they offer no panacea.

The electrical grid has already failed - even in parts of those cities - and soon all electric power will be gone as both transmission and generation fail due to a lack of sustainable maintenance and skilled labor.

And electric power - as much as petroleum-based power, modern agriculture and transportation of goods and produce - is necessary to maintain a level of civilization.

That, I'm afraid, is coming to an end."

Gomez paused, and in that pause, I asked, "So you believe we are doomed to reverting to a primitive society - or doomed over all?"

He smiled and said, "Not... exactly..."

"Well, WHAT 'exactly', man!" I said impatiently.

He leaned forward and said, earnestly, "You have to realize - as I have been espousing to these people here - that it is NOT enough to merely survive for the short term!

We have to consider the longer term - not just five, or ten or even twenty years out!

By that time, ALL infrastructure will fail. Canned goods will likely be contaminated or just used up. Petroleum power will not last - gasoline and diesel fuels have LIMITED storage life even in ideal conditions. Electrical power needs skilled technicians to maintain, and the ability to produce - eventually from raw materials - wires and parts.

Food will have to be grown and cattle raised. Predatory animals will become a great danger. Not to mention 'other' language speaker groups.

Arms - modern arms - cannot be produced using primitive techniques.

We need to find a way of sustaining a level of technology that makes modern life possible. Else - in a decade or two - we will revert to a primitive society, unable to build from the old."

He paused and took a breath.

I could see Penzo nodding, leaning forward, and listening intently. If our Penzo thought this man worth listening to, then, I too would listen.

I also saw, out of the corner of my eye, José, our resident scientist, looking pensive, turning his eyes upward as though seeing something he did not like.

I leaned back and crossed my arms. "So - what do you propose - and what have you been proposing to your group and, apparently, not convincing them? Else you would not have waited for us to show up."

"That's just it, don't you see?" he said. "I NEEDED you to 'show up'. Without you - or even a larger group than you - we would not be able to accomplish what I have been proposing."

"And that is?..." I said through gritted teeth.

He sat back and smiled. "What I propose we do is to go to one of the numerous military bases in San Antonio, Texas - AFTER visiting my old post in Del Rio. We need to obtain military armament and gather enough fighters from the surrounding areas - Spanish-speakers obviously - and prepare ourselves to take a location I know about that is ideal for survival.

We don't know what resistance - if any - we will face, but we must be prepared to take it by force!"

Penzo spoke, surprising us all. "And this place has sustainable power, manufacturing capabilities, high technology and protection for long term development?"

"Yes, it does. And more," Gomez answered. "It has the capability to sustain a very large group of survivors for decades - AND provide the means and technology to rebuild civilization."

"And what is this 'magical' place?" I asked, skeptically.

Gomez smiled and answered, "The Cheyenne Mountain Complex located just outside of Colorado Springs, Colorado."

VI. SAM - AT GORE'S FOLLY

I thoroughly disapprove of duels. I consider them unwise and I
know they are dangerous. Also, sinful. If a man should challenge me, I
would take him kindly and forgivingly by the hand and lead him to a
quiet place - and kill him.

- Mark Twain

GWEN CAME RUSHING IN and got Victor's attention.

It was unusual for her to come to what was becoming known as "The
War Room" without specific invitation, so we all knew it was important
news.

I had gotten the distinct impression that Gwen did not exactly approve
of our self-appointed leader. Nor would I expect her to - as a proven law
enforcement professional that had dedicated her life to serving the public
interest for a legitimately-established government.

Victor only pretended to be a law officer.

To this day I really don't know what he was B.E. - "Before Event." But I
would bet my life that "law" was nowhere in the job description.

He was too apt to act in what I could only describe as a... well...
WANTON manner - for the lack of a better word.

Oh, I bought that what he did was probably reasoned and logical, and,
ultimately, for the "greater good" - but I never doubted that he enjoyed it. I
had the feeling that he was as disengaged as though he were playing in a
video game. I never saw doubts, second thoughts, or remorse.

I'll admit that his "handling" of the work detail protestors had resulted
in "lubricating" the machinery of organization and discipline. But at what
cost of our collective souls - if there was such a thing?

I knew that he was fond of his "core group," but I never got the
impression that he was fully emotionally invested in any of us.

Janis had sought to disabuse me of this notion. When I told her my
impressions, she said in her "lady of the manner" tones, "Pish-tosh, my dear
Sam. He absolutely dotes on you!"

She saw my uncomfortable frown at that thought, and waved her hand,
"Not in THAT way, my dear. I believe he cares for you as a daughter - or a
SON," she added hurriedly before I could voice my protest. I clamped my
mouth shut.

She went on, her hand on top of mine, "You would never be in danger from him - nor, I suspect, either Jonas or myself - and that dear boy, Timothy - ummm - 'Gunny' - how I dislike that nickname!

In any case, we may disagree with him and point out his foibles, and basically refuse to do his bidding, but he would never do us harm beyond glaring and frowning fiercely at us."

She added quietly, "But I fear for any others."

I knew what she meant.

There was this guy that came in while I was expecting Floozer's group to show up. It had been two months since our conversation on Skype. Floozer's last words to me was to say, "I'll call you as soon as I crossover to the US and snag a cell phone. See ya, Sam! Stay loose."

He hadn't shown up.

I asked everyone that came in for my prescreening if they had heard of Floozer or his group of travelers. Some answered they had heard of him through the social media portal, but none had heard from him, or had seen him since.

I was pretty bummed, as I had felt a kindred spirit. It would have been cool hanging out and brainstorming with Floozer. He would have been a real resource for our community.

Anyway, I was screening this big dude - I think he had come from Ohio - and I asked him about Floozer. He had leaned over to me and waggled his eyebrows. I had never seen anybody do that in real life before.

He was this big, rangy football player type. A bit taller, and bulkier than Victor.

He said, "Honey, I'll be your Floozie..." and laughed, nastily.

I told him, "Hey, dude. I was a guy, Before the Event."

"That don't bother me none, honey," he smiled a nasty smile. "I had my share of pretty boys in the joint - and YOU smell WAY better!"

Before I could say anything, he went on, "Say... what are you, anyways? A Mex - a raghead, or somethin'? You don't look like a nigga gal to me... though I've had my share of brownie poon in my time."

Charming.

Sarge - Lori - had been standing by quietly and supervising the interview line. She - he - must have noticed something because he walked over with his hand on his sidearm. He loomed over us, and leaned over to get his giant black face in our line of sight.

"Anything wrong, Sam?" he said and looked over to the dude. Lori's - SARGE'S - voice is a low Darth Vader-like rumble.

The guy just leaned back and grinned, unafraid.

He told Sarge, "Me and the little lady was havin' a conversation, boy."

Sarge said, "I'm not a boy."

The dude was about to open his mouth and say something stupid, when I interrupted. I said, "That's okay, Lori. Let's just get this screening over."

The dude and Lori got into a staring match, neither being intimidated.

Which was stupid, as Lori - Sarge - outweighed this big dude by at least fifty pounds. And was a good 5 inches taller. And had a powerful sidearm on his belt.

But the dude wasn't cowed.

Sarge finally stood up, still glaring at the guy, and walked back to the door. He stood with his massive arms folded and kept looking at us.

The dude turned back to me and said, "Now, where were we little darlin'?"

We finished the intake interview with the guy being quite candid about what he had been.

He told me he had been in Chino (a prison, I presumed) serving 15 to 20 for second degree murder.

He was part of the Aryan Brotherhood prison gang, with all the requisite prison tats - including, so he said, a giant swastika on his neck. He said he missed his tats and that as soon as he could, he would "tat-up" this pretty college-boy body he now inhabited.

"Though I gotta admit, this here body is ever' bit as strong and quick as I was," he bragged. "This here boy was with the Ohio State Wrestling Team."

He claimed he had been an "enforcer" for the gang, and that he was looking for a similar position here - "... killin' all those Mex-Eee-Kans," he said. "Though I hear your head man may be one of the 'mud people', himself."

He said he had transitioned to the body in Columbus, or Cincinnati - or someplace - I forget which.

He had been confused at the beginning, but soon caught on. The folks he was with didn't "mess" with him, and he got to do pretty much what he wanted. He was bigger, stronger and willing to do violence. Just like before.

He had heard folks talking about this place and decided to come down.

"If I knew you'd be here, darlin'," he grinned, "I woulda been here sooner." He put a hand on my arm and I flinched away.

I blinked away tears of frustration and humiliation. Guys like this had always tormented me as a man. A geek and a nerd. Somehow, as a "woman" it seemed even worse. And the sexual undertones made me feel helpless and afraid.

I looked up and saw Victor standing there, behind him in the doorway. Victor was smiling, but the smile didn't reach his eyes.

He said loudly, "Is this clown giving you grief?"

The "clown" stood up very quickly and spun around. He was fast!

He looked like he was about to attack, but then stood still as he saw Victor's hand on his sidearm. Lori also looked prepared to draw, and Gunny walked in behind Victor carrying an MP5 loosely in his hand.

The guy un-tensed, forced a smile, and said casually, "You must be the big cheese."

"I'm Victor Vega," he said, "and you are done with this interview."

"I heard a' you. You supposed to be a badass," the guy drawled. "I think it's easy to be a badass when you're surrounded by your 'homeys' carrying guns."

Victor continued to smile coldly and said, "Is this the part where we exchange insults and I challenge you to bare fisticuffs? Dude, this isn't a movie. If I wanted to, I'd just shoot you."

"For what?" the guy said. "Am I horning in on your darkie girlfriend?"

Victor snorted a laugh and looked at me, puzzled. "What's his story?"

"Prison. Ayran Brotherhood enforcer. Inherited a college wrestler's body, so now he thinks he's a real badass, himself." I answered, feeling better and more relaxed with Victor on the scene.

He twisted around to look at me and said with a smile, "I was always a badass, you rag-head bitch."

"Now, now," Victor said, "Play nice."

This guy obviously had a screw loose.

He had told me that, previous to going to prison on a murder charge, he had made extra money fighting in underground, no-rules, anything-goes bouts. Sometimes they ended in death or permanent injury.

That's why he wasn't afraid of Victor. He knew Victor's current reputation and his past (former life's) experience in MMA. He thought sports rules were for pussies - and he didn't believe Victor's skills would be passed on to the person currently occupying his body.

And even if they had, he was willing to take on the smaller, lighter Sheriff.

Victor shook his head, sorrowfully. "Damn. This is so cliché."

He looked at Gunny and said, "Looks like I'll be working out early."

Victor invited the racist jerk into the gym.

I didn't want to watch, but I admit to being worried. I followed them into the gym.

Victor did not take off his boots, which was pretty unusual for him. He merely stepped onto the matted platform, after unbuckling his gun belt and handing it over to Gunny.

Victor walked up to the low platform and stopped by the racks at the far end that held practice wooden weapons and batons. Then he turned around to face the big guy that was just mounting the low stairs. The guy was grinning and rolling his shoulders in anticipation.

He said, "Don't you MMA boys fight barefoot and in your undies?"

Victor smiled, shook his head and said, mildly, "I'm good." He stood with his arms behind his back - obviously pretending unconcern.

Well, I was concerned. I walked around the platform to get a side view.

Victor had shown me striking techniques and defense, which I was (surprisingly) able to pick up rather quickly and easily in this athletic body.

Victor had told me that his mind was constantly at war with his body as he had been - in his former life - more of a kick boxer rather than a wrestler. The "Victor body" had been primarily a submission grappler who used kicks and punches to set up "takedowns" in order to choke out or submit his opponents using arm bars, leg locks and other crippling techniques.

In the sport. But was his "combatives" experience any different?

He had confessed having to reconcile his former self's "mental" propensity to depend on kickboxing with his new body's "muscle memory" of Brazilian grappling - which sometimes got in the way when he sparred with others. Sometimes with not very good results.

That had been practice fighting, which really didn't compare to his reactions in combat. Different deal.

My experience with Victor had taught me one thing: size matters.

This guy had height, weight, reach and sheer athleticism all over Victor. It just depended on who had retained and integrated fight experiences - mind and body.

Not sticking to the clichéd "bad guy in the movies" archetype, with no oratory or preamble, he immediately launched himself at Victor with a lightning fast kick to the groin and followed with an equally fast overhand strike.

At least that had been his intent - and it was a most effective attack.

But for one thing.

Look. I'm describing this as though I experienced it in "real time." That wasn't the case. It happened so fast that I didn't have time to register what I was seeing. It was like watching a scene using a strobe light.

Later, I was able to reconstruct it from my impressions (and subsequent nightmares.)

Victor did not block the kick by attempting to sweep the leg or to absorb the kick with his arms or legs. Instead, Victor brought out what he had been holding behind his back as he faced his opponent. It was a hardwood practice sword used by the Japanese to great effect.

He slashed at the guy's kicking leg, sweeping it in to smash the side of the calf and then slashed down viciously at the overhand punching arm, shattering it from wrist to elbow. I heard the meaty "thump" of the wooden sword as it struck the leg - it sounded like you would expect. But what got to me was the arm shattering. It literally sounded like a tree branch breaking under a sledgehammer.

The guy didn't even have time to scream in pain. He had planted his forward leg after it got slashed in order to put as much force as possible into his overhand punch. As Victor shattered the arm with the wooden sword, he immediately threw a side-kick stomp to the knee of the planted leg. The knee was also shattered, and was bent backward at an angle that was just gross.

Victor was apparently not through, as he drove the wooden "blade" into the already beaten opponent's liver, which bent him over.

Victor then used the momentum of the falling body to "tuck" the blade under the guy's armpit on the unbroken arm. As the crippled body fell, he grasped the other end of the blade with his free hand, did a twisting step over motion to straddle the shoulder, "sat" down on it, and used the leverage and torque to rip the guy's shoulder and arm beyond all repair.

When it was over, Victor stood up and said, "How's that for 'no rules'?"

He just let the sword drop on the mercifully unconscious opponent and stepped down off the platform.

Both Gunny and Lori were staring in shocked silence.

I had my mouth open.

Victor walked over to me and whispered, "Sorry."

He put a warm hand on my shoulder and I tensed up. After a few seconds, he walked out of the gym, having taken his sidearm back from the still shocked Gunny. Sarge - Lori - stared at him as he left.

Speaking over his shoulder, Victor told them to drag the crippled body out to the dump truck for bio-mass processing.

I'M WANDERING A BIT, as this next part is difficult for me. (As though the last part wasn't.)

As I said before, Gwen had rushed into the war room. I was there, along with Janis, Gunny, Jonas and a new guy, Paul, who had medical experience. He had been, Before the Event, an intern at a trauma center.

We hadn't needed doctors and nurses up to this point, as no one had (mysteriously) gotten sick in all the time we had been occupying Gore's Folly.

No sniffles; no flu; no food poisoning - and - as only the fit and healthy survived the event - no chronic diseases. But it seemed... odd to me.

Oh, we had our share of injuries - especially combat injuries and some off-the-wall accidents. The combat injuries tended to be fatal. High powered bullets tend to do a lot of damage. But there were cases where medical care could reduce fatalities.

We were discussing what equipment we should forage from a nearby medical complex in preparation for the likelihood of accelerated fighting - and therefore increasing the chances of combat related injuries - as more Spanish-speaking groups were moving into "our" foraging territory from south San Antonio, where they held sway.

Victor thought we should build our own trauma center and actively recruit people willing to be trained by our new intern as medics. I knew from my intake interviews that we had two ex-EMTs and three firemen. They would probably make up the core.

But we had not encountered a single nurse or doctor, other than this intern. We did have two former dentists that could be recruited and trained. There seemed to be a lack of dentistry needs amongst our preternaturally healthy group, so other than "body bag" duty, that would provide meaningful work for them.

Gwen showed up, looking more flustered than I had ever seen her. As Victor looked up and frowned at the interruption, Gwen said in a quavering voice, "We've taken casualties."

Janis gasped a small, "Oh!" and Victor said, "How many? Where?"

"Six KIA - 2 shooters, 1 driver, 3 supercargo. Four supercargo wounded but ambulatory. Ambushed along Loop 1604 west toward the town of Helotes. We were foraging a large storehouse and manufacturing plant for copper and brass."

She paused and looked at me. "We lost Lori."

THROUGH MY OWN SHOCK AND SORROW, I saw a change in the normal Victor expression.

This was a devastating blow for me, personally.

While I felt close to our core group, Lori - Sarge - that young, female soldier now residing in a hulking black man's body, was my best friend. He and I shared a bond of the shock and strangeness of being gender-swapped. She to a he, and I vice versa.

The awkwardness of that experience brought us close, even if our separate interests and specialties did not bring us together too often.

I knew Victor - as a former combat vet - respected Lori's accomplishments. They shared the combat veterans' experience that was unknown outside their circles. It was an exclusive club none could enter except by going through the trials of war.

But I hadn't expected the sheer anger on Victor's face.

As Gwen reported to him, his expression got darker and darker.

I really wasn't paying close attention to Gwen's report, but I reconstructed it later from what I heard after. My shock and sorrow was too deep at that time. But here is what she said, in essence.

Foraging Group 6 - as it was designated - was composed of 8 shooters carrying the following: three M16s, four MP5's, and one M240 machine gun, which was carried by Sarge - Lori - because he was so big that he handled it like a mere rifle, even though it weighed over 30 pounds loaded. That provided the group with massive firepower, if needed.

In addition, Group 6 had two drivers and two assistants (all armed with MP5s) for the "deuces" they drove. One shooter drove the accompanying vehicle. In this case it was an unarmored heavy duty pickup.

Eighteen workers/foragers, armed with pistols, were the "supercargo".

When Gwen mentioned the wounded, Paul got a look from Victor and immediately got up and out to see about their treatment. As he left Gwen shouted, "They're about ten minutes out." Paul nodded as he ran out.

The Group had just finished loading the foraged cargo when they began to receive fire from three directions. They had managed to push their attackers back, but not before receiving casualties. Sarge had been at the forefront of the pushback, sending massive amounts of fire from the M240, which he was shoulder-firing.

As they were loading the wounded and dead, Lori was hit.

Victor asked, "Head shot?"

Gwen shook her head, sorrowfully. "No. Center mass."

I didn't know why that was significant at the time, but I saw Victor's expression get even darker, if that was possible. He shook his head as if to deny what he had heard.

I found out later that Lori - Sarge - had not been able to be fitted with ANY body armor, much less the more effective Dragon Skin. He had been just too big. They would have had to stitch two sets together - but that was impossible.

Lori had suggested that they forget about it, but Victor had told him, "After this run, you and I will take a trip up to Camp Bullis. They might have SOMETHING that fits!"

Lori had laughed and said, "That's where my spec ops buddies took their survival training. Have you SEEN the size of the average special operations soldier? They're TINY! You'd have to put FOUR sets of armor together for me."

"Well.... We'll try anyway," Victor had said. "Besides, I want to take a look at the hardware that might be there. Sam hasn't been able to get an inventory - even with her super-duper code-breaking ninja skills."

Now it was too late. If Lori had body armor - even the lousy Kevlar - he might have survived a center mass hit.

VICTOR SHOOK HIMSELF and looked up angrily. He growled, "Who the hell was on Oversight duty?"

What Victor was asking was who was manning the satellite imaging to sweep real time for danger warnings. The "street cams" had failed along with the power grid months before. So he had me link up our dishes to receive the "Spy" satellite images that the U.S. had.

I had known that the Chinese or Russians had more coverage in the U.S. as our satellites were not generally used over our territories.

But, since I couldn't read or program in those languages, and low-level binary was too cumbersome to construct elegant "takeover" 'bots, we were forced to take over control of U.S. satellites that orbited over South America (for obvious drug enforcement purposes) and program them to "look" in our direction.

It wasn't ideal, nor could the composite images provide the kind of resolution we needed because of the "angle of sight". We were able to make do until I could figure out how to adjust the orbits - if that was even possible.

I told him, "It doesn't matter who, Victor. We only have one aperture view of about five miles, radius. And we had 7 groups out at the time. The odds of spotting this coming..." I shook my head and trailed off.

"Get down to the control room and find those bastards!"

I got up, feeling numb and headed to the elevator.

WHEN I GOT TO THE CONTROL ROOM, Bob was typing commands and watching the sat surveillance monitors. Bob was a guy that I had recruited - no doubt based upon his geeky worship of my accomplishments. He was *juuusst* obsequious enough to stroke my ego without going overboard. He had been a high level programmer at Oracle, and he knew of my exploits. He was just the kind of guy we needed to take over our security surveillance.

He looked up and said, "I know. I know. I'm tracking their movements. I adjusted the sweep when I heard about the attack."

I sat down in front of another monitor rather than watch over his shoulder. "Well?" I asked.

"I got 'em..."

I heard a "...but..." in there. I looked at him impatiently. "AND?!!"

"Well..." he said, irritatingly, "if it's any consolation, they had massively more casualties than our side - a LOT of bodies..."

I snapped, "It's not! Get on with it!"

"Well..." Again with the 'well', "We got bigger problems."

"Explain."

"Yeah... as expected they were part of a larger force. I was able to reorient the SAT feed and track their movement..."

"And?"

"And... I saw the track where they were headed. They headed west and south from Helotes on Loop 1604, then down to 151 and to Loop 410..."

I asked, "What's there?" dreading the answer.

He looked at me soberly. "Lackland Air Force Base."

"Damn," I swore softly. I knew the implications. I said, "Show me."

LACKLAND AIR FORCE BASE had, essentially, ceased to be a real "air base." It was the Air Force's site for enlisted basic military training for all service Airmen of the regular Air Force, Air National Guard, and Air Force Reserve. In other words, Air Force "boot camp."

Victor had little interest in exploring the base until I pointed out that it was the headquarters for the Twenty-Fourth Air Force (Air Forces Cyber Command) that consolidated cyberspace combat and support forces. In other words, it had the best military spec communications and computing platforms in the world.

That got his interest up enough to make it a priority exploration - after Camp Bullis.

Camp Bullis took priority because it potentially housed heavy weapons, special ops gear, transpo and armor. We hadn't got around to it, but we were planning on an exploration party the next week.

It was unlikely that Lackland had the same kind of weapons and ammo that Camp Bullis had. And what aircraft might exist, we wouldn't have the skills to mount a ground crew, armorers, not to mention, pilots. But they COULD have enough weapons and equipment to make it worth our while since it would have had a guard detachment and maybe an armory or two. So Victor had decided to make it priority # 2.

Looks like someone had beaten us to it.

And it was bad.

As I watched the feed, Bob zoomed in and focused on a pretty broad area where there seemed to be people and lots of movement and activity.

In front of the hangers by the old airstrip, vehicles were gathered, and we could see a MASSIVE number of people scurrying about loading things that appeared to be weapons and ammo. There were a number of HumVees and covered "deuce and a half" military trucks on the tarmac.

I whistled and said. "What's the VTAP estimate?"

We had taken the time to "borrow" an NSA program called Visual Threat Analysis Program, or "VTAP", when we hijacked the satellite. It was similar to the program I first used to estimate the number of dead at the beginning of the Event.

Bob turned to me and gulped, "Well... um... it shows about 300 transpo and about 4,000 personnel..." He paused.

I said, "Go on," unconsciously channeling Victor.

"Umm... they've got lots of machine guns. Big ones. I wouldn't know how to identify them without better resolution... but I got a printout of VTAP's 'best guess.'

I don't know one type from another, but I'm guessing it's bad."

It was.

I FINISHED MY BRIEFING for the core group in the war room.

I had included VTAP's estimates of the number of potential combatants we would face, as well as the kind and numbers of weapons that would be deployed.

VTAP included an estimate on deployment tracks and points of attack.

I'm definitely not a military person in any way, shape, or form, but I understood enough to be scared.

And what scared me more is that Victor, himself, looked scared. Some of the color had drained from his face. Gunny looked concerned and Gwen seemed awfully fidgety - not at all her usual self. All the other "non-coms" we had recruited looked uncomfortable.

And these were the people with enough sense and experience to be scared.

Janis was just wide-eyed. Jonas was staring off into space, lost in thought.

I finished by giving VTAP's estimate of the routes they would, with 90% probability, take to get here.

"The probability is 90% that they will split their forces to come over two different routes.

The easiest route out for them is to co-ordinate their departure from their location on base - which is currently easternmost - and take 151 to the junction on 410, then continue on 410 East until they hit Bandera Road.

One of the splits will continue on 410 then West on IH-10, while the other, smaller force, takes Bandera Road into Helotes to Scenic Loop Road to come up on our blind side."

"Classic pincer," said Jonas. I thought he hadn't been paying attention. "You think they know where the Folly is exactly?"

"Yes," Gwen said thoughtfully. "There's no reason to believe they don't have the requisite skills to hijack their own surveillance satellites, since they are at the heart of the US Air Force's Cyber Command."

"Not likely," I said. "The Air Force computers and programs will be fully encrypted and most certainly won't have 'Press 1 For Spanish.' No, I would have noticed any foreign acquisition, anyway."

Gunny spoke up, surprising us. He said, "That electronic stuff ain't needed. Good ol' HUMINT is all that's needed."

Hume what? We all looked at him. But both Gwen and Victor were nodding their understanding.

He went on, "Gwen - you remember those 'poachers' we shot in the nearby woods a while ago?"

Gwen nodded.

"We thought they mighta been 'Muties' out foraging for themselves since they were solo," Gunny said.

Gwen nodded again, and Victor's mouth pursed in sudden understanding. Which had me all beat to hell.

Gunny said, "They were wearing cammo. They mighta been spotters - and the ones we didn't spot might have the intel on us. I was trained to do that kinda job, myself."

"Damn," Victor swore softly.

Jonas suddenly barked out a laugh.

We all looked at him and he was smiling, gently.

"What's so funny?" Victor growled.

Jonas came to himself and looked around, sheepishly at us. "Sorry, mates. I just thought of something that may help." He kept smiling, which was, I thought, inappropriate at this particular time.

But Victor - who had grown to respect Jonas' intellect and problem-solving capabilities said, mildly, "Let's hear it."

"Well..." said Jonas, "I was just thinking it pretty ironic that we are in the 'Alamo City' and that we're facing an overwhelming force of the Spanish-speaking variety just like the old Battle of the Alamo."

"I don't see how that helps, Jonas," Victor said through gritted teeth. "The Alamo defenders all DIED!"

Jonas grinned and quoted, "...'Those who cannot remember the past are condemned to repeat it...' Let's learn from the past!"

"Are you suggesting we abandon the 'Alamo' unlike the original defenders, Jonas?" Victor asked, sounding genuinely surprised.

"Not at all, mate!" Jonas said. "I suggest we change the playing field - or the history lesson."

"Oookaay??..." Victor said, uncertainly.

Jonas asked, excitedly, "You know we've been having problems with Biomass overproduction - especially of methane and of fertilizer product - not to mention an overabundance of fuel?"

"Yeah, so?"

"Well, we decided to store some of the product well away from here. To that end, Gwen has procured all the heavy duty commercial dump trucks and cement mixers in the area. They're parked nearby and fueled up.

We're just awaiting the clearing of the route to the storage facility, some 20 miles east of here."

"Again... yeah, so?" Victor was getting impatient. As was I.

"What if we use that available equipment to blockade the routes, and give them a real surprise?"

Victor said, "I don't see how that would stop them for long. It'll bunch 'em up for a while, and we can set up crossfire killing corridors, but we don't have the firepower, the manpower, nor the ammo to do any real damage."

"That's just it! We don't have to stop them for very long," Jonas said, "Just 'funnel' them into a bunch! How do you think the Spartans took on the Persian Empire at Thermopylae?" Jonas said.

I said, "Uh... dude. I SAW that movie! The Spartans died!"

"So I suggest we turn this from the Alamo into Thermopylae - with a difference," Jonas said, looking at me, "- only this time Xerxes gets a BIG surprise and the Spartans don't get wiped out!"

BOOK FOUR: WAR

Prepare for war! Rouse the warriors! Let all the fighting men draw near and attack.

(Joel 3:9 NIV)

"In preparing for battle I have always found that plans are useless, but planning is indispensable."
— Dwight D. Eisenhower

"Everybody has a plan until they get punched in the face."
— Mike Tyson

"No plan survives contact with the enemy."
— Helmuth von Moltke

I. THERMOPYLAE

VICTOR WAS READING GWEN'S WRITE-UP of the battle orders as he rode in the SUV to inspect "Funnel Point Alpha" and found them a bit... too professional and obtuse. He understood the professionals' need to eliminate ambiguity, but...

He sighed and put aside his 'pad and clicked the power-off button.

In his mind, the "battle plan" was really pretty simple. He had to give it to Jonas and the mind that could take its problem-solving engineering methods to come up with a plan to give them a fighting chance, given their relative resource and materiel poor state.

The main concept was this:

Gore's Folly would take assorted heavy trucks - cement mixer trucks, dump trucks, big rigs with flat beds, and strategically blockade the routes that the enemy would have to take, considering the two large forces they had deployed.

Along the IH-10 route - which would have by far the biggest force coming against Gore's Folly - they would travel some 13 miles to a cross roads 6 miles past Loop 1604, which was the northernmost loop surrounding the entire city.

They would park the trucks sideways (two trucks, side by side, on a slant.) These would be on both sides of the Highway and on the access roads running parallel to IH-10 to provide extra heavy duty protection and blockading.

This junction had the advantage in that it had the density of buildings and shallow parking lots that could allow further blockading. The Gore's Folly defenders would set up fire teams on the rooftops to enable crossing fields of fire. If, and when, they received too much fire to make it survivable, they would come down and take to the side streets on the opposite side of the buildings and return to Gore's Folly to aid in defense.

The trucks would be parked in an inward pointing herringbone pattern in order to force the enemy convoys to "funnel" themselves to get through a narrow gap left on the main highway. This would cause them to bunch up, and cause the mother of all traffic jams with no way to unsnarl it.

This narrow "canyon" would allow the strategically placed Gore's Folly forces to create killing zones and fields of fire that would "attrite" the bunched up enemy forces while minimizing their own exposure. The enemy force would have no choice but to attempt to break through by bulling forward.

If they saw the blockade in time to react, they would be hampered by uncertain and narrow routes along side streets, which could prove to be an ambush disaster for them. It was either bull through or turn away.

The Gore's Folly troops would initially be deployed using motorcycles and dirt bikes for a quick get-a-way for the second phase of the plan. They would also be deployed using HumVees' and pickup trucks that had been selectively (and hastily) outfitted with pedestal-mounted machine guns in the back beds - much as were used in third world countries like Somalia, and were known as "Technicals."

None of the troops would be deployed using troop transport, in order to accommodate the hit and run style of this strategy.

The drivers that had driven the heavy trucks used in the blockade would be taken in retreat by the HumVees and the Technicals. There were not enough of these to accommodate everyone. The harsh reality was that, in defending the blockade, Gore's Folly troops would take casualties.

Behind the southernmost blockade of IH-10, there was another similar blockade of trucks. When the first blockade - "Funnel Point Alpha" - was breached, the troops would retreat behind the second line of trucks forming the blockade. This blockade was designated "Funnel Point Bravo" in Gwen's written Operations Orders. It was located some three miles up IH-10 West before it intersected with Loop 1604.

They would engage the "funneled enemy" at "Funnel Point Bravo" in order to kill as many of the opposing forces as possible to further "attrite" the enemies' equipment, personnel and ammo.

If, and when, the "Funnel Point Bravo" was breached, they would once again beat a rapid retreat, but this time back to Gore's Folly to aid in defense.

Hopefully, they wouldn't have to if the Plan worked.

The plan was essentially the same for the smaller enemy force "sneaking up" the back route on Bandera Road. Trucks would be deployed in much the same manner along Bandera - the difference being that they wouldn't have to cover 8 lanes of superhighway and, on either side, 3 additional lanes of access roads. Just one 4-lane city road.

Another difference was that the road was lined with trucks on either side. At the point designated "Funnel Point Delta," some three miles up the road, they would position an additional barrier of trucks to slow down and bunch up the enemy forces.

On the impending breach on either route of the secondary blockades, the Gore's Folly troops would retreat, and institute "Code Omega." That was going to be the trickiest part of this, since both defending groups would have to pull away rapidly from the attacking enemy to get to relative safety.

If Jonas' plan didn't work as hoped, Gore's Folly would be facing an attack that - despite their vaunted "fortified" status - they could not fend off, successfully. Jonas' modified Thermopylae would become another doomed Alamo.

II. THOMPSON - 2nd SQUAD LEADER

"It doesn't take a hero to order men into battle. It takes a hero to be one
of those men who goes into battle."

- Norman Schwarzkopf

I GOT TO THE ROOF of the building where my squad was already
settling in. I climbed the newly erected ladder that had been constructed by
our engineers on the Westernmost side. Luckily, the building was only three
stories high. But I reveled in what my new body was capable of.

The mere act of being able to negotiate the rungs of the ladder and feel
that I could go all day without tiring was a really magnificent feeling.

The building we were on was facing eastward on the starting point of
the "arrow" formed by the blockading trucks. The rest of my squad were
already spread out and positioned as the overhead SAT showed on the ops
planning map.

I joyfully leaped up the rungs, carrying my rifle on a back sling. Even
though I was no sniper, I carried a British L115A3 AWM Sniper Rifle
outfitted for the .338 Lapua Magnum, effective at over 1500 yards. It
weighed about 16 pounds fully equipped, and I carried about 1000 rounds
in a sling bag that weighed who-knows-how-many pounds.

It was no problem for this young, strong body. I felt as light as a feather,
even knowing I was going into battle.

Pre-Event, I had spent my days in a wheelchair as a quadruple amputee.
I had received my injuries in Iraq thanks to a "cleared" minefield.

The only thing I could think about, as I sat in the VA hospital, was how
I could end it all. I couldn't commit suicide without help. Hell, I couldn't
wipe my ass, even using those useless prosthetics they were always foisting
on me.

I don't mean to denigrate my fellow soldiers that suffered from PTSD
due to "experiencing too much." But some of them weren't even physically
injured - they should experience the pain and helplessness I felt being
unable to do anything without help.

At least they could go out walking, or running, or drinking, or doing
dope when the nightmare replays became too much. I couldn't even do
that. I could only sit there in my piss and shit feeling hopeless.

Do I sound bitter?

Well, now I'm not. I considered the Event a blessing from God - for which I was eternally grateful. Unlike the others, I had no qualms or confusion about what had happened to me. I considered it a joy.

Even when it became apparent that we were in a "language war," I accepted that as a small price to pay. So I was always smiling, even in the worst of it. My nickname was "Smiley" Thompson.

I had stopped smiling earlier today.

Being some of the few experienced soldiers or law officers at Gore's Folly, 2nd squad had formed the core of the convoy protection roster under the command of Gwen Philpot. She appeared so young, but I had come - as had all the others - not to judge the outer shell that people now wore.

We ALL appeared young(ish), but - in our former lives - we could have been anything from teenagers to octogenarians. And we could have been either gender, previously. No telling.

Such was the case with Lori - the "Sarge."

I had been on the convoy protection duty along with Lori this morning. Normally, I would not have been, as there were six other Groups out on foraging missions at the time that I could have led. Somebody with my experience would have been in command of some other shooter squad.

Lori - "Sarge" - had invited me along, saying that he wanted me to take command of 2nd Squad. Sarge had been assigned to aid Gunny in the training of new troops.

We had many more volunteers for this duty from inexperienced people after they had served on "body clearing duty" for any length of time. And we could always use more shooters - but not without training.

So, Gwen had assigned Sarge to the duty of training the new shooters - and Sarge had assigned 2nd Squad to me.

I was taking a familiarization run with Sarge, when the convoy was ambushed. It was something both Sarge - as her former self "Lori" - and I had experienced serving in the "Sandbox." The difference was that this ambush was not preceded by an IED attack, and the ambushers did not appear to have any experience setting strong fields of fire and effective kill zones.

They were like the amateurs I had fought in Somalia - more the "spray and pray" types. Little more than gangbangers. Even the rag-heads had known how to set up kill zones. These guys had no clue. So, we beat them back. Nevertheless, 2nd Squad and the convoy took casualties.

Sarge had laid down MASSIVE return fire with his shoulder-carried MG.

I knew that I, myself, had been responsible for at least nine enemy KIA, but Sarge had been a killing machine. Unlike me, Sarge did not have the Dragon Skin armor - or ANY armor, not even Kevlar.

I at least had the confidence that I could sustain any but the unluckiest of hits without harm. Sarge only had his guts.

Sarge and I decided to expose ourselves in order to draw fire to protect our fallen and injured.

The rest of the 2nd Squad Shooters were taking care of business and were engaging the retreating force and inflicting many more enemy KIA. Both Sarge and I began to organize the drivers and the supercargo into litter bearers.

I was facing Sarge as I saw his chest explode in a spray of blood.

Three tumbling projectiles thunked harmlessly on my body armor, having gone straight through Sarge's body. Sarge crumpled immediately, his massive frame already dead as the bullets blew out his heart and lungs.

That exposed the shooter, standing with an AK, doing "spray and pray" about 20 yards away in an alleyway by the warehouse. I hit him with a carefully placed three-round head shot.

But that didn't change a thing. Sarge was still dead.

I HAD VOLUNTEERED 2nd SQUAD for the most dangerous of the fighting positions - but not without cause. We - with the possible exception of 1st Squad, led by Gwen, herself - were the most experienced bunch. We had ex-SAS, U.S. Marines, Rangers and regular army guys from all over the English-speaking world. They had fought in every possible engagement - from Korea to Afghanistan.

We all knew how to handle ourselves in battle. We had no REMFs in our squads.

And we had these new, relatively young and fit bodies to help us do what we needed to do.

There was this one guy in 1st Squad that was forever bitching about how he had been robbed of at least 15 years, since he had been 22 before the Event (or, "B.E.", as Sam was always trying to get us to say.) Now this guy was in a 37 year old body. But I think his bitching was just that - bitching for bitching's sake - just like soldiers bitch all over the world.

Takes all kinds.

I hadn't climbed up for the joy of it, but I had to check out the newly erected ladder on the outside of the building. I had my second squad leader checking out the ladder on the other corner, away from the expressway. We needed two egress points if (when) it came time to bug out. We didn't have the luxury of waiting.

I had the squad take the inside stairs to the highest floor, then come up to the roof from the outside stairway access. That would not be a good way to exit when the feces hit the windmill. So, we had exit ladders built on the side of the building away from the enemy line of sight.

We had motorbikes and ATVs waiting at the bottom. I had carried most of the Heavy Weapons we would use in the ATV.

My squad had one Browning M2E2 (.50 caliber); two M249 Squad Automatic Weapons; two Barrett M107 .50 Cal Sniper models (in addition to my L115A3 Sniper); three ICS-190 GLM Grenade Launchers loaded with six HE projectiles, each, and 2 AT-4 light anti-armor weapons. The balance of the squad had their own M16s. All that, plus the extra ammo boxes that had been brought up by elevator.

At bug out, we would take what we could carry, and leave the rest behind.

What worried me most - other than running out of ammo (or that the enemy would have mortar capability to lob HE projectiles on our position) was that we had only two barrels for the .50 Cal Browning.

When the barrels got hot, they needed to be changed before they warped and became useless - and dangerous. So we would have to be judicious in our order of fire. We needed to use the Browning as basically anti-materiel suppression. Anti-personnel would be taken care of by the more precise weaponry - and the grenade launchers.

Our mission was simple - and was mirrored by Gwen's 1st Squad, sitting on a building on the opposite side of the broad highway, right on the access road. We were to engage the blockaded enemy troops on our section of the access road, and attrite as many personnel, and materiel, as possible. Since there was no way through the blockade on the access roads, we would force the enemy to retreat with their vehicles back to the flyover exit to join the main body of attackers.

The temptation of the "gap" left in the highway, coupled with strategic placement and concentration of crossfire mainly on the access roads, would "force" these troops to take the "easier" alternative on the main highway. Since we would not subject the highway to concentrated fire, this would be viewed as the best hope for a breakthrough.

We knew we would be subject to intense fire from both the access roads and the main highway, but we would be prepared using sandbag emplacements and concrete ledges to work behind. We also installed

SWAT ballistic shields braced by further sand bags.

The troops on the main highway would receive the greatest pressure as the enemy would try to concentrate their fire in order to breach the gap. The enemy would, of course, be impeded by the bunched up transports and personnel getting in their line of fire.

If we succeeded in making the enemy move to the main highway, we could then concentrate on doing as much damage to the enemy as possible.

If we received the "enemy breach" signal, then we would bug out and head back to Gore's Folly to support the defense of our Area of Operations.

Hopefully, the secondary blockade would further dampen the attack. If that blockade was then breached, the "Omega" signal would be transmitted for our troops to bug out as rapidly as possible before the REAL crap hit the wood chipper.

III. SAM'S LOG - GORE'S FOLLY

I WAS FEELING GUILTY. I felt a personal sense of failure at having not accessed the spy satellites hanging over U.S. soil.

What I had told everybody was that the only satellites I could easily access were the U.S. spy satellites in geosynchronous orbit over foreign countries. I could break into those and highjack them quite easily. And I did so with South America. The angle on the video feeds was a bit wonky, but workable.

There were other satellites I could hijack that hang over the U.S., but those were primarily communications and photographic. The example I gave to Victor was the Google Maps satellites which provide high-resolution aerial or satellite images. Most of the current satellite imagery is over 5 years old and updated infrequently, and not in real-time.

While it was true that I was handicapped by our inability to "translate" the foreign satellites' high-level code based in, - let's say, Cyrillic - I was really too lazy to try to use binary to decipher their code. It would be a long and tedious - and maybe impossible - job for me.

However.

Sigh.

I KNEW there were domestic spy satellites hanging over our heads. NSA and DEA projects had expanded in the Obama years to include domestic spying. I KNEW that.

But, pre-Event, I had been scared off of any THOUGHTS of hacking into those systems, post Snowden.

One day, sitting in my office at Google HQ, (I was actually playing the latest version of BioShock online, at the time) when two dudes showed up unannounced. They were in suits (natch) and I recognized the look. They were Feds of the humorless "Patriot Act" type.

They didn't bother to show ID, as their ability to walk in on a high level security wing at Google was ID enough.

I looked at them blandly, wondering what the NSA or CIA or Homeland wanted, now. I had been behaving myself (sort of) - at least, as far as these Feds were concerned. One of them merely withdrew a sheaf of papers from his coat pocket and showed them to me.

"You remember signing this?" the guy asked.

It was part of my "deal" to get out of going to Fed nerd prison. It stated that if I ever looked into classified government programs without specific permission or direction by whatever Federal agency was responsible, I would be subject to immediate incarceration at whatever hell-hole they decided to throw me into for the balance of my short life.

Short, because everybody (us hackers, anyway) knew that if the Fed chose to, they would "rendition" me to a facility in a Middle Eastern country that had no qualms about torture.

Gulp.

I said, "Yeah?..."

They let me know - without letting me know, you understand - that the U.S. was working on a system of "domestic terrorist attrition" that involved satellite systems such as those I had previously breached internationally. They were here to warn me that if I even LOOKED their way, on the domestic front, they would immediately enact rendition via the Patriot Act.

Gulp, again.

Okay.

Message received.

Aye, Aye, sir!

Yassa Massa!

They went away.

And I never looked.

But now I wish I had. I knew that if the 'Net were still up and running that I COULD have access to the secret programs using backdoor infiltration techniques I was quite good at. It would be a lot easier than attempting binary code programming on foreign-based high-level programming languages. But now there was no more 'Net.

So no more access via the 'Net.

But.

And this was important... BUT... there WERE intra-Satellite communication channels that ALL of our Satellites used in order to provide backup and redundancy and for informational cross-processing. In other words, the U.S. satellites could help each other out in a pinch.

I had access to the U.S. foreign deployed Satellites, so if I could identify those intra-Satellite protocols, I would be able to access the NSA, or whatever, spy Satellites right above our heads.

I had been afraid to try - pre-Event - and really had no compelling reason to. I had no need.

And post-Event, I had been more than willing to "make-do" using the access to the foreign SATs that I had - and too lazy to make the effort, else wise.

But now, with everyone going into the battle for our lives, there was ample reason to.

So, while everybody else worked on getting battle-ready, I worked on getting us "eyes."

But that would not bring Lori back.

BY THE TIME THE TRUCKS ROLLED AWAY and Victor was getting to go on his inspection run, I had broken through the communications protocols and had established control on the Satellite over our immediate sky.

I established control over the most relevant video feeds, and I was completely blown away by the resolution and clarity. Multiple camera "eyes" were capable of simultaneously transmitting live images in infrared and low light at resolutions that rivaled photographic film.

This was just the edge we needed. Too bad I had been too busy being lazy and hadn't got to it in time to - perhaps - make a difference with Lori.

I went to Victor as he was running around, preparing to go out and inspect the barriers on the main highway. Gunny was standing beside him looking more sullen than I have ever seen him. He appeared to be having as close to an argument as I have ever seen Gunny come to with Victor.

He was saying, "But, Cap'n… you'll need me out there!"

Victor looked at him and said (more patiently than I've ever heard Victor speak), "No, Gunny. You're needed here. I need you here.

I need you to set up the defenses for if, and when, it all goes to shit.

I need you to oversee the mounting of the Twins on the roof, and I need you manning a Barrett from high ground."

Gunny started to argue, but Victor cut him off, saying softly, "Please, Gunny."

Which rocked me. I'd never heard the word "please" come from Victor's mouth before. Gunny just nodded and went out the door, brushing by me.

Victor looked up at me with tired eyes. I could see the strain was getting to him. I imagine I looked like hell, too, but Victor surprised me once again by smiling softly - and I thought, rather fondly - at me.

Before we could say anything, Jonas burst through the door announcing, "They're in place!"

"The trucks?"

"Yeah, they're good to go!"

"Jonas… are you SURE about the ranges?"

"As sure as I can be, Mate, considerin' it ain't MY ass hangin' out there! But it'll be close. You have maybe… MAYBE… two-three minutes from 'execute'."

Victor nodded. He looked at Jonas, "Can we get away with minimal casualties?"

Jonas shook his head. "Maybe you can ask Janis' God for help on that one.

You know we'll take casualties, regardless. This all hinges on how many casualties the enemy's willing to take before giving it up - if they do."

"I know. I know," said Victor, slowly shaking his head.

I spoke up, "I think I've got something that'll help…"

They both jerked their heads up to look at me.

"We've got eyes now…" I said, "Really good eyes!"

IV. GWEN - 1st SQUAD LEADER

"As the hunter is hunted down, she slays her enemies on
sacred ground."

- Boadicea

"A good plan violently executed now is better than a perfect plan
executed next week."

- George S. Patton

I WATCHED AS MY SQUAD settled in, wondering how many
would die today. Or if I would die.

I'm not a soldier... I never was one. I was a law officer in a more civil
land than the one we were currently in, even Pre-Event.

I had led officers into dangerous situations. We had even faced vicious
gangs and small groups of terrorists. But that was with the full force and
arms of the Queen's own. I always knew, deep down, that I was NOT the
final front. My country - my people - would come together to help us in
overwhelming distress.

Now, I was expected to lead real soldiers - soldiers who had, in their
previous lives, fought in real wars where the engagement with the enemy
was to kill the enemy - not to arrest them.

I watched these quiet, professional men and women going about the
business of inflicting maximum violence on our enemies. They rather
reminded me of our own "action squads" (what Victor called SWAT) in my
native Cardiff. Their calmness masked the sheer human terror of what they
were asked to do.

They - as well as 2nd Squad - were the best, most experienced soldiers
we had. Both squads were on the rooftops in order to inflict as much
damage to the enemy as possible. We were the only fully experienced
squads. The balance were raw recruits whose only experience, if any, was
the guarding of foraging convoys. This kind of battle was well beyond their
ken.

They would be facing the brunt of the attack head on. Their advantage
was, hopefully, that the enemy would be hemmed in and too bunched up to
effectively engage our forces.

Those of us on the roof tops would do our best to harry the enemy with crossfire from our advantageous positions. The frontline positions themselves, while taking refuge behind a double wall of cement filled lorries as well as the occasional heavy dump truck filled with gravel, would put up their own crossfire to withering advantage.

At least, that was the plan.

But, as the saying goes, "Man plans... God laughs."

I WAS WATCHING ONE OF MY SNIPERS settling in with the very intimidating 50 Calibre Barrett rifle. He had it positioned on a tripod with sandbags all around it. It looked like a futuristic cannon. He worked and reworked the mechanism, inserting and ejecting the gigantic magazine.

He would peer down the 'scope and adjust little dials and fiddle with bits that were incomprehensible to me. He certainly appeared to know what he was doing.

My other sniper was not doing that routine. In fact, he appeared to be napping.

I think I trusted him more for that.

My "adjutant," George Bader, was the one I counted upon to provide the "soldier's" viewpoint, as opposed to the law-enforcement paramilitary view I was more used to. While our training was similar, I obviously did not have "battle" experience.

I was counting on him not to let me do foolish things that would put us all in peril.

Since we were positioned high atop a very large bank building, there had been no way for us to put external ladders on the outside face of that building, as had 2nd Squad. We had to rely on - and climb - internal stairs to the 14 story roof top. Even with our "new" healthy bodies that was a rough climb, given the amount of equipment we all carried.

That was the main disadvantage of this tiny dancer's body I now wore. While strong and fit, there was just so much weight I could muster. I had been limited to carrying my own personal weapons and toting two boxes of ammunition by the green handles. At that, I was still getting the cramps out of my arms and hands. But the balance of my squad didn't seem too worse for wear - even though they had made more than one trip, up and down those stairways, carrying heavy equipment, ammo and weapons.

Now, we were settling in to wait on news from Gore's Folly.

Jonas - with the help of that genius beauty, Sam - had set up a communications system for our purposes. Jonas and Sam had already set up the satellite dishes, previously - from which we were now receiving updated visual intelligence.

They had set up antennae for radio communications similar to what we police used around the globe, as well. We did not have access to encrypted and enhanced military-type radio 'comms that would be more useful under these circumstances.

Victor's SWAT van had been equipped for such, but we hadn't taken the time to locate similar equipment. Victor was always talking about going to the Special Forces training camp just north of Gore's Folly - but, again we hadn't found the time to do so. We COULD have located the local police and SWAT comms buildings and use that scavenged equipment at Gore's Folly, but again...

Now that laziness would put us at a disadvantage.

Or perhaps not.

Jonas and Sam had jury-rigged a communications system that included using our own cell tower. Gore's Folly had one sitting at the top of the hill, and Sam - with the help of one of our new recruits, who had been a Verizon (I assumed that was an American mobile company) network engineer - had activated it to use the mobile system for our own communications.

We could not, obviously, use the system to reach "the outside world" as the cellular networks had failed along with the power grid. But we could communicate with, and within, our little community using the familiar gadgets we were all used to.

This had the further advantage of not having a training curve, such as that required by radio 'comms protocol. Our mostly civilian community needed firearms training for defense on our foraging expeditions - not the 'comms training necessary for a protracted battle.

Until now.

They had rigged up communications for the field by providing "push to talk" handsets and Bluetooth earpieces. They had also divided up the field into communications "sections" to avoid confusion. They could relay information at a moment's notice, if needed.

Now we heard the 'comm Tech's voice in our earpieces, "Break, break. Break for general announcement. Hold one." And then, a pause.

Jonas' voice came on with his distinguishable Aussie accent, "Ladies and gentlemen on the front lines: the enemy has ceased mucking about at the airbase and are now departing on the projected route. Our Satellite images are quite clear, and VTAP is projecting the enemy group will move at a 20-30 MPH clip, putting them at their split point in 15 minutes.

Should the forces NOT split, you will be informed. ETA to Point Alpha is projected at 30 minutes after split and at Point Delta 40 minutes after same.

Be advised: they appear to have three Bradley Fighting Vehicles, but we have no details as to armament. Good news is that, as the slowest vehicles, they are bringing up the rear. In all likelihood, they will not be able to engage without fear of committing friendly fire.

We'll be back to you with further. Out."

"Well, shit," George said, shaking his head, "a frickin' Bradley."

"We can deal with that," I said, "we have two anti-tank weapons and 2nd squad has another two."

"Pardon me, ma'am," George replied, "But I don't think that's enough. Bradley's are hard to kill. And we don't have Anti-Tank rounds, anyway - just HE." He shook his head, sorrowfully. "I just wish we had an old-fashioned, third-world RPG to melt through that armor plate!

From up here, we won't be able to hit the sides OR the under plate with our AT's. Somebody's gonna have to go down there to try and sneak in a round or two."

Well. So.

I said, "Let's not worry on that bone, George. Let's stay positive."

George snorted, as was his right. I didn't know what I was talking about.

I WALKED TO THE EDGE OF THE ROOFTOP and peered at our funnel point.

Past the overhead bridge that crosses the main highway, cement and dump trucks were set up in a double line across both the north and south-bound lanes, to form an inward-bending vee-shape in order to "funnel" the enemy forces and to have them aim for a "break" in the line of trucks.

The plan was, as the enemy drove onto the "flyover" that ramped the eastbound traffic on Loop 410 onto the northbound IH-10 lanes, they would naturally "bunch up" into a slow moving mass as the feeder ramp narrowed.

IH-10 was labeled "West", but that was because the highway continued to the Western U.S. into New Mexico, Arizona and California. For now, however, it was due North on the compass.

That highway led in the general direction of Gore's Folly some 24 kilometers - or as my American friends would have it, 15 miles - down the road.

Partway there, however, we had another set of truck barriers just before getting to the "outer loop" of the city, which was designated "Loop 1604."

This was our secondary line of defense for when - or if - the first line was breached. We would retreat there for a time and hold the enemy back with heavy fire.

1st and 2nd squads would take the side roads on rapid vehicles to get to the crossroads bridge on Medical Drive, providing downward crossfire zones, while the main body would retreat up IH-10 to the truck barrier and set themselves up behind the line and drive two more trucks to close the gap.

When the time came and the signal "Omega" was sent, we would ALL withdraw as rapidly as possible to get to a "safe" zone.

That second retreat would be back to Gore's Folly.

We had covered the southbound lanes with a solid wall of trucks as a barrier, and had done the same across each of the feeder - or access - roads.

If the enemy chose to branch off to those access roads in order to speed up the traffic flow, 1st and 2nd squads' job would be to concentrate our fire on the feeder road personnel in order to force them back to the main highway - where they would bunch up even more, and be tempted to break through the slight "gap" left between the trucks on the main northbound lanes.

I looked down at these lines of defense, wondering what would go wrong.

Something invariably would.

"BREAK, BREAK. Break for Point Alpha announcement, only. Hold one."

Again.

I looked up as though it would help me to hear better.

Jonas' voice: "Ummm… mates. It appears as though the enemy forces are using only northbound lanes on 410. They have split off a smaller force on Bandera Road as predicted, and Point Delta has been informed they are coming their way.

Delta plan is optimal.

As for you blokes at Alpha, it appears as though you have about 15 minutes to make adjustments, if needed. Since the southbound lanes will not be used, 1st Squad positioning will not be optimal - and the 'surprise' packages will not be effective..."

Victor's voice: "Break, break. This is Victor...

2nd Squad, hold and adjust positioning to extend cross fire zones down the northbound lanes. Put your long range guns set to max, and the short range weapons, including HE launchers, to support close in. Be cautious of 'friendly fire' blowback. 'Ware your firing lanes.

1st Squad, plan is still optimal. Lay down fire as planned.

2nd Squad Leader, see if you can send one person down to move as many of the claymores as possible to 1st Squad's position. He or she will have to join 1st squad, or the main defensive lines, as time allows.

Squad Leaders, acknowledge. Over."

I pressed my talk button, "Gwen, here, acknowledged."

"Squad Leader Thompson. Acknowledged. Over and out."

Sigh. I said I wasn't a professional soldier.

Victor's voice, "Victor. Out."

After an awkward pause, Jonas' voice came back, sounding a bit uncomfortable.

"Ummm... this's Jonas again. Ummm.. I have a request from Janis to say... ummm... something to all the troops... uh... standby."

Then, Janis' calm, measured voice:

"I offer this prayer:

Our Father in Heaven, as these fine men and women go into battle, every person will beseech you each in his or her own way. Our enemies also in their own language - which so enrages us, but is heard by you as your loving children's' cries - will ask for your Devine protection and for total victory.

And now, we bow before You, Our Father. We offer our prayers as best we can, and we pray to You for those for whom You have not chosen to reveal Your true self. I pray You watch over these young men and women that are led into battle. Bring them home, safely, to us.

As it says in Your Holy Word, Lord, in the Book of Psalms:

'Blessed be the LORD my strength, which teacheth my hands to war, and my fingers to fight:

My goodness, and my fortress; my high tower, and my deliverer; my shield, and he in whom I trust; who subdueth my people under me.

Bow thy heavens, O LORD, and come down: touch the mountains, and they shall smoke. Cast forth lightning, and scatter them: shoot out thine arrows, and destroy them.

Send thine hand from above; rid me, and deliver me out of great waters, from the hand of strange children;

Whose mouth speaketh strange words and falsehood.

Amen."

As she clicked off, I heard many soft, answering "Amens."

V. BATTLEFIELD

Let your plans be dark and as impenetrable as night, and when you move, fall like a thunderbolt.

- Sun Tzu

THEY CAME AS PREDICTED, out of the east loop onto the off ramp leading toward IH-10 northbound. Since the off ramp was naturally narrower than the four-lane that fed it - and construction barriers (pre-Event construction was a constant in this town) narrowed it further - the enemy forces coming off the flyover were slowed down and bunched up, imitating Pre-Event rush-hour traffic snarls.

Victor watched, via his computer 'pad, the overhead view from the spy satellite Sam had hacked into. Victor smiled as he saw the groups of vehicles come to literal stop as the traffic bunched up. He could imagine the commander - whoever he was - probably sitting in one of the Bradleys wondering what the hell was up.

They presumably had electronic communications capabilities - they had been in one of the most advanced air bases in the world, after all. He imagined the conversations going back and forth from the lead vehicles back to the trailing ones several miles back. It would be in Spanish, of course - but the gist would probably be like this:

WHAT THE HELL? WHAT'S THE HOLD UP, THERE?

SORRY, BOSS. BUT WE'RE KIND OF HUNG UP ON THE OFF RAMP. AND PROGRESS IS A BIT SLOW.

WELL MOVE FASTER!

SORRY, BOSS, BUT FLUID DYNAMICS BEING WHAT THEY ARE, WE JUST GOTTA GET THROUGH THIS.

WHAT THE DEVIL DOES THAT MEAN?

WELL, WE NEED TO GET THROUGH THIS TURN AND WE NEED TO SLOW DOWN. THE RAMP CAN'T ACCOMMODATE FOUR ABREAST.

JUST GET DOWN THERE, ASAP!

YES, BOSS. DOING THE BEST WE CAN.

Or something like that. Or maybe not.

Sam was in his ear reporting privately.

"The off ramp is slowing them down and stretching them out for several miles. Some are at a standstill, waiting their turn on to the ramp.

I see several bodies directing traffic, trying to get some order as they try to move trucks from the far lanes over to the left."

A pause. Then, "Several of the enemy are diverting to the previous exit and taking the access road, which will put them in 1st Squad's fire zone - as predicted."

Yeah, Victor thought, and leaving 2nd Squad with little else to do than provide crossfire for the main blockade on IH-10.

There was no time to reposition the squad, and it would not have been a good idea, in any case.

"I see them!"

Victor looked up from the 'pad. His driver was standing beside the open door using the binoculars.

Victor got out of the car and squinted down the main highway. The off-ramp was not quite visible from here, but he could make out shimmering dots on the road.

"Break, break. Team Alpha. This is Victor. The enemy is in sight. No firing until I give the word.

Repeat. No firing until my signal.

All troops remain under cover. 3rd Squad on bridge, do not give your cover away until the claymore signal. Victor, out."

He saw his troops get down behind the double wall of trucks. He himself was carrying an M240B machine gun, with LOTS of ammo. He would position himself behind the double line of heavy trucks, which would provide plenty of cover. He now wore a full helmet, besides his Dragon Skin Armor. He only wished he could have equipped all his troops.

But he would be on the line - laying down heavy fire and seeking to do as much violence on the enemy as possible. Which was going to be plenty.

He just prayed that Jonas' plan would work. If not, they were as good as dead.

THE COMMANDER WAS GETTING IMPATIENT. Things were at a standstill, and didn't look as though they were going to improve anytime, soon.

He was sitting in the Bradley Fighting Vehicle at the back of the four lane column of vehicles, stewing.

He had ordered that a smaller force of vehicles - those that could be peeled off on the right hand lane - exit further on, and do a turnaround to enter the access road running parallel to the highway. This gave them a chance to flow traffic in a more expeditious manner.

That helped, but given how "bumper-to-bumper" traffic flowed with these restrictions, it still left them crawling forward. Some 400+ vehicles of all types - from HumVees to Troop Transport Trucks to plain utility pickups - were starting and stopping, but then just came to an abrupt stop. And they sat.

"Damn it," he said to the driver, "Get me the sub-commander!"

The crewman bent to his mic and spoke softly into it.

He turned around and said, "The sub-commander is on, sir."

"Fuentes!" the commander growled into his own comm set, "What the blazes is the hold-up NOW?!!!"

"Commander, we have spotted a barrier that runs across all traffic lanes. The barrier appears to be heavy trucks parked to blockade."

"A trap?"

"More like a defensive line, sir. Looks like a formidable one. Those are heavy duty dump trucks and cement trucks," the sub-commander reported.

"We are just out of effective weapons range, but we are not getting through here without a fight. I intend to send a fast scout forward to see what is waiting for us."

The commander sighed, and said softly, "Very prudent, Fuentes. Get back to me, soonest."

"Yes, commander. Out."

A VEHICLE BROKE OFF THE MAIN GROUP and came speeding down the highway weaving back and forth across the lanes. They apparently thought this was a good way to present a difficult target. They were wrong, of course, but Victor admired their desperate attempt at doing anything to change the inevitable.

They were imitating the dashing run that soldiers do to avoid snipers. But that was futile while driving a pickup truck against massed weaponry. The truck wasn't quite that nimble.

He felt sorry for them - almost.

Victor keyed his 'comm and said, "Victor, here. Hold your fire. All positions, hold your fire, even if fired upon.

Team leaders, clear?"

They all came on, one by one and acknowledged the order.

He went on, "I will do the firing - but DO NOT feel free to join in. Maintain your fire discipline and DO NOT engage until I give the order. OUT!"

Victor looked around. Most of the greenhorns were looking up at him with fearful eyes. This would be their first time in a real battle for most of them, even though they all had defended themselves in post-Event encounters.

He nodded to them and said, "Don't worry. I'll take 'em out. Just make sure you're not exposed to return fire."

"Yes, sir," some of them answered quietly. Victor nodded to them again, appearing calmer than he really felt.

Despite the last few months experience in "little" firefights with "Xeno-lingual" groups, Victor's last experience as a soldier in real combat was more than forty years in the past.

As a 19 year old fighting in Viet Nam, he had experienced the real terror that comes from having determined men looking to take his life or to seriously maim his body.

After a while, the mind adjusts... or breaks.

He adjusted by becoming hard and numb to the fear. He didn't - quite - break.

But over the last forty years he had... fuzzed... the memories of how that actually felt. To be in a battle that was as impersonal and uncaring as large battles often are was both psychically and physically draining. Hot, speeding, and invisible projectiles coming at you from no apparent direction were terrifying. He remembered the sound of projectiles hitting all around him, as impersonal as sharks crunching through a swimmer's leg.

He set his jaw, and moved to put his machine gun in the gap between the blockading trucks. The gap was actually pretty good and gave him a wider field of vision - and therefore a wider field of fire - than he thought possible.

The pickup truck - which had been outfitted as a "technical" by the enemy - had a Light Machine Gun (LMG) mounted on a swivel post. He could make out the markings, and just about see the machine gun mounted over the cab sparking and winking as it fired at their position.

His own M240B machine gun was loaded with armor piercing rounds - with a tracer loaded every five. It had a rated effective range of 1,100 meters on a tripod. But because he was firing it as only a bipod-supported shoulder mount, his effective range was basically cut in half.

And since he was not an experienced machine gunner, his own effective range would be even shorter. Let's say 400 meters.

But he could not take the chance to risk his maximum long shot with the vehicle approaching in a weaving pattern. So he decided to wait for the truck to be within 100 meters. It was hard as the enemy truck was firing its own LMG in the hopes of suppressing any return fire.

It was not quite effective, as firing ANY weapon from a moving, weaving and jouncing platform was really problematic. And finding the gaps, firing wildly at the blockading trucks was, at best, a lottery ticket win.

But the metallic thumps, cracks and pings - sounding like a hailstorm on a tin roof - had a psychological effect on the defending troops, especially as green as they were.

God knew it had an effect on Victor, himself.

He said, loudly (more for himself, really, and to appear the grand leader in control), "Steady, troops. And NO FIRING!"

He knew the seasoned squads would not have to be reminded of his previously broadcast order.

When the truck reached the point he had set in his mind, he breathed out slowly and...

Time slowed down. He could now make out the driver's face with its expression of fierce concentration on keeping up the weaving pattern while not overcompensating and tipping them over. He could read the fear behind the concentration, and he could see the white-knuckle grip the driver had on the steering wheel as he maneuvered the truck. Standing up on the bed of the truck, the gunner was crouched over the LMG in the correct two-hand firing position.

He was strapped to the truck with stabilizing belts, but was being thrown about, nonetheless. He was doing a good job of swiveling the machine gun on its mount and raking the truck barrier back and forth, hitting the hard metal surfaces of the truck sides. Many of the rounds were punching through the first metal layer as the gunner had armor piercing ammo loaded every few rounds.

He was firing in slow, measured bursts, conserving barrel life, as all good machine gunners should, while putting out effective suppressing fire. As the truck turned to the right to begin another weaving maneuver, he could see the gunner swivel the LMG.

The rounds appeared to be twinkling slowly to Victor's heightened senses, and the bangs and clangs of the bullets striking metal were harsh and metallic. He heard some rounds hit flesh as they struck 'lucky' through the gaps and where his people didn't hunker down well enough.

He took another breath as he saw the side of the truck as it turned again. He squeezed his own trigger, sending 30 Rounds in measured bursts. He saw the metal surfaces of the truck gouged with gigantic holes, and he saw glass splintering and saw the flesh of the driver and the gunner burst apart in bloody gobbets, before the truck rolled over and literally disintegrated before his eyes, sending bits and parts of metal, rubber and glass exploding across the roadway.

He stopped squeezing the trigger and took another breath, and...

... he came to himself, his ears ringing from the burst of rounds despite the earplugs he had so carefully inserted.

He heard two things, simultaneously:

Cheers from his troops - and the panicked cries of "Man down! Man down!"

SUB-COMMANDER FUENTES WAS CLEARLY NERVOUS as he watched his men weaving down the highway firing the LMG for all it was worth. Brave men.

He watched through binoculars as their bullets tore across the truck barrier. They were clearly in range, but he could detect no return fire.

Then he saw the splatter of metal and glass and then saw the truck roll sideways as it was torn apart by a seemingly invisible force.

He saw all this before he heard the distinctive rip-saw sound of return machine gun fire. Light travels much faster than sound.

He couldn't see where the return fire came from. He was chilled by the thought of disciplined forces holding their fire under orders - and then having only one shooter return fire and completely destroy the attacking vehicle as though swatting a fly.

Fuentes keyed his 'comm and said, "Commander. We have a problem."

My God, he thought, what kind of men were these?

VICTOR QUICKLY ORGANIZED HIS TROOPS to take the wounded and evac them back to Gore's Folly. Two men were wounded, mainly from bullet fragments that had struck the edges of the truck barrier and still had enough kinetic force to cause damage. A woman lay in a death sprawl, her chest and back blown away by the round from the attacker's weapon. It had gone right between a gap.

He decided to leave the dead woman where she was as a reminder to the others to obey orders. She had obviously not been able to resist looking and had not hunkered down as Victor had ordered. To have been struck in the chest, she would have to have been standing to peer through the gap.

Stupidity was definitely a capital punishment offense in this new world.

Victor shook his head angrily.

He keyed his mic. "Break for Sam. This is Victor, over."

"Sam, here... nice shooting... er... over."

"We got two for the doc on the way. Have him ready. We got one KIA. Over."

"Sorry. That's... bad. Over."

"Yep... Sam, you got eyes on the enemy? What does the Sat show? I don't have my 'pad with me, so don't bother to feed. Over."

"Umm... yeah. They seem to be holding back. The formation has quit building up, but the access road group is flowing up to... just... at the point where your guys are held up. Over."

"Break for 1st squad leader. This is Victor. Do you have eyes on your formation? Over."

"Gwen, here, Captain. Affirmative. Our spotters have optical view. Over."

"Break for 2nd squad leader. Do YOU have eyes on our formation? Over."

"Thompson, here. Affirm, Captain. Our spotters and snipers all have optimal sight lines. Over."

"Break for Victor. Gwen, here. Over."

"Go ahead, Gwen. Over."

"Uh... Captain, my shooters wanted me to let you know they, too, have optimal sight lines. Over."

"Thank you, Gwen... Squad Leaders: prepare your long range to sight in on random. Only your long range. Clear? Over."

Silence. A pause.

"Break for Victor; Thompson here. Understood. Over."

"Gwen here... um... sorry... Break for Victor. Gwen here. I THINK I understand, Captain... but what do you have in mind? (pause)... Uh... Over."

"Just have your long range ready to engage random. Be ready on my mark. Your snipers will know how to engage for effect. Trust them, Gwen. Squad Leaders: Acknowledge. Over."

"Thompson: clear, Captain. Out."

"Gwen: Umm... clear. Will wait on your mark to engage. Out, as well."

"Victor, out."

THE COMMANDER WAS GETTING THE DETAILS from his Sub-Commander.

It had not quite gone as expected, but the result was the same. He had fully expected to lose the scout vehicle - but not before getting more of an idea as to the forces behind the blockade. All they had gotten was the fact that ONE machine gun was defending the barricade - but not what kind.

He sighed. He began tapping his front tooth with his fingernail, lost in thought. It was a habit he had brought over from his previous life.

He heard his Sub-Commander's voice in his ear phone, querying, "Commander?..."

"One moment, Sub-Commander. Stand by for orders," he replied.

He turned to his driver - a senior non-com with plenty of battle experience in Angola, fighting for the damnable Cuban Communist Army. The Commander was no fan of communists - but what matter, now? All that counted was competence and experience. The young man before him - appearing no more than in his late twenties - had been translated from a seventy-five year old crippled veteran of the wars in Africa.

So useful.

"Jorgé. I think we need to risk at least a quarter of our forces attacking the barrier - fully engaging them head-on. What are your thoughts?" he asked.

The non-com frowned and replied, "I would be more comfortable if we had the Bradley's and that firepower leading. That's what I think,

Commandant."

"Hmmm... no..." he said thoughtfully. "Before we go to the trouble of re-arranging this traffic jam to get by, we need to know it is not wasted effort. We are far from the exit ramp."

"Commandant - we can do both. Send the forces to attack and in the meantime prepare the Bradley's to lead any further attacks. It will be getting dark in a few hours, sir. We cannot afford to waste time," he advised.

The Commander nodded, thoughtfully and said, "Good advice, Jorgé."

He keyed his mic and spoke to the Sub-commander: "Fuentes. New orders..."

"Yes, Commander?"

"I want you to send 1/3 of your forces on the highway, and on the side road access, to attack the barrier. You will align the attack vehicles in a staggered formation so as to clear your lanes of fire.

We want to eliminate the possibility of friendly fire and bring as much fire-concentration on the blockade. You will also dismount 1/3 of your ground forces and have them in skirmish lines, taking cover behind the attack vehicles.

You are to remain behind and direct the attack via your comms.

Secondarily, you will move the remaining vehicles up, just up to effective range, and create a lane to receive the support of the Bradley's for attack support. We will work on clearing this traffic jam to move the Bradley's up and get them onto the ramp.

How long will it take you to organize the attack, sub-commander?"

He heard silence. He appreciated Fuentes was probably getting advice from his senior people.

"Commander... my people tell me we have to reshuffle our vehicles in order to maximize the effectiveness, as you ordered... and we have just the person to do the job. He's a logistics expert and..."

"Never mind the details, Fuentes," the Commander interrupted. "Just give me an estimate!"

Again, silence for a beat. Then, "Commander, we estimate... 15 to ... 20 minutes."

"Fine, sub-commander. See to it. Radio when you begin the attack. Over and Out!"

VICTOR HEARD FROM SAM. "Victor this is Sam."

"Go ahead, Sam."

"You have activity."

"Tell me."

"Um... they appear to be rearranging the HumVees and 'Technicals.' I think they're gonna attack!"

"Roger, Sam. I was expecting that. They're pretty jammed up to be effective. Keep an eye out and feed me the Sat view."

"Okay. Out."

Victor picked up his 'pad.

What Victor saw from the overhead view was not surprising.

They were rearranging the stacked-up vehicles by moving them back and forth, and sliding in one for another, like a sliding-tile puzzle game where interlocking tiles have to be arranged to reveal a picture.

He could see one man directing the traffic flow and actually doing a pretty good job of it. He was standing on the highway and pointing to a truck or to a HumVee, and pointing where they needed to go. He was apparently arranging the vehicles to maximize their attack lanes and minimize any friendly fire zones.

Behind this activity, he could see a HumVee with a man standing up in the turret that had an M240 mounted on it with a protective plate. Ouch! That would bring plenty of firepower to the game. The other Hummers had smaller caliber guns - mostly LMG's - obviously retrofitted on these U.S. Air Force vehicles that would not have been armed at this Air Base.

So the one hanging back must be the forward command, as it was 'haughtily' surveying the action going on around them.

The 'traffic cop' was doing too good a job. Victor had an idea.

"Break for 2nd Squad. This is Victor. Over."

"Thompson, here, Cap'n. Over."

"Thompson, do your Barretts have eyes on the traffic conductor? Over."

"Affirmative. We have 'im five-by. Over."

"Can your shooter take him with a big 'splash'? Over."

A pause. Ten or so beats, while Thompson talked it over with his sniper equipped with one of the .50 Caliber Barrett Sniper Rifles.

"That's affirm. Shooter understands what you want. Over."

Victor smiled thinly. Gotta love professionals!

"Roger. On my mark, have your shooter take him out messy. Clear?

Over."

"Roger. Awaiting your mark, over."

"Do you also have eyes on the Hummer about 200 meters back equipped with the .50 Cal? I think it's the forward command. Over."

A pause while the spotter scopes scanned. Then, "Affirmative, Captain, but line of sight is not - repeat - NOT optimal. Over."

Shit!

Then, "Break for Victor. This is Gwen. Over."

"Go."

"Victor, one of my shooters has direct line of sight on that HumVee. Do you want both the driver and the man in the turret taken? Over."

"Negative. Negative. I want the head man alive, for now. But I want the driver taken out for effect.

Squad leaders: listen carefully. No firing other than these targets, except on my command. Tango 1 will be the conductor directing traffic. Tango 2 will be the Command HumVee driver. Clear? Squad Leaders, Acknowledge. Over."

Both acknowledged the order.

Victor smiled. It was time to prod the bull into charging.

SUB-COMMANDER FUENTES WATCHED the rearrangement of his attacking forces with great satisfaction.

The man directing and setting up the firing lanes for the attack was a genius. His name was Vicorío Fuentes-Garza (no relation.) He had proved his worth as a logistics master, time after time, and had an intuitive grasp of what he called "the Laws of Fluid Dynamics".

He had, in fact, tried to organize the departure from the Airbase, and had warned of this pile-up now jamming their effective attack. The Commander had ignored his warnings and had waived him away impatiently. The departure had been taking a long time to organize as it was, and this man was advocating further delays to optimize the trip.

The Commander's shortsightedness was now - as the Americans would have it - "biting us on the hindquarters."

It really lost the flavor of the thought in Spanish - the phrasing didn't quite capture the nuance he - not quite - remembered. He missed having other languages to call upon for their own delightful way of expressing concepts. Now, in this world, he couldn't bear to try to dredge up those languages.

Sub-Commander Fuentes watched Vicorío standing on the Highway as he, himself, stood in the turret of the HumVee, admiring the man's deft, orchestra-conductor like movements directing the vehicles to their own attack patterns. Fuentes smiled, recalling a movie he once saw about the great American General Patton.

As the scene unfolded, the great World War II general was taking over as a traffic cop when he became disgusted with a muddy traffic jam involving tanks. God only knows that the COMMANDER wouldn't deign to...

THUNK-SPLAT!

He watched, not comprehending what he was seeing.

It seemed to him as though Vicorío's head had become suddenly surrounded by a muddy pink and gray mist. It covered him from the shoulders up, and he appeared to be bowing, jerkily.

As the mist pattered down and out, Fuentes could see that man's head had disappeared in that cloud. Vicorío's body fell bonelessly to the highway.

"Sniper," Fuentes thought - almost calmly as he registered the sight. His body tingled as the thought rolled around his head. He found he could not move his body. Or shout a warning to his men, as he should have done. He merely stared at the sight of a man with his head completely disintegrated by an invisible force.

It was terrifying.

THUNK-CRASH!

This time he felt the force of the blow going through the windscreen on the driver side of his HumVee. He knew what was happening, as a meaty, bloody smell permeated the vehicle, wafting up to him as he stood in the turret.

His gunner, who had traded seats with Fuentes to give him a better view of the operation, was screaming up to him to get down - to get back inside.

Fuentes looked down at the screaming man and then across to the driver. The driver appeared to be relaxed - leaning his head against the window as though to take a long siesta.

But the man's entire chest was gone, blown to bloody shreds in line with the oversized hole in the windscreen.

But the driver wasn't taking a nap. He had his head leaned over because all his upper body was gone, except for a string of gristle and bone that was connected to the shredded mass.

"That explains it," Fuentes thought, as his gunner kept screaming urgently.

"... TANGO 2 DOWN.."

Victor heard the update from the calm-voiced sniper.

"Ready to execute RANDOM on your mark. Over."

"Stand by."

Victor decided to wait for the helpless feelings and terror of the moment to sink in for the opposing forces. He knew that fear and anticipation would cloud their minds.

That's where his people had the advantage.

The U.S. and U.K. had been constantly engaged in a real war, globally. The opposing forces would mainly be composed of Spanish-speakers who really hadn't been on the battlefield for decades. They might have been exposed to violence in their world, but a real war was different than police versus gang action. Even political insurgency and drug wars were different.

Only the odd Spanish-speaking American who might have served in the War on Terror in the last decade - and there might be a few of those, as Hispanics of any flavor made up a great percentage of the U.S.'s standing army - would have an inkling.

The rest would be in shock.

It would serve to wait a beat or two to have the word disseminated to the ranks of the sight of a man's head disappearing and another's body blown in half by a seemingly invisible force.

The long range shots had the advantage of the event preceding the sound, as the projectiles where hypersonic. And maybe the crack of the weapons couldn't be heard above the rumbling of engines massed on the highway. Mysterious and frightening. The hindbrain would react before the forebrain.

Now Victor decided that it was time to rain down lightning bolts from Zeus.

He keyed his mic, "Execute RANDOM."

FUENTES WIPED THE SWEAT OUT OF his eyes with the back of his sleeve. He was crouched down behind the HumVee hoping against hope that he was not in the line of sight of these very effective snipers.

His gunner was dead, having decided to take Fuentes' place behind the .50 Caliber BMG mounted behind armor plate in the turret. Apparently, he thought he would be safe behind that armor, and wielding back the equally massive rounds coming at them, but at a massively greater rate.

After his gunner pulled him back into the cab with his dead driver's smelly body inside, fresh firing from the invisible snipers was just starting, in an apparently random way. Which made it all the more the frightening.

Death from anywhere. Invisible. Uncaring. Arbitrary.

That had always made snipers a very effective weapon in any war.

Snipers had been known to keep whole platoons pinned down.

These snipers - and there had to be a large number of them - were picking targets at random. Like a video game. Snuffing out lives like it was merely a building of points.

No apparent strategy or purpose. Just having fun with it. Doing a head shot here. Cutting a body in half, there. Going through armor plate, just because they could.

His gunner had gotten behind the BMG and started sending out rounds - not at the truck barrier - but at the rooftops where he thought the snipers' perches may be. This was apparently the right thing to do.

The BMG put out a racket - and drew attention.

The gunner was killed when an armor-piercing incendiary round punched through the plating; destroying the gun - and the gunner.

Fuentes was trying to explain the situation to the Commander. They were pinned down by sniper fire, and needed to withdraw - out of range. But that meant that the vehicles bunched up behind him would have to retreat backwards.

Meanwhile, his troops were being slaughtered in no particular spot. One here, another four meters behind, yet another 1/4 kilometer to the left...

The Commander was yelling in his ear to press the attack. To make room for the Bradleys - to MOVE his goat-fornicating ass! Just DO Something!

They were dying anyway! Attack and die for something! Attack!

So they did.

VI. SAM - COMMS CONTROL

*Make every move count. Pick your target and hit it. Perfect
concentration means effortless flowing.*
-- Masirib Jeff Elliott

I WATCHED THE SCREENS, ANXIOUSLY - resisting the urge
to bite my nails.

I couldn't imagine myself down there, on the battlefield.

It was easy for me to pretend this was all a movie - seen from above and
in great detail and resolution. Or maybe a realistic videogame, where the
blood mist and gore were just spectacular CGI special effects.

But I knew better. Those were my friends - my new family - facing
unspeakable terror.

I even felt sorry for the enemy - I could not hear their foreign speech
and I was, therefore, not enraged by any post-Event "xeno-lingual" phobia.

Why was this happening? For what? It was senseless.

Yet when I watched the dead body of one of our soldiers fall in the
bloody spray, her back exploding as a machine gun projectile blew through
like an invisible fist, I was jubilant when Victor's return fire shredded that
pickup truck and its two occupants. I felt the same vindication as when a
hero finally gets the villain in a movie.

But in reality, there were no heroes, here - nor any true villains.

I reported the enemy's status to Victor after the oncoming attack vehicle
was destroyed. They now appeared to be arranging their trucks and attack
vehicles in a pattern. It looked like it was designed to give them maximum
sightlines to attack our people.

There was a man that appeared to have control over directing the traffic.
I zoomed in on him, and I was about to tell Victor about this guy when I
heard on the 'comms:

"Break for 2nd Squad. This is Victor. Over."

"Thompson, here, Cap'n. Over."

"Thompson, do your Barretts have eyes on the traffic conductor?
Over."

"Affirmative. We have 'im five-by. Over."

"Can your shooter take him with a big 'splash'? Over."

What the heck was Victor up to? That wouldn't stop them.

Jonas came over to stand beside me from where he was monitoring the Bandera Road operation. Vic, our new tech, was running the Sat Views for him. There was little activity on that front, so he listened in on "my" ops.

I looked up at his grim face. He was frowning and his eyebrow was furrowed.

I asked, "What the hell's he up to?"

"Psy-ops," he answered. "Our boy seems to know how to inflict terror strategically."

I knew what "Psy-ops" referred to. I read stuff just like anybody else. I wasn't that uninformed.

It was what the military defined as: "Planned operations to ... influence ... emotions, motives, objective reasoning, and ultimately the behavior of foreign governments, organizations, groups, and individuals." (Actually, I looked it up on my wiki servers.)

Jonas held up a finger to halt more discussion as we both listened to Victor's final instructions.

I asked Jonas, "But again... what's he up to? And what the hell is 'RANDOM'?"

He was staring at the monitor which was split into various views, showing the enemy forces up and down the highway (Man! There were a LOT of them!); the man directing the rearrangement of the enemy attack pattern; the two sniper perches; the Bridge (which was camouflaged at the moment); and Victor's truck barrier.

Jonas shook his head and said, "He's gonna force 'em into attacking before they're ready ... and you're not gonna like it."

I looked back at the monitor and frowned, "But what..."

The man directing the traffic suddenly dissolved in a pink mist. At least his head did, and he dropped to the ground in a tangled heap.

I heard, "Tango 1 Down." I recognized Thompson's voice. I gaped open mouthed at the scene in front of me. It was surreal.

"Jonas..." I began. He interrupted and said, "Zoom in on the lead Hummer."

I did, and the scene resolved to a view of the HumVee. There was a glimpse of two people in the cab through a slight angle on the windshield. I could see a man standing where the "moon roof" would go in a regular car. Only this "car" was equipped with a long-barreled machine gun, sitting behind what looked like armor plate.

The dude was staring at what had happened to the man who was directing traffic. He appeared not to be able to take it in. He was just standing - right out in the open.

I fully expected him to be next. I tensed - but, no.

The windshield below him on the driver's side suddenly imploded, and I could see a red color splashed against the splintered windshield like someone popping a balloon filled with red dye. The man on top looked down through the moon roof and, although I could not see his face as he looked down, I could imagine him gaping at what had just happened to his driver.

I also saw the hands of the passenger pulling at him urgently as if to get him to get back inside, out of the line of fire. But, in reality, there WAS no place out of the line of fire. Maybe this was what Victor had in mind.

I heard Jonas breathe out, "Masterful."

"What?" I asked, looking up at him. He just shook his head at stared at the screens. I went back to looking.

By the time I looked back the man had gone into the interior of the HumVee. Everything was suddenly still, and I could see people coming out of their transportation, gaping like rubber-neckers staring at a traffic accident. Some of them were stepping on running boards and craning for a better look. Some of them seemed to be screaming out information or news or worried questions.

That made them all the more human to me. They were reacting in bewilderment, just as I would. Those nearest the dude who was now headless and bloody on the highway tarmac were staring in frozen horror.

A few minutes passed.

Victor's voice: "Execute RANDOM!"

A pause.

Then... a red splash where a body had stood up craning for that better look. Then another 100 meters or so away where a girl was standing looking bewildered before becoming bloody shreds; another further away bursting through another windscreen with the bloody balloon effect splashing against the shattered glass... and another ... and another... and...

Like deadly raindrops splashing heedlessly, invisibly - randomly... bringing death to both the wary and unwary.

I was horrified. Now I knew the meaning of "Random."

VII. THOMPSON - 2nd SQUAD

We sleep safe in our beds because rough men stand ready in the night to
visit violence on those who would do us harm.

- George Orwell

MY BOY TOOK OUT THE "TRAFFIC COP" and 1st Squad took
out the HumVee driver through the armor glass of the windshield.

Both perfectly executed shots. I was looking through my own 'scope -
and I knew I couldn't have made that headshot. I could - maybe - have put
one center mass using my British Sniper rifle.

But the terror-inducing .50 cal round striking like invisible lightening
had no substitute for spectacular effects. It was a psy-ops officer's wet
dream.

I knew most of the snipers in my old unit in the "Crotch" were not in
favor of using that equipment as anti-personnel. Marine snipers generally
favored the finesse of the M40A5 chambered for the reliable 308
Winchester or the 7.62 NATO round.

I agreed, but for Victor's purposes of terrorizing the enemy and putting
pressure on them to cause bad decision-making - it was perfect.

I approved.

I had my squad prepare for the "RANDOM" execute order. I decided
to participate and gain some much needed practice with this unfamiliar
weapon.

It was a sweet machine. The L115A3 was chambered for the .338 Lapua
Magnum and has ballistics comparable to the .50 BMG my boys were using
- but with lesser power. It COULD punch through armored glass - but not
through armor.

But the Barretts could - and the boys had extra mags preloaded with the
.50 Caliber, Armor-Piercing-Incendiary Cartridge, if needed. I figured I
would leave any hard targets up to them.

Anyway, we all sighted in different targets. I decided to have fun with it,
and not sweat it too much.

I had my machine gunners and my small arms shooters check their
readiness for the inevitable. But they were, for the main, sitting back to
enjoy the show.

There was a shocked silence and stillness in the massed crowd of vehicles after the first two shots. After a while, we noticed their people moving to get a better look at the goings on.

Some people were standing on truck beds and running beds and relaying info and rumors - soldiers love rumors - to their buddies.

I imagined:

WOW! DID YOU SEE THAT?!!! MARK MAC'SPIC JUST GOT HIS FRICKIN' HEAD BLOWN CLEAN OFF!

HOW YOU KNOW? DIDJA SEE IT?

HELL YEAH, I SAW IT! HIS HEAD WAS - JUST A KINDA RED MIST - AND THEN HE FELL DOWN ON THE HIGHWAY! MAN, HIS HEAD'S JUST GONE!

GETTA OUT THE WAY! LEMESEE! LEMESEE!

DAAAMMMNN!

WHAT NOW? LEMESEE!

MAAAANNN! THE BOSS' HUMVEE JUST GOT HIT. I CAN SEE THE BLOOD SPLATTERED IN THERE! MAN OH MAN!

LEMESSEEEEE!

Something like that - only in Spanish. But soldiers were soldiers. Greenhorns and Vets. Human nature. That curious monkey brain that loved to watch train wrecks - or former Disney teen stars' blow-ups.

I sighted in on a target, myself. I picked a guy, nervously biting his finger nails. I hated that habit.

He bounced up and down in my scope, in time with my heartbeat. I was no sniper, but I qualified as "Rifle Sharpshooter" and as "Pistol Expert", which didn't make a whole lot of sense, to me. It seemed to me that I should be a whole lot better with a rifle than a pistol - but there you are. But with this piece of equipment, with no crosswind, I should have no trouble holding my own. But I would leave the really long shots to the experts.

I heard Victor on the 'comms, saying: "Execute RANDOM!"

My heart started beating faster, and my sight picture bounced all the more. All around me - and across the highway at 1st Squad's perch - I could hear the big guns crack as the shooting gallery began. I took a deep breath, held it, and sighted in. I squeezed and... the Tango went down. A perfectly-executed head shot.

I looked for another target, and found the driver of a troop transport - her eyes wide open, and her mouth the same. One through the windshield and she was gone.

I continued to pick targets slowly, leisurely, and at random.

It was sweet.

VIII. SKIRMISH LINE

Never interrupt your enemy when he is making a mistake.

- Napoleon Bonaparte

FUENTES WATCHED AS HIS TROOPS ATTACKED THE BLOCKADE, moving slowly, to provide cover for the dismounted troops firing small arms. The 'Technical's' were firing their LMGs and the HumVees their larger Squad Automatic Weapons. At this distance, only the machine guns had any hope of reaching the blockade - but the M16's carried by the troops could reach it at their furthest range - but not with great effect. It just made them feel better to provide "suppressing fire" - even if it did little good.

The machine guns were seemingly doing a better job of it since no return fire was coming their way. But Fuentes was no fool. Their enemy maintained outstanding fire discipline, and their last tactic had been transparent to him.

They had used their long range snipers to great effect. But the enemy's idea was to provoke, rather than deter. If Fuentes had his way, they would have retreated and found a more advantageous battleground.

But the Commander had not seen fit to take his advice. He wanted an attack NOW!

Fuentes could see behind the enemy thinking. Their sniper tactic had his people cowering behind any cover they could find in order to get away from that frightening barrage.

It was as daunting an attack he had ever been in - and he had been in some daunting ones, indeed.

He had been on the receiving end of mortar fire and artillery barrages that seemed to go on and on with no hope of let up. The explosions and the chest compressing 'WHUMPS' would take both breath and courage away from even the strongest. The whistling hot shrapnel was the added spice to the terror.

Here, in this sniper action, the invisible, silent maiming and death coming at random times and places added a new dimension of terror. He - an experienced (and, he hoped, brave) soldier - had also cowered behind his HumVee, hoping that silent death would not reach out to him. His gunner had braved the fire to engage the enemy with the biggest weapon, the .50 caliber machine gun mounted in the turret - and had paid with his life - and with the loss of that weapon.

He wished the Bradleys had been here to take the brunt of the attack and to reach out to the blockade with their 25 millimeter Chain Guns and their heavy machine guns. They would be virtually invulnerable to any fire they received.

But Fuentes knew enough not to underestimate an enemy.

Nor to underestimate the ego-driven stupidity of the generals and colonels that directed all battles from the rear.

His Commander - no exception - had ordered his people to the attack. Ignoring the cost in lives that this approach would cause was never a concern for these types of men. And Fuentes, for his part, was not one to disobey orders.

So he ordered his troops to attack the blockade - knowing fully that some surprise awaited them.

It stood to reason. The enemy had provoked this hasty action. He could also see the genius of creating the artificial canyon where they could be caught in a deadly trap. The effectiveness of their sniper fire zones had proved this.

He waited to see what the enemy had up their sleeves.

And he dreaded it.

THOMPSON WATCHED THE MASSED TROOPS APPROACHING THE BLOCKADE, firing for all they were worth.

Victor had ordered a deliberate sniper cease fire in order to encourage the enemy to brave getting to their vehicles to commence their attack and approach. It had worked, as the enemy had organized themselves into a hasty formation and was currently approaching the blockade firing all guns.

The smart ones were firing in measured bursts in order to preserve ammo and barrel life. Machine guns firing at a rapid rate would have to change barrels as they got red hot in order to avoid warping. Just a fact of life - and war. But the inexperienced ones were firing with no discipline and would risk misfires - or, in worst cases, blowbacks.

But that was their own lookout.

All 1st and 2nd Squads had to worry about was keeping their heads down through the undisciplined enemy fire. 3rd Squad was no problem as they wouldn't engage until the signal was given. They were all cozy in their limestone colored Ghillie Suits and jury-rigged cammo covers.

But the front blockade line sitting behind the trucks was getting the brunt. Most of those front line blockaders cowering behind the double wall of massive steel trucks were fairly inexperienced, and Victor would have a hell of a time maintaining fire discipline.

No doubt he had threatened to shoot anyone not complying with his orders. And everyone knew he was good about sticking to his word, Thompson thought with a smile.

VICTOR HAD THREATENED ANYONE WITH DECAPITATION should they break fire discipline.

His orders were simple: do not move from your assigned position; do not fire until ordered to; keep the approaching enemy in your sights and be prepared to unleash Hell.

He went up and down the line to reinforce the order.

He knew it would be hard, especially listening to the metallic WHUMPS and cracking PINGS of high velocity rounds striking the blockade. He had his most experienced troops underneath the massive trucks where they would be fairly well protected by the double wheels and heavy rims. They had deflated the tires in order to protect from blowouts, which could prove as dangerous as small explosives.

These troops manned the LMGs and the spare M240s from under the heavy trucks.

He wanted to wait until the enemy was deep inside the "vee" formed by the blockading truck line.

But he was feeling antsy himself. He had to count on Sam and Jonas to give the word.

He gritted his teeth. It was hard. So hard.

He got down on one knee and peered through the gap he had assigned to himself and rested the bipod of his M240. He rechecked the large box magazine that held the M13 ammo belt, folded for optimal feed. He had six spares. A lot of ammo.

Man, they were close! Where the hell were Sam and Jonas?

He fought down the urge to call them. He was breathing hard. The enemy was seemingly right on top of them!

Shit! What the hell was Sam doing, anyway?...

But it was Jonas' voice: "Break for Victor!... Go!"

Victor: "All lines...... fire at will!"

THE WALL OF FIRE COMING FROM THE BLOCKADE OF TRUCKS AND the rooftop snipers and machine guns seemed to stagger the attacking vehicles like a fighter taking a body blow.

Fuentes watched as his troops took the return fire that splintered metal, glass - and flesh and bone. Some of the trucks taking direct fire were gouged by the high velocity rounds - the metal gaping in wide circular holes and the glass of headlights, windshields and side windows splintering and blowing out - tinted red. Tires blew, and engine blocks spewed smoke and steam.

Infantry, instinctively taking cover, went down in vicious crossfire. The vehicles behind the leading front were not immune. They also received damage, and were forced to stop out in the open.

His own reserve was receiving fire - although probably not on purpose. The weapons used by the enemy had the ability to fire at over a mile - and the projectiles that were aimed at the attacking force sometimes missed and hit his reserve lines.

He heard metallic "thunks" and splintering glass and sometimes a scream or two.

He did not have the fire discipline installed in his troops. Sometimes one or two of the "Technicals" in the reserve line opened up with their own return fire - oblivious, in their panic, that they were probably shooting their own troops from behind.

When that happened, Fuentes screamed into his comms for the reserves to cease fire! This happened too many times - and in one case, a gunner standing on the truck bed manning a machine gun would not - or could not - listen. Fuentes repeated his order to cease fire many times before he decided enough was enough.

Fuentes drew his sidearm and made this way back to the offending shooter. He walked around to the back of the pickup and aimed his 9 MM handgun at the back of the gunner's head. He pulled the trigger and blew the gunner's brains out through the front of his skull. Blood and brains splattered on the truck cab.

The others soon got the message.

VICTOR FIRED HIS M240 THROUGH THE GAP, occasionally feeling the "thump" of a stray round hitting his advanced armor. His troops weren't equipped with Dragon Skin, and he knew they were taking casualties. He heard the occasional thunk of a round hitting flesh and sometimes a cry. Sometimes a death scream.

Sometimes a cry for mother. What makes dying soldiers cry for mother? It's really weird and, by observation, universal.

Of course it's hard to hear over the din of machine gun fire, motor noise, bullets gouging through metal…

3rd Squad had already revealed themselves on the crossover bridge some twenty-some-odd feet over the highway and 100 yards behind the line.

They had uncovered their heavy machine guns - a couple of BMGs and four old-fashioned Browning .30 Caliber 1919A4 Machine Guns they had found at the back of the Gun Smithing Store. Still serviceable and still deadly.

And being used to great effect by 3rd Squad who had removed the guns from their sand colored tarps and were putting out a massive wall of fire.

Victor decided that it was time for the next move.

He keyed his mic and said, "Break, Break, all Squads. Initiate grenade launching. Squad leaders acknowledge!"

He got that acknowledgement.

A few minutes later, even over the din of the fire fight, he heard the distinctive 'thooo-umph' sound of the grenade launchers. And a few seconds later, High Explosive Grenade Rounds were falling on the attackers across the highway and the access road.

That should shake them up!

FUENTES WATCHED THROUGH BINOCULARS as high explosive rounds began falling over his attacking troops. He swept the binoculars up to the rooftops and saw the hand held launchers being wielded by the enemy.

He recognized the MGL-140 grenade launcher being used. It fired 40 mm HE grenade rounds that would devastate his forces. These had a kill radius of about 16 feet, and they were being launched in an expanding spread. His troops were being slaughtered and his attack vehicles torn to smoldering shreds.

The Commandant be damned!

He keyed his mic, all communications protocols forgotten, and yelled, "Retreat! Retreat! Get the Devil out of there! Bail out and run back!"

He saw the dismounted troops running back in disordered panic. The attack vehicles not bothering to turn around, but hitting reverse as quickly as possible to come back the 1/2 mile on the highway away from the barrier.

The running figures were abandoning weapons and ammo to make the half-mile run as quickly as possible. The Commander would be furious. But the Devil with him!

"Come on, come on!" he mentally urged his troops.

The firing had stopped as the troops retreated - and the grenades quit falling around them. There was a lull. Maybe the opposing commander was taking pity and granting mercy on the survivors. Bad strategy - as those troops would be sent again as the Commander showed up in the armored fighting vehicles.

But maybe they didn't know about the Bradleys. The question remained - just HOW did the enemy know when and where to set the blockade so effectively.

Did they have drones in the air? That was impossible.

Still, he felt hope.

Until he saw a series of explosions coming down the highway as though someone had set a string of firecrackers wired in sequence.

"Oh, God, no," he thought. "No!"

VICTOR GRINNED AT THE CARNAGE and at the sight of the retreating troops.

He keyed his mic and said over an open channel, "Fire in the hole!" and set off the planted Claymores strung across both sides of the highway and the access road.

THE CLAYMORE MINE HAS A HORIZONTALLY CONVEX PLASTIC CASE, shaped to deliver the optimum distribution of fragments at a 55 yard range. Internally the mine contains a layer of C4 explosive behind a matrix of about seven hundred 1/8-inch-diameter steel balls set into an epoxy resin.

When the Claymore is detonated, the explosion drives the matrix forward, out of the mine at a velocity of 3,937 feet per second breaking it into individual fragments. The steel balls are projected in a 60 degree fan-shaped pattern that is 6.5 feet high and 55 yards wide at a range of 55 yards - half the length of a football field.

The force of the explosion deforms the relatively soft steel balls into a shape similar to a .22 rim fire bullet. These fragments are effective up to a range of 110 yards.

The fragments can travel up to 270 yards. The optimum effective range is 55 yards at which the optimal balance is achieved between lethality and area coverage, with a hit probability of 30% on a man-sized target.

Gore's Folly had strung a Claymore mine every 40 yards along both sides of the highway and along the access roads to an approximately half mile distance from the truck barricade. They were wired to detonate sequentially about the speed of a running man.

FUENTES LOOKED AT THE STRING OF EXPLOSIONS coming toward him and engulfing his retreating troops. He had a thought that sent a strange tingle through his body.

He looked around him and to the left of the highway, which was divided by the ubiquitous concrete barriers. He saw the small sand colored curved block that could be easily overlooked as a lighting fixture or some other innocuous piece of highway detritus.

It had been deliberately colored in the limestone color so prevalent in this part of the country, and so easily overlooked.

He had time to think, "Oh…" before the world went white…

SAM SAW THE DETONATIONS ON THE SATELLITE FEEDS. The VTAP Program was reporting a 99.9% probability of 310 enemies KIA and 50 Vehicles destroyed.

She hung her head as those around her let out whoops of joy.

IX. RETREAT

You may have to fight a battle more than once to win it.

- Margaret Thatcher

THE COMMANDER'S BRADLEY FIGHTING VEHICLE HAD JUST CLEARED THE RAMP along with the two other Bradleys when he got the word on the radio that Fuentes and most of his force had been destroyed.

His disbelief was profound and he sat there staring at the smoke from the detonations that was blowing down the highway toward them. His senior non-com, Jorgé, was speaking angrily - urgently - into his microphone and pressing his ear pieces against his head as though to hear better.

Jorgé swiveled in his seat to report. "It appears the enemy forces created this blockade in order to funnel our forces into a Claymore mined trap," he said.

He went on, "Apparently they spaced out Claymores along both sides of the highway, and the right hand access road, to nearly a kilometer. Our forces were annihilated..."

"Pincha Madre!" The Commander slapped the panel in front of him. "We should have had the Bradleys leading the charge and pounding the crap out of them! We're armored! Claymores are dandelion fluff to us!"

Jorgé was astute enough not to point out that sub-Commander Fuentes had advocated just that.

The Commander sat back in his chair fuming. Jorgé knew better than to interrupt his thinking.

After a few minutes, the Commander sat up in his chair decisively.

"Jorgé, you will give the following orders:

1. Have our remaining forces gather behind the Three Bradleys.

2. Our Bradley's will lead the charge when the smoke clears.

3. We will strafe the rooftops with the 25 mm Chain Guns, before going to the blockade.

4. We will attack the enemy barricade with our Heavy Machine guns and the Chain Guns.

5. No other vehicles will fire, unless they have clear line of sight on an enemy target.

6. No troops are to dismount, and troop transports will remain out of range until we have cleared the blockade.

Is that clear?"

"Yes, sir," Jorgé replied, and turned back to the communications console to issue the orders.

VICTOR AND HIS FRONTLINE SQUAD STARED at what they had wrought.

There were no cheers or shouts of jubilation. Only the cries of the wounded could be heard. As the smoke blew down the highway away from the blockade, carried by a steady south wind, they saw the damage they had inflicted on the enemy.

HumVees and pickup trucks outfitted as 'Technicals' were riddled with holes from the automatic fire and with the devastating results of the claymore ambush. Dead enemy troopers lay strewn about like bloody road kill as far as the eye could see.

Here and there, a prone, bloody body - not recognizable as a human being - writhed in agonizing death throes. Victor had never seen the like - in real battle or in the movies.

He heard Thompson's voice in his earpiece, disregarding comms protocol and saying, softly, "Jesus." It sounded like a prayer. "Do you think they'll give up?"

Victor watched as the smoke swirled away, revealing the massive Bradleys now facing the blockade, and the mass of fighting vehicles lined up in staggered rows behind.

Victor answered, "No."

THE BRADLEY IS EQUIPPED WITH THE M242 25 MM CHAIN GUN which fires up to 200 rounds per minute, as its main weapon. The gun contains ammunition in two boxes of 70 rounds and 230 rounds each for a total of 300 ready rounds and carries 600 rounds in storage. The weapon has an effective range of 3,000 meters depending on the type of ammunition used.

It is also armed with a M240C machine gun, with 2,200 rounds of 7.62 mm ammunition. M2 infantry Bradleys, which these were, also have turreted firing ports for a number of M231 Firing Port Weapons providing a button-up firing position to replace the top-side gunners, which makes them invulnerable to Claymores or regular heavy automatic weapons fire.

Looking at the vehicles through his binoculars, he could see the 25 mike mikes aligning with the rooftops.

Staring at them, Victor keyed his mic for a general announcement. "Break: all rooftop squads. This is Victor...... Execute Bug Out! NOW!!!"

THOMPSON WAS BENT DOWN CARING FOR ONE OF HIS WOUNDED who had caught an unlucky round, when he heard Victor's order.

What the hell?...

He went over to the ledge to look out over the gathering enemy. He saw three Bradleys leading the parade. He picked up his spotter scope.

And he saw the auto cannon swivel up to his position.

He turned around rapidly to his squad and yelled, "Get the hell out, NOW!" before the 25 mm rounds reached up blowing through the ledge wall and through his Dragon Skin Armor like a fire hose through tissue paper and blew him to bloody shreds.

GWEN MANAGED TO GET HER SQUAD SCRAMBLING to the far side of the multistory bank building before the giant rounds began to tear great gouges from the sides and glass of the building.

She was yelling, "Go, go, go... leave it! Leave it!" as her team tried to gather armaments and ammo. They dropped everything and ran to the back internal stairway when they heard the projectiles violently tearing through concrete, steel, and glass.

She prayed they would make it to the stairs… She prayed SHE would make it!

She ran as though Satan himself was after her.

JORGÉ LOOKED UP TO THE ROOFTOPS through the viewport as the chain guns ceased fire. The devastation was impressive. These Capitalist Yankees could sure build weapons, he had to admit.

He turned to the Commander and said, "Rooftops neutralized. Begin the forward attack, sir?"

"Yes, Jorgé," he said with satisfaction. "You may order the attack"

VICTOR WAS RACING TOWARD THE MEDICAL DRIVE crossroads and overpass. The first blockade disappeared from sight two miles down the road, obscured by natural dips and curves as well as by distance.

It was actually a "turnaround," rather than an actual overpass leading to a cross street bisecting each access road. It was ideal because it was surrounded by thick reinforced concrete and "limestone" brick walls.

The walls began a fairly long distance down the highway and climbed claustrophobically to surround the highway on both sides going up 30 feet from the highway. Pre-Event construction had also closed off lanes with impenetrable concrete "Jersey Barriers."

The Bradleys would not have enough room to come down the highway side by side. And if they tried to smash, or go over, these low barriers - designed to even survive encounters with semi-tractor trailers - they would get stuck and become vulnerable to attack by anti-tank weapons.

It made an ideal funnel point for a secondary ambush.

And, of course, the enemy would know that.

In fact, Victor was counting on it.

THE COMMANDER WAS PLEASED THAT THE BRADLEYS

had so easily "parted the Red Sea" of their own wrecked and smoldering vehicles. They were now able to engage the Heavy Truck Barrier with their 25 MM Auto-cannons and Heavy Machine guns.

They punched great, gaping gouges from the metal beds of the dump trucks and through the concrete carriers that were so recognizable with their distinctively shaped containers.

Some of the dump trucks had been filled with gravel or dirt. Many of the cement trucks were at least partially filled with set concrete to provide more protection for the enemy. This proved to be no problem for the 25 mm Chain guns and their rate of fire.

Anyone taking shelter behind those trucks would be as likely killed by flying debris as much as the actual projectiles. So much for the enemy's "defense plan."

The racket inside the Bradleys was deafening - but that was because of the machine gun fire. The electric belt-fed auto cannon were relatively quiet compared to the explosive power the large projectiles delivered.

The Commander ordered a cease fire when he saw the work of devastation wrought by the Bradleys on the truck barrier.

Pieces of truck parts and metal were strewn at least 20 meters out from the blockade. Holes were blown straight through the sides of the heavy metal monsters. No one taking cover behind the trucks could have survived.

He said to Jorgé, "Order Ortega to go through the gap left by the enemy and report."

"Yes, Commandant," Jorgé replied, and he relayed the order to one of the other Bradleys.

They waited as the vehicle maneuvered through the zig-zag opening. As it passed the barrier, they could see the Bradley through the holes they had blown through.

The vehicle stopped and idled.

The Commander frowned and said, "Well?!!"

Jorgé bent to the communications console.

He turned and reported, "Commandant. There is no one there. A few dead bodies, but it appears that the enemy retreated without bothering with their dead."

"Humpph!" the Commandant grunted. "Not surprising. I'll wager some of the dead were only wounded when we attacked, and they didn't take the time to evacuate their people," he said, disapprovingly.

Jorgé shrugged. He had seen - and done - worse in Africa.

The Commandant pursed his lips. "We will go through the gap - first the Bradleys, then the attack vehicles with the infantry transports bringing up the rear.

We will go up a half kilometer and stop to check our formation. With decent spacing, all materiel should be well past the barrier.

Issue the order, Jorgé."

"Sí, mí Commandate!"

SAM WATCHED THE SATELLITE FEEDS as the enemy forces breached the now useless barrier. She was worrying on a thumbnail as she noted Victor and the others driving rapidly up the highway, about two miles past the first barrier.

Jonas was back monitoring the Bandera Road operation, as it had quickly come to a head. There were losses - she'd heard that much.

Jonas was cussing up a storm - then she heard him say, "Oh... sorry, Janis."

Sam looked up and saw that Janis had come up beside her and was facing the monitor. She had her eyes closed. Her hand was up slightly toward the monitor, as though giving a blessing. Her lips were moving silently in prayer. Whether for the dead or the living there was no telling. Probably for both.

Her mouth quirked in a slight smile at Jonas' apology. She kept her eyes closed and said, "It is not something Our Lord has not heard before, my dear Jonas," and went back to her silent prayer.

Jonas stayed silent.

Sam, for one, felt better for Janis' quiet presence. She was the one person she felt closest to - after Lori's death. Had it only been early this morning? So much had occurred since then. It was now getting late evening. The sun would be down soon.

The enemy had lined up in formation and the Bradleys were stationed about a half mile up from the blown-apart barrier. They were apparently waiting for the rest of the formation to clear the barrier, before moving on.

What if...

Sam's thought was interrupted by whoops and cheering at Jona's station. She and Janis turned to see what the fuss was about - but they were at the wrong angle to see the monitor from there.

Jonas was grinning and said, "Wait for it!... One thousand One... One thousand Two... One thousand ..." when he got to about one thousand eleven, there was a muffled thump that shook the foundations of this massive building.

Jonas let out another whoop.

A MASSIVE "THUMP!" SHOOK THE COMMANDER'S BRADLEY from the ground up.

"Sergeant, are we taking fire?" the Commander asked sharply.

"No, Commandant. That was from far away," Jorgé answered. "Permit me to go outside and observe."

The Commander gave his assent. "Watch out for any traps, Jorgé."

The sergeant nodded, unbuckled and stepped through the hatch to stand on the highway. His troops were staring to the west where a pillar of smoke was rising. He swept his binoculars to look over the green hills. A black mushroom cloud was roiling upwards, at least 10 or 15 kilometers away.

He keyed his mic and reported to the Commander what he observed.

The Commander asked in a slightly panicked voice, "Nuclear?"

"No, sir. Wrong color. That is a chemical explosion - maybe a munitions dump?"

"That doesn't make sense," the Commander said.

"No, sir. It does not," Jorgé agreed.

The Commander was silent.

Then, "Well, that is somebody else's lookout. Now we have a mission to complete," he said. "Get back in and let us complete our objective to destroy the Gringo nest."

"Yes, sir."

SAM KEYED HER MIC and said, excitedly, "Break for Victor! This is Sam."

"Go."

"Victor - they're on the move!"

"Roger. We're moving out now. Tell Jonas to get ready. Over."

"Um... yeah. Roger. Over and Out."

"BLOCKADE UP AHEAD, SIR," Jorgé said.

"No worries, Sergeant," the Commander said jovially. "We can handle that. Carry on."

Jorgé said nothing. Something was nagging at him.

He peered out to the left, scanning for that "something."

Then it struck him.

"Commandant!"

"What is it Sergeant?"

"Sir, there are a lot of dump and tanker trucks parked along each side of the highway!"

"So what? They were probably planning more blockades."

"No, sir. They seem too evenly spaced along our route."

"What are you saying, Jorgé?"

"We have to stop, Commander. We have to go back!"

The Commander yelled, "Go back?! Are you crazy? We are invulnerable in these Bradleys."

"Sir. I think we are in big trouble!"

VICTOR WAS FLYING DOWN THE HIGHWAY, and crossed the safe point. He keyed his mic. "BREAK, BREAK, BREAK! This is Victor! Execute Omega!"

ON A MILD SPRING DAY IN APRIL OF 1947, the SS Grandcamp was in port at Texas City, Texas.

Its cargo was 7,700 tons of ammonium nitrate.

Using the standard chemical data for the decomposition of ammonium nitrate gives a result of 2.7 kilotons of energy released. The US Army rates the relative effectiveness factor of ammonium nitrate, compared to TNT, as 42%. This means the blast equivalent would be 3.2 kilotons of TNT.

The cargo exploded, killing 581 people and injuring over 5,000.

Forty-eight years later, in that same month, Timothy McVeigh drove a rented truck full of a mixture of fertilizer and diesel fuel to the Federal

Building in downtown Oklahoma City. The explosion killed 168 people and injured more than 680, as well as damaging and destroying many surrounding buildings.

One third of the Federal building was destroyed by the explosion, which created a 30-foot wide, 8-foot deep crater next to the building. The blast destroyed or damaged 324 buildings within a 16-block radius, shattered glass in 258 nearby buildings, and destroyed or burned 86 cars around the site.

The effects of the blast were equivalent to over 5,000 pounds of TNT, and could be heard and felt up to 55 miles away.

That was one small truck.

GORE'S FOLLY HAD LINED TWO MILES OF IH-10 WEST, from the first blockade to the second barrier, with fifty trucks, each loaded with fifteen tons of a fertilizer and diesel fuel mixture.

On Victor's order to execute "Omega," a cellular signal was sent out from the Gore's Folly cell tower to the fuse mechanisms buried in the fertilizer-laden trucks.

Four miles of IH-10 West were obliterated, along with all the crossroads and buildings in a 7 mile radius.

The attacking force disappeared in that gigantic blast.

The mushroom cloud was much larger than the one seen West of IH-10 towards Bandera Road, and was felt all the way to Lackland Air Base Command.

THE VTAP PROGRAM calculated with a 100% certainty that all 3000 enemy personnel were killed. Along with all of their vehicles - including the "invulnerable" Bradley Fighting Vehicles and their formidable weapons. They were, in fact, vaporized.

> Battle not with monsters, lest ye become a monster
> - Friedrich Nietzsche

BOOK FIVE: AFTERMATH

*When you go out to war against your enemies, and see horses and chariots
and an army larger than your own, you shall not be afraid of them, for the
Lord your God is with you…*

- Deuteronomy 20:1

I. LAUGHLIN AIR FORCE BASE

RIVERA WAS FUMING AS HE looked for Gomez.

He was not used to being kept waiting. After getting to Laughlin Air
Force Base in Del Rio, Texas, Gomez - and, irritatingly PENZO (of all
people) - had taken it upon themselves to inspect every inch of the base.

When they had gotten there, they found scores of dead - but not from
the event. Apparently the air base had a great number of English-Speaking
survivors. But the surrounding town of Del Rio - and Pierdes Negras across
the border - had greatly out-numbered the air base survivors.

There had been a pitched battle between the two groups - the base
personnel armed with military weapons and the Spanish forces armed with
U.S. Customs, Border Patrol, and Mexican Federalé weapons, which were
not inconsiderable.

The battle that ensued was a Pyrrhic victory for the Spanish-Speaking
forces. They had utterly destroyed the assets that were most valuable:
electric generation, weapons, food and most of the shelter.

But what had chapped Gomez's butt was the almost total destruction

212

of the airplanes and the tarmacs and runways. Fires and explosions had taken most of the useful buildings - and the all important munitions dumps. Those had obviously gone up in devastating blasts that had destroyed all but the furthest buildings and all of the airplanes parked on runways.

There was also evidence of post-event crashes as planes were on approach or take off as seizures and transfers hit. That accounted for most of the damage to the runways, tarmacs and the parked planes.

Miraculously, there was one intact T-6B Texan attack craft built for close ground support in Afghanistan. Further, this particular prop driven plane was armed with two Hellfire missiles, along with a .50 caliber machine gun and belted ammunition.

That's where Rivera found Gomez and "his team," examining the plane.

Besides Penzo, he was accompanied by the lone pilot he had been able to locate amongst the group that crossed the border with them. His name was Creflo DeLeon. He was from Belize, and, thankfully, Spanish had been his natal language. While not Military, his pre-Event occupation had been flying tourists around in an old propeller-driven plane that looked very much like this military equivalent.

As Rivera walked up to the group, he heard Gomez saying, "... and we don't have a real ground crew - or for that matter, armorers - to check the condition and usefulness of the plane."

DeLeon scoffed and said, "Colonel, I HAVE been my own ground crew..."

"But not on a military aircraft bearing munitions!" Gomez retorted.

"No, but it can't be that much different..."

"Gentlemen!" Rivera loudly interrupted.

They all looked at him. Gomez bearing a thin-lipped smile, Penzo, his usual poker face and DeLeon frowning and just barely rolling his eyes. Rivera had caught the fact that this DeLeon did not think much of him. He should have brought Abdul along and put this fellow in his place.

But he was under the Colonel's protection - and Gomez was too valuable to get rid of - at least until they got into Cheyenne Mountain and unlocked its potential. Only Gomez could accomplish that. Rivera would bide his time.

But Penzo's attraction to the Colonel bothered Rivera. He did not know where the inscrutable man's loyalties lay.

"Gomez," he said, refusing to address him by title, "did you get the report from our brethren in San Antonio?"

"I heard," Gomez replied blandly. "Unfortunate. But what does that have to do with us? You are calling them brothers and we haven't even met them," Gomez said with his careful and slow Spanish, as though trying to pick out the right words.

Gomez had explained that his Spanish vocabulary was rudimentary, even though it was his natal language, having grown up speaking English. He could put things in context, but it was hard for him.

Rivera said, "Don't you care that the Gringos destroyed over four THOUSAND of our people?"

"It seems to me that our 'brethren' went looking for a fight," Gomez said with a shrug, "and they got one... besides - as you know - I considered myself an Hispanic 'gringo' in my previous life.

We can just bypass San Antonio altogether and hit military installations in New Mexico and Arizona on our way. We'll pick up people and equipment, I'm sure."

"Well, let me appeal to your military side, then," Rivera said. "These people destroyed a valuable asset that we could have used to take Cheyenne Mountain! The Lackland people are telling us they used up most of their arms and materiel on the attack.

And the gringos probably used atomics!"

Gomez snorted and laughed. "Doubtful. The... signs...?" he turned to Penzo for help.

"Signatures," Penzo said, helpfully.

"Ah... yes... 'signatures'... were chemical rather than nuclear. No 'atomics', as you put it, just a good old-fashioned..." again he paused to look at Penzo for help. This irritated Rivera, no end.

"... an I.E.D.," Penzo supplied, "... ún Dispositivo Explosivo Improvisado."

"You're saying a roadside BOMB did that?!!" Rivera exclaimed.

Gomez smiled. "Not JUST a roadside bomb - but probably a whole lot of bombs loaded into those trucks that the 'gringos' put across as barriers. I heard San Antonio's report on that. They probably loaded up a bunch of... ca-ca...? ... feces...?"

"Fertilizer," Penzo supplied.

"Ah... yes... fertilizer! ... Fertilizer and diesel fuel. Just like Oklahoma City."

"What???"

"Never mind, Rivera. It's no concern of ours."

"No concern?" Rivera said, "Do you really want these people at our backs as we move to take Cheyenne Mountain?"

That silenced Gomez for a bit.

Then he said, "You may have a point…"

Rivera 'harrumphed' in satisfaction.

Gomez turned to DeLeon and said, "How would you like to take this baby up for a test flight… and maybe get in some target practice and send a message to the 'gringos'?"

"Excellent!" DeLeon said with a wide grin. "When do we go?!"

"Just you, DeLeon," Rivera said. "The colonel is much too valuable to risk."

Gomez studied Rivera's face, taking in the meaning.

He said, "Do our 'brethren' have the co-ordinates of the enemy's headquarters?"

"We will ask," Rivera said with a slight smile.

II. GORE'S FOLLY

AFTER THE VICTORY THERE WAS LITTLE celebration.

They had lost too much.

Other than congratulating Jonas on his fine plan, Victor had not spoken to anyone but had merely retreated to his room. Maybe to catch up on much-needed sleep.

Jonas lost himself in the bowels of Gore's Folly - perhaps checking and fine-tuning the output of the Biomass System.

Gwen - having survived her real first battle - retreated into herself, reliving, again and again, those terrifying moments with her squad's building being chewed to pieces. The mad dash to the stairs, with the building shuddering at each rapid fire of the 25 mm shells.

She dreamed about the race from the building - urging the squad to hurry, hurry! Hurry away on side streets to put as much distance from what was coming as possible.

Away from the terrifying concussion and flash that was felt in the bones and compressed the lungs. Away from that horrible hot wind that threatened to overturn their vehicles.

Then making their way back to Gore's Folly in the darkness - made even darker by that giant, black mushroom cloud.

Janis puttered around her roof top agri-plot, talking to the plants - or, perhaps praying. Or both.

Gunny kept busy organizing new scavenging forays and training the newbies.

Sam mourned.

AFTER A FEW DAYS, things got back to "normal."

There was planning and discussion on expansion. More recruits were joining up from the East and North Country.

Victor held court in his war room and listened to all the ideas to check off as many of the items on Sam's Book of Lists. Jonas had many ideas on construction, expanding their grid to power nearby buildings and to fortify Gore's Folly.

Victor and Gunny were putting together a plan to raid Camp Bullis as soon as possible.

Sam worked night and day to improve the VTAP programming to increase the warning system. They wouldn't be caught napping again.

Janis prayed.

"VICTOR!" Sam called.

Victor looked up with a smile, which faded as he saw the panic in Sam's eyes.

"I just got an updated feed from VTAP after expanding the watch parameters," Sam said.

"Okay," he said softly, questioning.

"VTAP is now checking activity in a wider radius than just the metro area."

Victor made a circular motion with one finger as if to say, "Get on with it!"

Sam swallowed and said rapidly, "Well it seems that a very large force - numbering up to 6,000, according to VTAP estimates - crossed the border at Laredo, Texas and has now arrived at Laughlin AFB in Del Rio."

Victor sat up and asked, "How far is Del Rio?"

"Well, about 3 hours by car, but a large group like that would take days to organize and get here, if that was their intent..."

"Great," Victor interrupted, "So we'd have plenty of time to pull another Thermopylae on them..."

"No, Victor!" she yelled. "They've launched an attack plane - and will be here in a half hour!"

THEY GATHERED AROUND THE VTAP console and monitor. VTAP had identified the plane as a T-6B Texan attack plane. 90% probability that it carried two under-wing Hellfire missiles and a forward .50 Caliber Machine Gun.

It was on a trajectory to arrive in less than twenty minutes.

Victor asked Gunny, "What damage can it do with two missiles?"

"Plenty, Cap'n. But you also gotta worry about strafing from the air. We loved 'em in the Sandbox. They were bad-guy killers."

Crap!

"Recommendations, Gunny?"

"Well, sir - won't do any good to have the troops out taking potshots. I suggest we get them all at the lower level. These here buildings are pretty dam' solid. Should be safer there."

"I agree. But, Gunny... we can't just let 'em go at us like a two dollar hooker."

Gunny grinned and said, "Never suggested that, Cap'n!"

"So?"

"So we man the Twins you had me install on the rooftop and get any BMGs left over from the ambush... which is just one, if I recall."

Victor frowned and acknowledged it was so.

"Also get the shooters to man the two Barretts we have left. Gwen lost hers, but Thompson's group managed to get away with theirs - even if they lost Thompson."

Gunny frowned and went on, "But, Cap'n - it'll be hard as SHIT to hit."

"Well... maybe we'll get lucky, Gunny."

"Lucky would be to have a couple of Stinger Missiles... maybe next time," Gunny said.

They were both thinking of their procrastination on the Camp Bullis raid.

WHEN IT WAS OVER, they lost part of the solar panel grid to a Hellfire missile. It was meant to take out Gunny's position manning the Twin .50 Cals on the rooftop. It overshot.

In a second pass, it had more luck taking out the BMG shooting at it from the fourth floor. The missile hit dead on, killing both the gunner and the shooter two floors below, using the Barrett.

They lost no other personnel.

The pilot was obviously a civilian, untrained in the strafing method used by these planes. He only managed to take great gouges from the building façade and some of the balconies.

Victor was standing out on the lawn shooting upward with his M240 as though shooting skeet.

No one even managed to come close.

The plane quit buzzing them when it ran out of ammo - then it flew away, mockingly wagging its wings.

Victor and Gunny agreed. Time to raid the Camp Bullis Arsenal.

It was time to take the fight to them.

APPENDIX I: MAPS

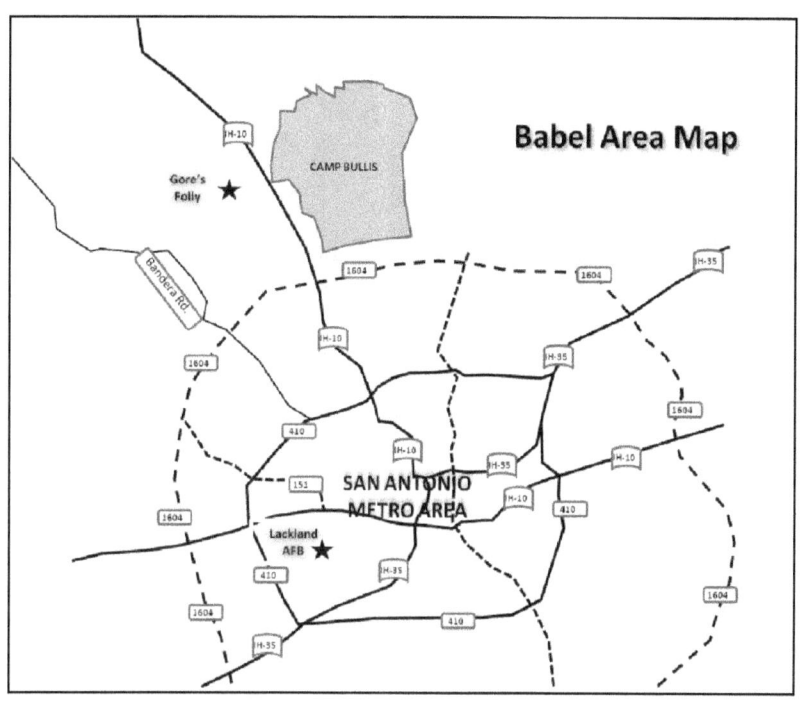

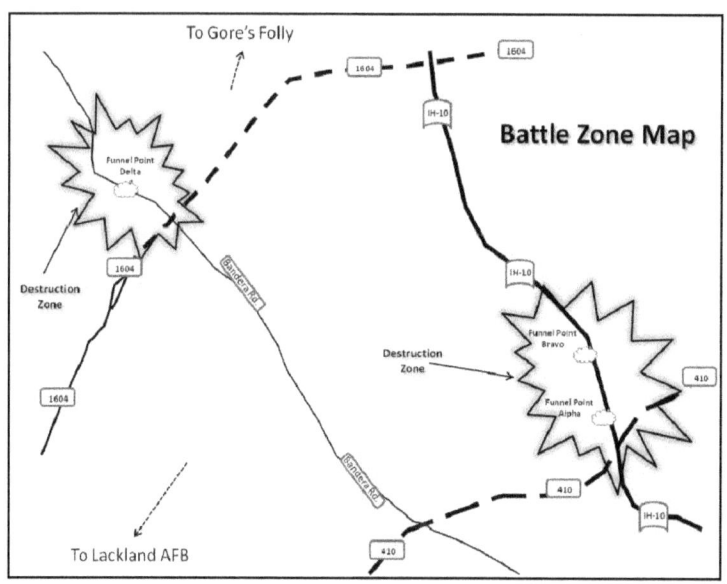

FREDERICK GARCIA

APPENDIX II: WEAPONS IN ORDER OF APPEARANCE

Pistol

The FN Five-seven pistol was developed as a companion pistol to the P90, the Five-seven shares many of its design features: it is a lightweight polymer-based weapon with a large magazine capacity, ambidextrous controls, low recoil, and the ability to penetrate body armor when using certain cartridge types.

Cartridge

FN 5.7×28mm

Pistol

The M1911 is a single-action, semi-automatic, magazine-fed, recoil-operated pistol which served as the standard-issue sidearm for the United States armed forces from 1911 to 1985. It was widely used in World War I, World War II, the Korean War, and the Vietnam War.

Cartridge

45 ACP cartridge

Rifle (Carbine)

Colt Commando 733 - The first carbine version of the M16 assault rifle appeared under the name of CAR-15 in 1965, and was intended for US Special Forces who fought in Vietnam. The original M16 was simply shortened by cutting the half of the length of the barrel (from original 20 inches to 10 inches) and by shortening the butt stock by another 3 inches. Specifically, "Colt Commando" currently refers to the ultra-short 11.5-inch barrel assault rifle of the Model 733 series. By comparison, the M4 Carbine has a 14.5-inch barrel, while the M16 assault rifle series has a 20-inch barrel.

Cartridge

5.56×45mm NATO

Rifle

The M16A4 rifle was standard issue for the United States Marine Corps in Operation Iraqi Freedom after 2004. In the U.S. Army, the M16A2 rifle is being supplemented with two rifle models, the M16A4 and the M4 carbine, as the standard issue assault rifle. The M16A4 has a flat-top receiver developed for the M4 carbine, a hand guard with four rails for mounting a sight, laser, night vision device, forward handgrip, removable handle, or a flashlight.

Cartridge

5.56×45mm NATO

Submachine Gun

The SIG MPX is the only submachine gun is available in several selective fire configurations for military and police use, as well as in semi-automatic only civilian-legal carbine version. This submachine gun is intended to compete with the famous HK MP5 submachine gun.

Cartridge

9x19 mm Luger/Parabellum, .357 SIG or .40 S&W

Shotgun

The Remington Model 870 is a U.S.-made pump-action shotgun widely used by law enforcement and military organizations worldwide.

Cartridge

12 gauge, 16 gauge, 20 gauge, 28 gauge, or .410 bore

Pistol

The Glock 17 is a 9mm short recoil-operated locked breech semi-automatic pistol. The Glock 17 feeds from staggered-column or double stack magazines that have a 17-round capacity (which can be extended to 19 with an optional floor plate) or optional 33-round high capacity magazines.

Cartridge

9×19mm Parabellum

Pistol

The Beretta M9 has been the standard sidearm of the United States Navy, United States Army and the United States Air Force since 1985, replacing the Colt M1911A1.

Cartridge

9×19mm Parabellum

Rifle

The AR-15 is based on the 7.62 mm AR-10, designed by the Fairchild ArmaLite Corporation. The AR-15 was developed as a lighter, 5.56 mm version of the AR-10. The "AR" in all AR pattern rifles stands for Armalite Rifle. Most U.S. civilian models are semi-automatic and used for hunting and self defense. They can, of course, be modified.

Cartridge

.223 Remington, 5.56 NATO

The .458 SOCOM is a relatively large round designed for a specialized upper receiver that can be mounted on any AR-15 pattern lower receiver. The 300-grain (19 g) round offers a muzzle velocity of 1,900 ft/s (580 m/s).

It is very powerful and is sometimes used to bring down feral hogs in Texas.

Rifle

The AK47 is a selective-fire, gas-operated 7.62×39mm assault rifle, first developed in the USSR by Mikhail Kalashnikov. It is also known as a Kalashnikov, an AK or in Russian slang, Kalash. It fires a heavier round than the M16.

Cartridge

7.62×39mm M43/M67

Sniper Rifle

The M40 is a bolt-action sniper rifle used by the United States Marine Corps.

Cartridge

7.62×51mm NATO

M32 Grenade Launcher

In 2005 the U.S. Marine Corps procured 200 US-made Milkor MGL-140s, designating it the "M32 Multiple shot Grenade Launcher" (M32 MGL, or M32 MSGL). The US Marine Corps M32 version is equipped with the M2A1 reflex sight. The MGL is a low-velocity, shoulder-fired 40 mm grenade launcher with a six-round spring-driven revolver-style magazine capable of accepting most 40×46mm grenades. The spring-driven cylinder rotates automatically while firing, but it must be wound back up after every reloading.

Cartridge

40×46mm grenade

40×51mm grenade (XRGL40)

Machine Gun

The M60 is a belt-fed machine gun that fires the 7.62 mm NATO cartridge (.308 Winchester) commonly used in larger rifles. It is generally used as a crew-served weapon and operated by a team of two or three individuals. The team consists of the gunner, the assistant gunner and the ammunition bearer. The gun's weight and the amount of ammunition it can consume when fired make it difficult for a single soldier to carry and operate. The gunner carries the weapon and anywhere from 200 to 1000 rounds of ammunition. The assistant carries a spare barrel and extra ammunition, and reloads and spots targets for the gunner. The ammunition bearer carries additional ammunition and the tripod with associated traversing and elevation mechanism, if issued, and fetches more ammunition as needed during firing.

Cartridge

7.62×51mm NATO

Machine Gun

The Browning M2 is an air-cooled, belt-fed machine gun. The M2 fires from a closed bolt, operated on the short recoil principle. The M2 fires the .50 BMG cartridge, which offers long range, accuracy and immense stopping power. All .50 ammunition designated "armor-piercing" was required to completely perforate 0.875 inches (22.2 mm) of hardened steel armor plate at a distance of 100 yards (91 m) and 0.75 inches (19 mm) at 547 yards (500 m). The API and APIT rounds left a flash, report, and smoke on contact, useful in detecting strikes on enemy targets; they were primarily intended to incapacitate thin-skinned and lightly armored vehicles and aircraft, while igniting their fuel tanks.

Cartridge

Current ammunition types include M33 Ball (706.7 grain) for personnel and light material targets, M17 tracer, M8 API (622.5 grain), M20 API-T (619 grain), and M962 SLAP-T. The latter ammunition along with the M903 SLAP (Saboted Light Armor Penetrator) round can perforate 1.34 inches (34 mm) of HHA (face-hardened steel plate) at 500 metres (550 yd), 0.91 inches (23 mm) at 1,200 metres (1,300 yd), and 0.75 inches (19 mm) at 1,500 metres (1,600 yd). This is achieved by using a 0.30-inch-diameter (7.6 mm) tungsten penetrator. The SLAP-T adds a tracer charge to the base of the ammunition.

Pistol

Heckler & Koch is offering the MK 23 on the civilian market and law enforcement as the MARK 23. The models for the U.S. market initially came with a 10-round magazine, to comply with the U.S. Assault Weapons Ban. The ban has now expired, and the civilian Mark 23 comes with the same 12-round magazine as the government variants, except in a few states that enforce their own bans on magazines larger than 10 rounds.

Cartridge

45 ACP cartridge

Machine Gun

The M240B is the standard infantry medium machine gun of the U.S. Army. It is also in service with the U.S. Air Force, Navy, and Coast Guard. It comes configured for ground combat with a butt stock and bipod, though it is also mounted aboard ships and small boats. It is almost always referred to as an "M240 Bravo" or even just "240" verbally, but always written as M240B.

Cartridge

7.62×51mm NATO

Light Machine Gun

A light machine gun (LMG) is a machine gun designed to be employed by an individual soldier, with or without an assistant, as an infantry support weapon. Light machine guns are often used as squad automatic weapons (SAW).

Cartridge

Varied

Sniper Rifle

The L115A3 Accuracy International AWM is a bolt-action sniper rifle manufactured by Accuracy International designed for magnum rifle cartridge chambering. The Accuracy International AWM is also unofficially known as the AWSM (Arctic Warfare Super Magnum), which typically denotes AWM rifles chambered in .338 Lapua Magnum.

Cartridge

.300 Winchester Magnum and .338 Lapua Magnum

Sniper Rifle

The Barrett is a .50 caliber, shoulder fired, semi-automatic sniper rifle. The long effective range, over 1,800 metres (5,900 ft) (1.1 miles), along with high energy and availability of highly effective ammunition, allows for effective operations against targets like radar cabins, trucks, parked aircraft and the like. The Barrett can also be used to defeat human targets from standoff range or against targets behind cover. However, anti-personnel use is not a major application for any.50 BMG rifle. Although, it has been used most effectively as a psychological weapon due to its powerful punch.

Cartridge

. 50 BMG .416 Barrett

Chain Gun (Used by the Bradley Fighting Vehicle)

The M242 Bushmaster is a 25 mm chain-fed auto-cannon. It is used extensively by the US armed forces in ground combat vehicles. It is an externally powered, chain driven, single-barrel weapon which may be fired in semi-automatic, burst, or automatic modes. It is fed by a metallic link belt and has dual-feed capability. The term "chain gun" derives from the use of a roller chain that drives the bolt back and forth. The gun can destroy lightly armored vehicles and aerial targets (such as helicopters and slow-flying aircraft). It can also suppress enemy positions such as exposed troops, dug-in positions, and occupied built-up areas. The standard rate of fire is 180 rounds per minute. The weapon has an effective range of 3,000 metres (9,800 ft), depending on the type of ammunition used.

Cartridge

25 millimetres (0.98 in) caliber

Hellfire Missile (Used by the T-6B Texan Attack Plane)

The Hellfire is an air-to-surface missile (ASM) developed primarily for anti-armor use. It was originally developed under the name Helicopter Launched, Fire and Forget Missile, which led to the acronym 'Hellfire' that became the missile's formal name. The Hellfire missile is the primary 100 lb-class air-to-ground precision weapon for the armed forces of the United States and many other nations, and is considered a proven tactical missile system, as it has been used in combat since the mid-1980s.

VEHICLES

HumVee

The High Mobility Multipurpose Wheeled Vehicle (HMMWV), commonly known as the HumVee, is a four-wheel drive military automobile. Primarily used by the United States military, it is also used by numerous other countries and organizations and even in civilian adaptations.

"Technicals"

A technical is a type of improvised fighting vehicle, typically a civilian or military non-combat vehicle, modified to provide an offensive capability similar to a military gun truck. It is usually an open-backed civilian pickup truck or four-wheel drive vehicle mounting a machine gun, light anti-aircraft gun, recoilless rifle, or other support weapon.

T-6B Texan Aircraft

The T-6 is a single-engine, stepped tandem, two-seat primary trainer aircraft that entered service in 1998. The T-6A combines features typical of a primary trainer with the very low fuel consumption and overall economy of a turboprop, while simultaneously providing 50 percent more overall thrust than its predecessor

The B version has a weapons control computer and six wing hard points for mounting bombs, rocket pods, or machine guns. This inexpensive and nimble two-seat aircraft provides a clear view where a highly trained enlisted fire support coordinator can ensure safe and effective fires on the enemy   below.

www.ingramcontent.com/pod-product-compliance
Lightning Source LLC
Chambersburg PA
CBHW070610130626
46556CB00001B/329